WALLABY

Other Wallaby Books by Andre Norton
Moon Called

WHEEL OF STARS
by ANDRE NORTON

A WALLABY BOOK
Published by Simon & Schuster
NEW YORK

Copyright ©1983 by Andre Norton
Illustrations copyright ©1983 by Chris Miller
All rights reserved including the right of reproduction in whole or in part in any form.

Published by Wallaby Books
A Simon & Schuster Division of Gulf & Western Corp.
Simon & Schuster Building
1230 Avenue of the Americas
New York, New York 10020

WALLABY and colophon are registered trademarks of Simon & Schuster

First Wallaby Books printing March 1983
Published by arrangement with Tom Doherty Associates
10 9 8 7 6 5 4 3 2 1

Manufactured in the United States of America

Printed and bound by The Murray Printing Co.

ISBN: 0-671-47001-9

WHEEL OF STARS

The author wishes to acknowledge her very great debt to Sandra Helton, who was so kind as to provide the astrological material used herein— including the horoscope.

1

Down in the pocket-sized strip of meadow the dawn wind was whirling leaves about. One fluttered up, to catch on the side of Gwennan's knitted cap. She pushed her chin deeper into the folds of her heavy scarf. Even this chill could be forgotten as she stood at last, half-wedged between the two rough stones, her attention fixed on a third and tallest one standing still higher on the mound, stark against the paling of the sky.

Simple formations of nature, these three? She grimaced behind her scarf half-mask and for the hundredth time—the thousandth—denied that to herself. Would it happen as she had hoped—could it so happen again? She was as certain of what she had caught a faint glimpse of three weeks ago at this same hour as she was that she stood now in this place.

The books — how she had combed books, studied the speculations of those who had been laughed at, derided, even persecuted in their time by "authorities" who held tightly to accepted views because the foundation of their own schol-

arship was based on conventional accepted—
accepted what?—merely more speculations if
one dug deep enough and far enough.

Now! The light—it was right—as it encased the
tall stone and—

Gwennan could have cried out. Perhaps she did
croak hoarsely into the folds of her scarf. Her
impression had *not* been imagination. There were
those scratches along the pillar of stone, far too
regular to be any freak of nature, too strange to
be—what? Only in the half light, at this hour had
she been able to see them. Were she to go forward
now and strip off her mitten, run fingertips down
that surface, could she also feel what her straining eyes told her were there?

To think so was the beginning of action. Her
bare flesh shrank from the cold but she did not
care. She touched—and then jerked away. It had
been instinctive, that withdrawal, after the sensation of feeling something which was not of the
rock, not born of the chill of air—not of—

She touched again. The oddness was gone. Just
as ripples spreading from a pebble dropped into
a pool were quickly spent. Now she strove to
trace those lines. Ogham? That forgotten tongue
written in scratches carefully placed above or
below a line, or runes with their sharp angles?
She had searched the books. No, those marks she
saw—had seen (already they were fast being lost
into the stone's secret, hidden by the change of
light) were nothing she could identify.

Only she *had* seen them. They *had* been there!
She would come again and again— Trespassing?
Gwennan looked beyond the upstanding fang of

rock to the woods below. There among the trees showed a slanting roof, as grey and grim—and seemingly near as old as these three pillars of stone.

She was, Gwennan assured herself fiercely (striving to hide her disappointment that the moment of revelation had again been so brief), doing no harm. The custom of nearly three hundred years as far as the town was concerned, made this untouched, untrodden land for the villagers. Yet no one had ever said in so many words, that the battered stone wall bordering the lane protected a forbidden territory.

Being born of the town, accepting as the town accepted, she had not realized for years how strange was the history of the valley. Not just because of these stones which had drawn her from the first time she had sighted them, but also because of Lyle House.

Back in 1730, when the first of the settlers from the coast pushed up the White River, away from the sea lands with their storms and bleak winds, hunting better farming—Lyle House had already stood here. Who built it and when? If any of the newcomers had asked that they had quickly set bonds on their curiosity.

For here were the Lyles already in residence, with them a handful of Indians, also a score perhaps of dark-skinned servants of another race—silent, never mingling with the newcomers. Yet the Lyle of that day who had been master had done nothing to forbid settlers. In fact, from time to time, help had come from those grey walls to strengthen not only the small beginnings of a town but to aid separate individuals.

Gwennan's school had taught the old conventional myth of Columbus and his famed discovery in its approved history books. Only in the present day men knew more. Before that Italian adventurer had taken sail there had been hardy fishermen from England trolling along the coast, venturing ashore to dry their catch before going home, keeping a careful secret of the rich waters. There were the longboat people, too. No longer could their visits be denied when a village of theirs had been recently uncovered. Before them—who else?

What of the ruins in New Hampshire—the many "root cellars" dug, walled with stone, carefully constructed — used by encroaching later settlers for the prosaic service which now gave them their name? All that had been found then had been ascribed to Indians. Those identifying the remains never attempted to explain why nomad hunters built walls of stone and shelters of a strange form when they themselves dwelt in short held camps.

Who were the Lyles and why had they found their way here? There were the legends of a pirate who had brought upriver his treasure and the remnants of his outland crew to found a small kingdom. But, however they had first come, they were a part of this land in a way that the later settlers quickly grasped and did not openly question. It was also true that the town and the outlying farms were never raided during the Indian wars, that certain of the Indians themselves had, on occasion, taken refuge with the Lyles. War had not come here—only modest prosperity. There was a mill built with Lyle gold—and oddly enough also a school, concerning which the Lyles had made only one stipulation, strange for those days, that the daughters of each household share equally with the sons in any learning dispensed there. Still, any influence the family might have exerted was always indirect—they did nothing to alter the ways of life the townspeople had brought with them.

Often, too, during the succeeding years, the big house was empty, save for that small core of servants (who apparently married to provide future generations to take up their duties as their elders aged and died). The ruling Lyle might disappear for a space. Sometimes there would come the news that there had been a death abroad. Sooner or later another member of their silent clan would arrive, to competently take his or her place, and life would continue as it always had. It was a woman who was the Lyle now. Gwennan had seen her only recently in person.

They called her, after the fashion which had come down from the first settlers and which the townspeople now found so familiar that they never questioned the oddness of such a title in this most plain-speaking of countries, Lady Lyle. There had never been any children known in residence at Lyle House, any marriages and families which might ensue were always in foreign parts. However, it was well known that each new head of the house in features and bearing resembled closely the one he or she succeeded. The family bred very true.

Gwennan had only lately begun to wonder at the minor mystery—how a family who had dominated the land for so long had also managed to efface themselves so thoroughly. She had been completely fascinated by Lady Lyle. In the first place, she herself had never met another woman who matched that gangling height which made her so self-conscious all her life.

She, herself, had always topped all her contemporaries at school and hated her own thin stretch of body. But Lady Lyle was a proud forest pine of a woman, with a great white braid wound around her head—forming so massive a crown of hair that she could never wear more than a knotted scarf to cover it. She walked with a presence such as Gwennan imagined a queen regent might have displayed in those other days when royalty ruled instead of reigned.

Though Gwennan had little in her own narrow life to give her any standard of judgment. As Nessa Daggert's niece her social life had been very meager. Any widening of physical horizons had been strictly curtailed. Miss Nessa had headed the town library, her whole life centered upon her duties there. She had taken Gwennan (very reluctantly, but from the strict sense of inbred duty, upon the death of her young and footloose, wandering parents) to raise. By town standards she had done her best for the child—adequate, if plain, food, clothing which was fashioned according to Miss Nessa's standards of what was fit, and the instilling of a moral code which was already being challenged by the outside world, made the sum of her contributions.

There had been no college for Gwennan. By the
time she graduated from high school (and she had
not been counted in any way a scholar since she
was apt only to apply herself to subjects in which
she was interested and to let the rest slide by),
Miss Nessa was already prey to the wasting dis-
ease to which she refused to surrender. She determined to hold the reins of her small place in
the world until the end and Gwennan became, as
a matter of course, her hands and feet, her ears
and eyes.

There had been no desire for rebellion on the
girl's part. Not only had duty been well established as a motif of life, but she had come to
really fear anything beyond the narrow round of
her own days. She had always been a social mis-
fit, and secretly she had found her inner escape
—books.

There *was* a drive in her, she had begun to
realize that. Though as yet it was formless. She
read — how she read — history, reports of ar-
chaeological discoveries, everything concerning
strange finds which could not be fitted into the
accepted pattern vouched for by the experts.
Oddly enough Gwennan had never been stimu-
lated to try and fit herself to become one of
the seekers of the unknown. Perhaps she questioned too much accepted theories. But, though
outwardly she was Miss Nessa's dutiful niece and
willing assistant, inwardly she measured, questioned, sought.

Once she had dreamed. This morning here, between the stones, memories of those dreams
stirred faintly. She thrust them fiercely aside.

When she had been quite young she believed everyone "dreamed real" and she had talked freely—only to be accused of telling lies, until she realized the danger of strangeness, and readily agreed that she had "made up" this adventure or that.

Not since her early teens had the dreams come, and, in the end, she had been glad. For the latter ones had been of nightmare quality producing fear which terrorized her until she had built a wall against them.

When Miss Nessa had died two years ago she had left Gwennan her house, a very minute sum in the bank (for in spite of her Spartan fight, the illness had eaten up much of what she had stored with strict economy) and her place in the library. The town, having been used so long to have Gwennan deputize for Miss Nessa, simply voted her on into that position. The only change in her life had been that her salary was a fraction higher and she was thus enabled to add to her precious collection of books.

Full daylight had arrived to bathe the stone and hide the marks. Gwennan pulled on her mitten and turned—to freeze. She was no longer alone.

The man who approached so silently had not climbed the mound, rather stood at its foot, gazing somberly up at her. He was tall—and he was a Lyle! His face carried Lady Lyle's features —bolder, harsher, more hawklike—still with the family signature plain to read.

In spite of the cold his head was bare, inclined backwards a little to better watch her from beneath half-closed eyelids. The hair, above skin so weathered that even in this season it was still brown, was a thick cap, golden bright even in this early light, cropped shorter than was the custom at present.

Those eyes so intent upon her were of the same brilliant, gem blue as Lady Lyle's. Gwennan shifted her feet uncomfortably. She was a trespasser, and dealing with a Lyle on his own ground was a little daunting.

"Who are you?" His demand came bluntly.

Gwennan refused to yield to her own uneasiness. Instead she moved away from the rock pinnacles.

"Gwennan Daggert." Her name would probably mean nothing at all to him—she was trying to think of an excuse to offer for being here. To betray her secret was more than she would ever do.

"Gwennan Daggert," he repeated. "And what brings you here, Gwennan Daggert?" Now his eyelids lifted as he favored her with an insolent, challenging stare. Perhaps he had every right to do so.

"Chance—" She could not seem to think fast enough.

He laughed. "Chance?" His head moved slowly from side to side in negation of her lie. Yet there was another change in his expression, as if a shadow had drifted away to reveal him more completely. There was a difference which she sensed, a kind of raillery, as if he held her so stupid he could coax her into other lies.

Gwennan was surprised at her own idea. Having had so very little contact with young men, she could believe that her social ineptitude might well betray her into the wrong guesses of the meaning of a lift of brow, the slight movement of those firm, rather narrow lips which were now shaping a smile she did not like.

In fact she found the whole man disturbing. This was like being confronted by a person who— Gwennan gave up. She had no time to search for small shades of strange emotions. Instead she wanted to get away—to be free and alone, out of the presence of this unknown Lyle.

As she reached the foot of the mound she discovered she must again look up to meet his eyes. Tall as was Lady Lyle, this man of her family was even taller. For the first time in her life Gwennan felt oddly small, somehow fleetingly like another person—as if this was a shadow of another meeting with one in complete command so purposefully disturbing. Approaching him she felt she was closing in upon something, in its way, as strange and hidden as the stone which had drawn and centered all her innermost curiosity for so long. Yet this was a man—flesh and blood, standing very much at his ease.

"Gwennan Daggert." Again he spoke her name, only something in the sound of those two words was not right. The girl felt as if he spoke them in another language, accented them wrong—was trying so to— She shook her head at such a fantasy, or thought that she did.

"You are addicted to dawn walks, then?" His mocking smile grew more pronounced. "Even in this weather?" Now he gave an exaggerated shiver. "You are a hardy people, of course, you Downeasterners."

Gwennan possessed firm self control once more—safely back in the mold Miss Nessa had formed. "We tend to be." She had, she hoped, mastered any sign of that momentary uneasiness which had troubled her. "If I wish to walk it must be early in the day. I have a job." She held up her wrist, peeled back the cuff of her mitten to consult her watch, "and—"

His brows, several shades darker than the hair, which was more and more impossibly golden as the sun began its slow rise, lifted a fraction. "What kind of a job which begins at this hour? It is not too far past dawn—"

"Late enough for me to be on my way." Her reply was short, curt. She might be unduly rude but she could no longer control that shadowy emotion she did not understand. The uneasiness which spread from him to lap about her grew ever stronger. That there was a second Lyle, unknown to the town, was strange in itself. There had never been any talk of Lady Lyle's having a son—or was this man within the age range to be her son? Gwennan thought she was no good judge of that.

A strange Lyle—still that mere fact should not produce such a feeling in her. One of—fear? What had she to be truly afraid of? She trespassed here, that was true. However, merely walking across a field to watch the sun rise between three stones—that was no crime. She had disturbed nothing, done nothing. Why did she feel guilty, threatened—as if he had some good reason to mistrust her?

"To where?" Still he smiled.

She *had* been right—there *was* a mocking note

in his voice. He appeared to find her amusing. Gwennan stiffened. That curl of fear was swept away by a flash of inner anger. She decidedly did not like this man. Just as she admired Lady Lyle, so, in the same measure, she disliked this relative of hers—no matter what relationship he might bear to the mistress of Lyle House.

"To the library." No reason to make any secret of who she was or her own life. The town was close-knit—more so in winter when the few summer folk were gone, and those of the old families drew together, inhabiting, in a way, a fortress against what might be a blasting season.

"The library?"

Again he picked up her words, a habit she was beginning to find irritating. She swiftly chose to foster that irritation as a kind of barrier against any other emotions he stirred to life within her. "But surely that does not open so early. I believe my aunt said noon on most days. I know she is planning to visit you later today—"

"There is always plenty of work to be done even when we are not officially open," Gwennan returned primly.

She was almost tempted, in order to prove to him how very ordinary and normal was life (now *why*, another part of her demanded, was this necessary?) by listing all those numerous small tasks which were really never quite finished no matter how one labored. Also she was hungry—a single cup of coffee drunk in haste in the dark while standing by the kitchen stove was not her usual breakfast. She fully intended to stop at the side door of Mary Long's bakery for some blue-berry muffins—to be toasted and enjoyed for a quiet hour while she read a waiting pile of professional journals.

"Ah, yes, work to employ idle hands which one hears of—though not so much these days. It would seem that Waterbridge keeps to the old ethic. Good—or bad." He made her a small mock bow, yet he did not move from directly before her. Short of shoving him out of her path, or making a very noticeable sidestep, she had to remain where she was. Gwennan was debating that latter choice when his hand darted out toward her head.

Instinctively she ducked, then flushed when she saw the leaf caught between two of his fingers. For all his talk of the cold he did not seem to feel the bite of the weather unduly, for, in addition to his bare head, he wore no gloves, and the front of his knee-length coat hung unbuttoned. Once more he laughed.

"What are you afraid of, Gwennan Daggert?" He took a fraction of a step closer. To her mortification, the girl moved hurriedly back. There was nothing but good humor in his expression as he held up the leaf, twirling it about on the small stem.

"I assure you," he continued, "I do not eat little girls, not even when I find them where they are not invited. Little girls who wear leaves on their heads—as if they are dryads or nymphs—"

This was a kind of teasing to which she could not respond. What made her freeze, feel awkward and uncomfortable? It appeared to her to be mainly his overt mockery. Again anger warmed her.

"I certainly do not suppose," she put into her

voice all the icy reserve she had learned from Miss Nessa, "that you do. I am well aware that I am a trespasser. As such, please accept my apologies, Mr. Lyle. It will not, I assure you, happen again!"

No, it could not, she told herself. Yet how could she make herself stay away from that tantalizing stone, the riddle which would not let her go? She longed to glance up over her shoulder at the finger of the middle rock, yet she felt that to do so would in some manner let him know—learn—in a way invade what was entirely her own.

He dropped the leaf. Again his hand moved, this time he grasped her right wrist, imprisoning it in a hold she thought that she would not be able to break even if she struggled—which pride would not allow her to do. While he never stopped smiling with those thin lips. Still, deep in his eyes, there was something else which denied any lightness to that smile. Gwennan did not want to understand what lay behind that shadow —she only wanted free of him. But she would not struggle to throw off his hold.

Then his voice changed. It became deeper, harsher, as if he strove to put into it the power of some imperious command:

"What *were* you doing here? Did *she*—?" The tip of his tongue flicked across his lower lip. "What does *she* want with *you?*" There was a distinct flare of scorn in that. He loomed over her almost as if he were growing before her very eyes, becoming larger, something greater and stronger than the man she had first seen. No, she must not let her imagination range that way!

"I have not the least idea," Gwennan sought to retain her composure, "of what you mean. If the 'she' you mention is Lady Lyle—"

"*Lady!*" He broke in, and it seemed to the girl that his dark skin grew even darker, as if blood flooded close beneath its surface. "Lady!" He made of that word something which sounded both an epithet and a protest.

"Mrs. Lyle, then," she corrected. "The town has always used 'Lady' as a term of respect—it is a tradition for your family. A tribute this time, I imagine, to the impression she makes upon people. But, at any rate, I do not understand you. I do not know her at all. All we have ever spoken of, and that was most briefly, was books—and the first time for that was last Thursday. She has only recently been coming to the library, at all.

"As for *my* being here," Gwennan was at last emboldened to give a quick jerk which freed her wrist, taking two quick steps to the side, "that is also a simple matter which has nothing at all to do with your family. I walk often in the early mornings—especially at this time of the year. And I like the woods—"

His demanding eyes swept from her to the mound. Almost as if in that glance he said aloud he had not found her in the woods, rather in a place which, for some reason, was not to be invaded. At that moment Gwennan would have willingly suffered any mockery, or even anger which he wished to summon, rather than ever tell him what had really brought her here. That would remain her secret—one which perhaps she would never be able to solve if the tall stones now became forbidden territory.

"And now, good morning, Mr. Lyle." She turned abruptly, strode firmly away, not looking back. Though she carried with her the unhappy feeling that he might be following her, determined to see her safely off Lyle land, back to that world where her kind should stay and live their quiet, narrow little lives.

"Wait—!" His raised voice was urgent. Gwennan would not run, but her walk approached a trot. She heard the swish of the grass about her legs, perhaps too loudly, it might be echoed by sounds proving that he, too, was on the move. She —was—not—going—to—run— She—was—not—

"Tor!"

Not his voice this time, rather a clear hail from farther away.

Gwennan, startled, did glance back. He *had* started after her, just as she had feared. Only that call had halted him, so that he half turned towards the mound. Out of the woods which screened all but the roof of the Lyle House, moved a tall figure wrapped in a hooded cloak. Gwennan did not need to see the face half hidden by the folds of cloth to know that this was Lady Lyle.

Embarrassment made her hot. She had been unhappy at being subtly challenged by the younger Lyle, but to be seen here by Lady Lyle— that was even worse. To be caught acting like a spy! She frankly took to her heels, pausing only in her dash when she came to the wall over which she must climb to reach the lane. On the other side of that barrier she halted, forced herself to wait until her heart stopped beating so fast, rubbing her mittens across her face, wondering why she was shaking so. This whole encounter seemed to have a serious meaning which she did not understand. She swallowed twice and started towards town at a brisk but steady pace, trying to concentrate on the day ahead and not what was immediately behind her.

Still all morning, though Gwennan strove to occupy herself only with what was to be done, her thoughts showed an unfortunate tendency to wander. She had to resolutely keep her back to the shelf of those books which were her own private research materials. She *had* seen those markings. That fact was far more important than the disturbing meeting with Mr. Lyle. Was he going to remain at Lyle House? If so, would she ever have another chance to complete her own investigations at the stone? The swing from hope to disappointment made her more unhappy than she could ever remember before. She might have been bodily pulled out of her neat little shell of a life, in which she had always been so sheltered and comfortable. Now she was being made to venture into the strange and unknown which she had always shunned, unless it lay on the printed page where it could be safely confined and enclosed when one wanted no more of brain-taxing questions and speculations for awhile.

Gwennan sat at her desk and found herself drawing over and over those strange lines which curved or hooked (were they subconsciously remembered from the morning's half sighting—or just what her imagination was offering her?). She crumpled the paper, threw it forcibly into the waste basket, then made herself select the books for the school class due in this afternoon.

Yet memory clung. She felt a prickling of skin, an unease, as if some dreaded action lay before her. Though she sternly told herself that this was a very stupid piece of self-delusion, as she would eventually prove.

2

Gwennan unlocked the library door promptly at twelve-thirty for old Mr. Staines who shuffled with a grunt of greeting to his chosen chair near the register. There followed a flurry of children on their way back to school. Her attention was fully captured by their demands. A half hour later Lady Lyle came in, her slim body muffled in that same soft dark green-gray cloak she had worn in the early morning. In the full light of the room Gwennan could see the hollows in the older woman's pale cheeks, making more prominent her well-formed nose, and the ridges of delicate bones. She looked more fragile than the girl had remembered her from only the week before. Had she been ill? Still she walked as firmly as ever, held herself proudly erect. Was she coming to face Gwennan with the sin of trespassing?

However, she spoke with a note of warmth the girl had not expected:

"It seems odd after all these years not to see Miss Nessa," she said. They might have been friends, comfortable in a long-held relationship.

Still those smiling lips were blueish—was she perhaps a heart patient—? Though who really knew anything about the Lyles? Now she produced a list, holding it out to Gwennan.

"I cannot hope, I fear, to find any of these on the shelves, they are perhaps too specialized in subject matter. However, Miss Nessa once told me that there exists a system of ordering books from other libraries, to be read on loan—"

Gwennan studied the spiky writing which at first glance seemed almost to be in some foreign language, until under close examination it became more intelligible. As she read, her first faint uneasiness strengthened. Was this list a subtle method of informing her that she had not only been discovered trespassing, but that the reason for her morning invasion of Lyle land had been guessed? She made herself pick up her pen and check four of the six lines on that scrap of paper.

"These are already here—on loan. It may be possible to extend that—"

"How very fortunate!"

Was she being subtly baited? Best make sure by confession on her own to bring matters at once to a head.

"They are a personal order—for me."

She dared to look directly at the other's worn face. There was nothing of that covert mockery which had shown so clearly in the young man's expression. Instead there was something of eagerness in the large eyes above dark smudges which gave the impression of weariness or ill health.

"You are interested then in such discoveries? But that is good! Though I have known many queer corners of the earth I was not aware until recently that there have been more such things recently brought to light—or at least into print.

"It could mean—" she hesitated, still staring so intently at Gwennan that the girl felt this woman was silently demanding from her some answer which she needed—needed, more than just desired. "What was your opinion of this particular one?" she asked abruptly, sharply, requiring an answer, even as an instructor might have done from a shy pupil. She leaned forward, making Gwennan aware of a strong spicy fragrance, and with her gloved finger pointed to the third title on the list.

"The one about the leys, and the possibility that such reported monsters as Nessie, and even UFOs might be associated with those?" Gwennan fended off a direct answer as she strove to make up her mind. She never discussed her private reading with anyone. The Lyles were noted travelers, citizens of the world at large. They represented such knowledge as could not be matched by anyone else Gwennan knew. "The authors," she continued clearly, "appear to make out something of a case in favor of that point—though they do not commit themselves to any of the several conclusions they offer at the end of the book. They leave you a choice."

"After stating known facts," Lady Lyle nodded. "I wish I could talk with those two young people —really talk. But what do you think? Which choice was yours? You surely have thought of what you read."

Gwennan braced herself. Here it was coming—
the questions, or perhaps the rebuke—for her
early morning visit. Only that did not seem to
interest Lady Lyle at all. Instead she was adding:

"You were the one who went backpacking to
hunt standing stones. Mr. Stevens mentioned that
his daughter spoke of it—"

Gwennan flushed. A summer ago when she had
so longed to be able to talk to someone, she had
half forgotten the penalty for being "different."
Yes, she had spoken to Nancy Stevens one day
when the book which had inspired her own single
and very amateurish attempt at discovery had
lain open on her desk and the other girl had appeared to show enough interest to ask a question
or two. She had learned her lesson when a
garbled account of her "stone hunting" had
drifted back to her. Just another of the freakish
differences which had cut her off from the town.

"Yes," Gwennan answered shortly, all her defenses up at once. "And I also trespassed. I have
visited your standing stones."

"What do you think of them? That they are just
rocks planted by the glaciers, as most authorities
have assured us?"

Just as anger had given her the courage to face
up to that other Lyle, so did determination give
her the courage not to be overpowered by this
one or forced into dismissing lightly what she did
believe was the truth. Let them both laugh at her
if they wished.

"No, I think they were set there for a purpose."

"I know they were." Lady Lyle had dropped her

voice, those four words uttered hardly above a whisper. "Such things have fascinated me for many years. Perhaps you would care to discuss the subject further when there are no interruptions. This is very short notice—rude perhaps—but would you care to come and have dinner with me tonight?"

Gwennan hoped she had outward possession enough not to show her utter astonishment. As far as she knew only two of the townspeople ever visited Lyle House—Mr. Stevens, whose legal practice sent him there at intervals, and a Mr. Warren, a summer visitor nearly as reclusive as the Lyles themselves, reputed to be a writer and collector of books.

She swallowed and then held firmly to her newly found boldness. "I would be very pleased. These books," she turned and swept them off the shelf behind her desk, "I was going to return them in the Friday delivery. But I shall call this afternoon and ask the loan extended for two weeks. At the same time I shall order the others—"

"Thank you." Lady Lyle nodded as if something momentous had never happened at all—as if it were very usual that the village librarian be personally invited to a house which had been a mystery for generations. "We dine at seven. My—my young kinsman will call for you."

"Oh, no!" Gwennan was jarred out of her carefully built shell. "I mean—there is no need for that. I am used to walking and certainly it is not far."

The tall woman no longer smiled. Her eyes

were still searching—watching Gwennan closely from under the shadow of the hood she had just adjusted to cover her head once again. "You do not find walking after dark in the lane disturbing?"

Gwennan laughed. "Of course not! Everyone walks, especially with gas prices as high as they are now. Anyway I do not have a car—"

Lady Lyle smiled once more. "But, of course. The frugal life—waste not, want not. In this modern world that is refreshing. Very well, if that is what you wish. Only, Miss Daggert, I would suggest that you do keep to the lanes—to cross fields in the early dark—"

Gwennan's hands tightened on the paper with the list. A mild way of commenting on her trespass? She must keep to her resolution of the morning then—no more visits to the stones—no matter how strongly they seemed to draw her. The Lyles need never again fear she would intrude upon their territory.

"The lanes, yes," she made careful answer. "They have—"

"No traps." She was astounded at that odd comment. Lady Lyle added nothing to that. Sweeping up the books, she had turned and gone, before the girl could thank her.

In Gwennan, surprise at that unlooked-for and abrupt invitation turned to an eagerness which she had not expected as the day passed. Lyle House was said to display a number of treasures brought back from the many journeys of the family. Stevens had several times spoken of it as a veritable museum. She longed to see that for herself. But she eyed her small wardrobe with open dissatisfaction when it came time to dress.

For all she knew the Lyles might live as formally as those rare and strange creatures she had viewed in some of the magazines the summer people donated to the library at intervals. She had only one good suit, no dress really suitable for such an occasion.

Now she zipped up the plaid skirt, tucked in the too-often-wandering tails of the blouse, and shrugged on the velvet jacket which was her one extravagance, meant to do duty for years to come. The soft material was of a warm rust shade she delighted in, and she smoothed its sleeves before she applied her finishing touch—fastening down the small frill at the blouse throat with the cameo which Miss Nessa had left her.

By six the daylight had already deepened into dusk. When she set out at half past that hour Gwennan put her flashlight into the deep pocket of her outer coat. She was glad of her boots, and as the wind plucked at the edge of her skirt she wished she had a long cloak like Lady Lyle's.

Miss Nessa's house was on the edge of the slowly growing town. Once it had been a farm dwelling. There were no street lights here, and out of habit Gwennan's eyes adjusted to the gloom. So she did not use the torch yet as she followed the road. Any traffic this far out was limited, and she could easily hear a car coming.

The paved street changed abruptly into a narrower road which had been surfaced when the Lyles brought the first motor car into Waterbridge at the time of Gwennan's grandmother. Though the air was crisp the night sky was clouded over, perhaps enough to dull the full moon which should be rising soon. The girl thought fleetingly, as she scuffed through the drifts of leaves, that it would be interesting to view the standing stones by moonlight. Somehow she had never visited the mound by night, now she wondered why—when it was too late to try such a venture.

She had nearly reached the two tall pillars marking the turnoff to the woods-hidden house itself when Gwennan became aware of a difference in the shadowed land. The night was unusually still. No wind now swept through the long weeds along the ditch, nor tumbled fallen leaves. There were no bird calls. The silence seemed almost to press in upon one. In her pocket her hand closed about the rod of the torch.

But she pushed away that rising uneasiness. There was certainly no reason to feel this way. She had walked this road many times, both night and day. Right before her was the entrance to the Lyle drive. A few steps along that and she would see the house which was not there masked by bushes—just a few more steps.

Out of the dark puffed a fetid stench, powerful enough to hit her like a blow. Not a skunk—no. This was stronger, more vile than anything she had met before. Putrid uncleanliness narrowed into an invisible blast which could have been aimed directly at her. She gagged, and, for a horrified second or two, thought she was going to be violently ill.

Something dead—?

Gwennan brought out her flashlight, thumbed its button. The beam of bright radiance made her blink as she pointed it down the private road. Striving not to breathe too deeply of that foulness the girl hurried on. Nor did she look from one side to the other, refusing to give way to any touch of fear.

The stench was lessening at last. She must have passed its source. This was the hunting season, and, though the Lyle's land was posted, there were always careless hunters who wounded an animal and did not follow, so that their victim stumbled on to die painfully and lingeringly.

Yet surely the carcass of such a kill would have been found by those in the house before it reached such a state of decay. She could not understand why it had not been buried. Also— she found herself listening—though she could not have said for what. The sound of her own boots crunching gravel of the drive was all to be heard. And that—so loud a sound—too loud— Why? Gwennan's breath came faster.

She rounded a hedge of leafless bushes, to see lighted windows ahead. Though she continued to use her torch as she neared the front door where the massive hand-wrought hinges of another day were black against aged wood. A knocker of intricate design centered the wide planks and she lifted that, unintentionally making such a clatter as to embarrass her.

The door swung open almost at once and light blazed out to enfold her—as if it alone could draw her inside. She came thus into a center hall totally unlike any part of a dwelling she had seen before, holding so much to catch the eye that she was not aware of the one who had opened the way into such a storehouse, until he spoke.

"Miss Daggert—so you *are* a fearless explorer —daring even the night."

It was Tor Lyle himself, of course. His golden head still appeared, even here, to draw light, glitter. She would not have believed that hair could take on such a metallic sheen. It was the more vividly alive perhaps because he wore a jacket of dark velvet over a black, turtlenecked shirt. Around his neck was a golden chain, its brilliance dimmed by that amazing hair. It supported a pendant covered with a tracery of lines so entwined that any pattern was too involved to follow without close examination.

Behind him the dark wainscoting of the hall walls was broken at intervals by niches, each of which was arched by concealed lighting to display the objects set within it. Gwennan caught glimpses of small statues, of plaques, once a strip of what was either strangely woven or embroidered fabric. This was indeed a museum!

Her host might have had the ability to read her awed thought, for he flung out one hand in an exaggerated flourish to indicate the closest of those niches. It held a slender figure of grotesque fashioning in the form of a woman whose lower limbs melted into what was clearly the rough barked column of a tree. Her upflung arms were half branch, small leaves depending from the tips of her fingers, while her long hair swirled above her head to form more strings of the same cleverly formed leaves.

The whole was in soft color, the leaves green with a faint sheen of gold at their edging, while the body, in its most human part, was wholly of that precious metal yet with a ruddiness added. The tiny eyes in the female's oval face were open, and some trick of the niche light caught a glint there, gem-hard in brilliancy—while the features of her near-human countenance held an expression mingling wild ecstacy with age-old sadness.

Gwennan stared, caught by all the imagination which she had so suppressed through the years from childhood. To her—though it was undoubtedly done by some trick of the clever lighting—there was a suggestion that those leaves trembled, that there was a faint rippling of the hair. It was as if she looked through a window or peephole into another world where abode forms of life far removed from all which she knew, yet in its way life which was permanent and intelligent.

"Ah, so you like Myrrah?" That question broke the spell the figure had laid on her. Gwennan blinked, flushed. She had allowed her naivete to show—which was irritating and she disliked him the more for reading her so quickly, for his subtle mockery at her open wonder. There was something in him which she continued to sense as vaguely wrong, slanted, which, in a way she did not understand, threatened her. But she was not able yet to define her emotions. Rather she shied from this unusual probing which part of her mind appeared to want to do.

"Myrrah?" She made a question of that name.

"Fair daughter of trees—what men once called a nymph." Tor Lyle turned his attention apparently wholly to the figurine, for which Gwennan was glad. "A fine piece of work, is it not? We do not even know the artist. However, viewing it one can believe those old legends that once even trees possessed souls (if one might term them that) and could manifest another identity at will. You have viewed Myrrah—now come and tell me what you think of Nikon. They may not have been modeled by the same artist—but there is a kind of likeness in technique—yes, there is a decided likeness."

She followed him to the next niche. There was a second figure, not this time half rooted in a massive trunk of wood. Instead its lower limbs were well apart, bisected in an entirely human fashion. Only where the feet might have been there were elongated appendages—toeless—resembling broad flippers. The skin was silver in hue and the concealed light skillfully revealed tiny overlapping scale which clothed it. It leaned a little forward, its arms outstretched in a curve as if to embrace something. Those slender arms ended in paws from which extended huge claws, cruelly displayed as if preparing to rend what the creature strove so to reach. To add to the impression of menace, the head was also hunched between the wide shoulders and the whole impression was one of avid desire to attack.

The head was a troubling mingling of caricature of human and simian. There was no hair, but rather a ragged crest of skin running from the mid point of the low forehead to the nape of the neck, standing erect. Those eyes were bulbous, the nose flat, with only a hole to mark its position. While the slightly gaping mouth, above a nearly chinless jaw, was open to show white points of teeth which gathered and reflected the light with unwholesome clarity. It was monstrous, a nightmare thing, alien as the nymph, but wholly evil in its aspect.

"Nikon," again Gwennan repeated the name. She frowned, trying not to look too closely, even though it drew her. If these were legendary creatures of mythology it was a series of legends new to her. She recognized neither name.

"Yes," once more mockery was in his voice. The girl half expected him to break into laughter at her ignorance. "Now there is—"

"Miss Daggert—" The cool, yet welcome sound of her own name was like a small, clean breeze in that dark place. It banished the influence she was half aware Tor Lyle could exert at will.

Gwenan turned, relieved, on the verge of a small new happiness, to greet her hostess.

As the young man, who now actually appeared a little diminished in his glitter, the mistress of the house wore a long velvet gown. The robe-like garment was simply cut, without any ornamentation. Still it added to her stature—almost having the character of the classic garb of a priestess far removed from the world in which Gwennan moved—the world which lay outside these thick walls around her now.

It was grey and caught in about her waist by a twisted cord of tarnished silver. Around Lady Lyle's neck a chain of the same dulled metal supported a disc surmounted by the upturned horns

of a crescent—both lacking the intricate embel-
lishment which complicated the pattern of a sun
disc worn by Tor.

"So—" she glanced beyond Gwennan now at
her young kinsman. The girl who had never considered herself particularly observant, nor attuned to others' moods, was aware of a strain. As
if, between these two, there was discord which
could only be feebly sensed, perhaps never open
to such action as she herself might understand.

Now Tor appeared to yield ground willingly,
though Gwennan was still convinced that the
mockery had not vanished from either his eyes or
the curve of his mouth. He stepped back, allowed
Lady Lyle to sweep the girl with her into an ad-
joining room. Biding his time—why had that particular thought crossed her mind now? Gwennan
had only an instant or so to question before she
became the willing guest — the ensorcelled visitor.

For ensorcelled she was, dazzled, charmed as
never before. They dined, Lady Lyle at the head of
a dark, old table, seated in a chair with a tall
carven back, seeming more and more to wear the
guise of a queen enthroned. Gwennan felt lost in a
similar chair, her fingers now and then slipping
along its arms, aware of the twisting of carvings
she did not have a chance to see plainly.

Tor Lyle was opposite her across that spread of
wood on which crystal and fragile china, silver,
cobweb lace and linen made islands. Nor did he
once break into the conversation which Lady Lyle
maintained, though he drank constantly from a
tall stemmed goblet, small sips of an amber-

colored wine, which Gwennan had tactfully refused. From Miss Nessa's household all such indulgences had been banished and she mistrusted her own reaction to that particular offering.

At her refusal Lady Lyle had nodded, almost as if she had approved and Gwennan noted gratefully that she herself had not allowed her own waiting goblet to be filled.

No, Tor Lyle did not speak. His eyes, a little narrowed as they had been at their first meeting by the mound, went from Gwennan to Lady Lyle and back again. He might be a man confronted by some puzzle which it was very necessary that he solve.

Having finished their meal, the mistress of the house once more led the way into another room, again wall-panelled. The wood had been painted, and the colors were freshly bright as if age had never touched. A brush, wet-tipped, might just have been raised from a last curve. There were figures pictured, which were wholly human, behind them the rise of cities and towns—some drawn with that lack of perspective which had never troubled artists of the past. They seemed to flow from one stretch of wall to the next, and Gwennan guessed that all were meant to follow the thread of some story, for she marked one of the same figures in action from one panel to another.

Only she was not given any time to study this, for what Lady Lyle promptly laid out on another table were very modern photographs. These looked starkly bare when one had seen the walls.

At a glance Gwennan recognized the places which had been so filmed. Three were of rocks which she had noted on her own one short trip of exploration.

Lady Lyle nodded, studying the girl's face closely.

"Yes," her voice was eager, alive. "These are what we should seek. See, these lie directly on a path which is laid so—" With an impatient whisk of the hand she brushed the pictures to one side, producing a map on which was drawn a scarlet line, so deeply red as to seem alive. Still the rest of the map was brown with age, other lines on it much faded. Gwennan had to peer very closely to make out a few landmarks she recognized. This was certainly a section of the valley—but one which showed nothing of dwellings and farms with which she was familiar.

"Drawn so," her hostess was continuing. "It intersects with another from the north—"

Yes, there was a second line, again much faded, its color a palish pink.

"And so you see where is their intersection? It lies at the stones—the meadow stones!"

"I never looked to the north." Gwennan dared to put out a finger tip to trace that other, much older, faded line. "These marks—" surely those dots were not age spots but had been set there for a purpose—"they are also stones?"

"At this hill notch there is a triangular rock. It is mounted to point so—" Now it was Lady Lyle's finger which stabbed down at the old map. "It is supported upon three small stones and the balance is correct. Let your experts who talk of glacier deposits make what they can of that!"

"Leys—" Gwennan's interest was caught now. "And where they intersect—"

"Places of added force! Just so. There are such sites—much greater perhaps. Stonehenge is one, Canterbury with all its legends as a sacred place. Even more—Glastonbury. All these mark interceptions of the leys. This one is but a simple conjunction compared to those. The leys are lines of magnetic force—that is already halfway proven —or relearned. Eventually those who have argued this truth for years will be vindicated. Once, we believe, men and women knew how to summon such forces, to harness them. They controlled powers of which men today cannot begin to conceive." Her words came faster and faster, her pale face showed a small flush as if blood gathered there in proof of her earnest belief in what she said. "Lost—" her hand no longer moved across the map, but lay limply, palm down upon its edge. She drew back a little in her chair, her eyes closed, and she breathed quickly, short panting breaths.

Gwennan was on her feet, alarmed, reaching for those limp hands, grasping their chill flesh quickly. It was plain that Lady Lyle was ill. She looked beyond the half-fainting woman to where Tor Lyle had lounged, taking no part in their inspection of the map. Nor did he move now— even when it was so apparent that his kinswoman needed help.

"She is ill! Dr. Hughes should be called!"

The young man shook his head. That smile was back, shadowy about his lips, and his eyes remained half veiled. She longed to shout at him.

When he got to his feet it was not to come to the woman whose labored breathing was now harsh in the room. Rather he went to pull a cord which hung near the huge fireplace. Lady Lyle stirred a little, opened her eyes to look straight into Gwennan's. There was no color in her face, while in the girl's hold her two hands were colder, seemingly more limp. The older woman drew a deeper breath—then another. She smiled, a small ghost of her earlier welcoming smile.

"Did I alarm you, child? This is nothing. When one has lived as long as I, sometimes even a small indulgence in excitement brings its toll. Do not worry—I shall quickly be myself again—"

Gwennan released her hands as one of the dark, silent serving women entered. She placed before her mistress on the table a tray bearing a single cup—one which appeared fashioned from a curved horn, so small that the beast from which it had been taken could not have been larger than a cat. Lady Lyle put forth her hand slowly, picked up the unusual cup and drank its contents. When she put it down empty she sat up with energy, looking fully alive and able again.

3

A wild crack of thunder sounding directly overhead sent Gwennan cowering among the bed
covers. Outside the window a flash of lightning
followed. Then came another sound not unlike an
explosion. That bolt must have struck some tree
not too far away. Again thunder rolled.

Only it was not the fury of the storm which had
awakened her. She had come instantly out of
sleep, as if summoned by a call. Just as it was
more than thunder and lightning for which she
listened—or tried not to listen—now.

She swallowed. A stronger sense of fear than
she had ever known kept her taut and tense.
Fighting against rigid terror, Gwennan was able
at last to move, to sit up in the midst of her tangle
of covering, to reach out to switch on the bed
lamp—fervently thankful when it worked. She
feared that storm damage might have left her in
the dark.

Rain beat against the walls. She sat, shoulders
hunched, still listening, pulling the upper quilt
shawlwise around her. It was very cold. In the

fall she always closed off the upper rooms of the old house, moving into the small downstairs bedroom which shared a wall with the kitchen.

Lightning—another crash of thunder. There was something else—for which she could not find words. Gwennan slipped from the edge of the bed, not pausing to put on her waiting scuffs, padded across the rag carpeting towards the bathroom, her guide the faint glow of the night light there. As she switched on a second lamp, there came another fierce roll of thunder.

Water flowed as she filled the drinking glass, looked at the mirror above the washbasin. Her hair hung in limp, sweaty strands. The flesh of her face looked both puffy and unusually pale. Gwennan drank and wondered if now, when she was so thoroughly awake, it might not be well to heat some milk.

Bad dreams. It must have been the building, the breaking of this storm which had given her the one from which she had so suddenly roused. She could not remember any details now. Only that she had awakened gasping, her nightgown sweat-dampened, her body aching. Her heart still beat fast, and all the rationalizing she tried to summon could not banish the remains of pure terror.

Fear—of what? She had known such storms all her life—though this one was late in the year. Suddenly she gripped the edge of the washbasin, holding to it tightly as an unexpected dizziness struck her. The sensation went as quickly as it had come, but left her weak and unsteady—and more afraid.

"There is nothing wrong—" she told herself, trying to speak calmly. "Just a storm— There is nothing wrong!"

Steadying herself with one hand against the wall, fearful of a return of that strange giddiness, she made her way back to the bedroom. But not to bed. Instead she stood just within the circle of light thrown by the reading lamp, staring about her at all the familiar things which loomed half in, half out of the shadows. There were her clothes laid out on a chair, ready for morning— the book she had nodded herself to sleep over— her small clock, its hands pointing to the hour, just hard on three.

Nothing was out of place, nothing different from what it was every night of the winter season while she used this room. Why should there be? Now she settled herself on the edge of the bed, pulled absently at the covers about her.

Fancies—not to be trusted. She had deliberately allowed too much to stimulate her imagination lately. Gwennan jerked up a pillow to support her back, unable as yet to lie down, having no desire to turn out the lamp. The book— perhaps if she read for awhile—

Only a part of her mind was too alert, had already turned in another direction. She was thinking of the acquaintanceship which had begun so abruptly and in its way altered the stolid round of her existence. Her first visit to Lyle House had not been the last, and each time she went there it was like being drawn deeper into enchantment.

For some reason Lady Lyle had fostered a re-

lationship which surprised Gwennan. What had
the girl to offer in return which would be of any
interest to a woman whose world was so far removed from hers—so utterly alien to everything
Gwennan had ever known?

A village girl of very limited formal education
—one without any claim to easy manners, certainly nothing beyond the very ordinary. It would
appear to anyone that Lady Lyle would consider
her the last person to cultivate. Looking back
now, Gwennan could hardly believe that it had
been only three weeks since she had first walked
into the treasurehouse the Lyles had so long
made their headquarters. She had seen much
there since, marveled at all those grey stone walls
sheltered. Each room she had been invited to
enter had been a new revelation—such as the
library with more ancient maps, older books—
even illuminated parchments which had been
freely unrolled for her to marvel over—volumes
so old that they had been fastened with locks of
rust-pitted iron or tarnished silver. A drawing
room with glass walled cases, chests, cabinets—
holding great and small rarities so crowded together that it was difficult to distinguish one
from the other. She had been fascinated, completely captivated—yes—enchanted in the old
sense of that word.

Though in fact she had never been given much
time to do more than attend to Lady Lyle herself,
her attention claimed fully by her hostess every
time she passed through that fortress-like doorway. She answered questions, was skillfully
drawn out to talk. It was never until she was once

more free of that house that she even realized
how skillfully and fully details of her life had
been confided to Lady Lyle, and how very little of
her hostess she ever learned in return.

There had been questions about her parents—
and for those she had had little straight answers.
Miss Nessa, as Gwennan had early learned, had
possessed very little liking for the man her much
younger sister had married. He was a footloose
wanderer Miss Nessa had insisted in a few rare
outbursts. That he and his wife had died in the far
southwest on their way to some foolish piece of
desert exploration was no more than was to be
expected. She had done her duty in accepting the
child of that misalliance and making very sure
that Gwennan was not encouraged in any ways
which approached such shiftlessness.

From that patchy knowledge of her own origin,
Gwennan had been led, by astute and compelling
conversation, to enlarge on her private interests.
Finding for the first time someone who shared, or
seemed to, her secret and timid attempts to learn
things which no one in the village would understand, Gwennan talked and talked—sometimes,
she was sure afterwards, uncomfortable with a
sense of shame, far too much—being too asser-
tive. It was as if when she was with the mistress
of Lyle House she was being offered a key which
would unlock a door she had long sought.

Luckily, for she still distrusted and disliked
him, Tor Lyle was not there. He had vanished
without any explanation on his kinswoman's part
shortly after Gwennan's first visit. Probably he
had departed on one of those journeys to which

men of his blood were so addicted. Lady Lyle appeared in no way to miss him.

Tor Lyle. Gwennan slid down farther on her pillow support—she knew she had no talent for social graces. Everytime she had met him she had been more and more painfully aware of her failing. Not only that she was physically plain, overgrown, awkward, a nonentity, but he mocked her silently. She was also very sure that he disliked his aunt's continued interest in her. However, it was also plain that Lady Lyle was ruler in that household and only her desires were of importance.

So—well, even if it ended tomorrow and Lady Lyle would be gone also, she had had this much—so much to think about. She was—

Gwennan stiffened, sat tense, one hand going to her mouth, her eyes wide. The storm had blown itself away to a distant muttering now. But the window was still tightly closed. Then how could she hear that—a strange shuffling as if feet never quite lifted from the ground broke into those branches so carefully banked just last week about the foundations of the house as insulation against the winter—the generations-old system the village followed from fall until spring. She turned her head slowly. Fear was with her again —stronger—weakening—flooding her mind, affecting even her body. The window—a square of dim light—

There—

Gwennan could not move, to draw the shallowest of breaths was an effort. She learned then that there is a terror so great that the edges of it mercifully cloud the mind. Maybe she actually blacked out for a moment—she could never afterwards be sure. Slowly she became conscious of her sweating body rigid and chill, her hands gripping the edge of the quilt so tightly that her fingers ached.

Red—red *eyes!* Yes—she was sure of the eyes. The head in which they were set—that remained only a hazy, darkish mass. But those eyes—like the coals of a hearth fire blazing steadily—fastened on *her*. She shivered, her body yielding to the ice of pure terror. Horror—a hatred so raw it was never meant for any human being to front, that—all of that—was in those flame eyes!

This was no dream. Out there in the night hunched something which was not of a normal world. Bears had been reported seen in the woodlands—even a cougar had been sighted last year— This was no animal—it was more—apart from anything she knew—or could sanely believe in.

Gwennan uttered a small sound, close to a moan. The unknown creature was watching her— it must be—she was fully exposed to sight by the light of the lamp. She listened for more crackling of the foundation brush, for the sound of splintering glass as it broke its way in to her. That—that thing was a hater. She had no doubt of that.

How long Gwennan huddled there waiting for attack to follow she did not know. At first she could not even move, the threat of the eyes held her motionless. Then, making the greatest effort she had ever known in her life, she started to crawl down the other side of the bed, as far as she might get from the window. Afraid to try to stand lest her legs buckle under her, she reached one of the bedposts, clung to it.

The telephone—help— She tried to think, as, with a second great surge of effort, she made herself look away from the window. To reach the phone she would have to get across the short hall, into the kitchen which was also, country-fashion, the sitting room.

Gwennan crumpled forward, on hands and knees now. She put all her strength into crawling across the cold floor, winning inches at a time. Then the darkness of the hall enfolded her. She had to heave herself up to claw at the latch of the kitchen door before she could fall through into that other room, still warmed by a well-banked wood fire.

Sobbing for breath, she used the edge of the much worn old sofa as a support, lurched from that to the chair by the small window table. Collapsing into that, her hands shook so she could not at once drag the phone to her. Nor could she at first discipline her fingers to dial— making three vain tries before she managed in the dark the combination which meant an emergency call.

"Sure was somethin' out there all right, Gwen —smashed all those branches under the window flatter'n a wheat cake. No rain did that, and I never heard of no bear comin' this far into town —not in years anyhow." Deputy Hawes leaned against the table while Gwennan poured a second brimming mug of coffee. "Trouble is the ground's

just too hard hereabouts since that last frost—
even after the rain—to show us a good print. Sam
is goin' to bring over the dogs come sunup. What
gets me is that stink—never smelled anything to
match it before. 'Nough to churn a man's insides
crossways, that is. Never heard as bears stunk
like that—worse'n any skunk as got his dander
up. You know, Gwen, t'aint safe maybe you livin'
here all alone. Kinda cut off, too. The Newton
place is a good bit away and there's that there big
hedge between you, cuttin' off a good sight of
your place. You can't even see their house—" He
gestured at the window where the gray light of
morning showed now.

"An' if we've got a bear roamin' around—"

Gwennan pulled her flannel robe tighter about
her throat. She had made a great effort and regained outward control before Ed Hawes had arrived. At least he had not seen her near-reduced
to idiocy as she had been earlier. He was two
years older, but they had ridden together on the
school bus to the high school at the center. Ed
Hawes did not possess much in the way of imagination as she well knew, but perhaps that was a
quality one was better off without in the present
instance.

She had been most careful in her report. The
red eyes—yes—but she had kept quiet about the
abject terror those had awakened in her and the
feeling of utter evil which she had afterwards
recognized as part of that fear. Now she was
thankful that there did remain physical traces of
the prowler and she had not been wrong in
calling for aid against something which was not

— Not what? Gwennan refused to allow herself to follow that train of thought.

"Why would a bear look into a window?" she wondered aloud.

"Well, now, that maybe ain't as queer as you'd think, Gwen. Some bears are curious. I heard of one two summers ago that prowled around a camp up near Scott's woods—gave a tourist a scare when he poked his head in to watch her dress just as calm as you please. Could be it was attracted by your light and just took a look-see. Sam's hounds, they'll pick up its trail— They are smart dogs. Mighty good coffee, Gwen, I'm obliged. Got to call in from the car now. I'll wait around for Sam—gettin' so much lighter now maybe I can see somethin' more myself. That stink—that's what really gets me. Bears maybe ain't rose bushes but they don't never smell *that* bad!"

He went out and Gwennan hurried to her bedroom to dress. With Ed around she was emboldened to go to the window. Yes, the branches beneath it were crushed by something which had weighed a good deal. The terror was gone, leaving behind it a dull anger, a little for her own complete breakdown, and the rest for the thing which had caused it.

Shrugging into her coat and pulling a scarf about her head she went out. The smell! She swallowed hurriedly as she rounded the corner of the house. It was that same disgusting stench she had met once before—on the night she had first visited Lyle House. Had that thing been abroad then? If so, she had been lucky not to meet it!

Though the branches were crushed down there were no marks on the ground except one or two shapeless, scuffed places. And the odor was such she could not make herself go any closer to observe those.

A pickup truck came noisily up the road and she heard the excited barking of the hounds. As it drew to a stop beside the patrol car, Sam Grimes got out, spoke to Ed, and then dropped the back end of the truck and whistled out the three dogs who yapped and milled about, nosing into the drifts of leaves. He slipped on leashes and drew them through the gate towards the house.

He did not get far. The excited yapping changed abruptly, became a howling. While the dogs pulled back, dropped to their haunches, straining away with the same determination as Sam showed in urging them on. He shouted commands and the howling stopped—becoming a whining complaint such as Gwennan had never heard any animal voice before. The hounds dropped belly-low to the ground as Sam continued to jerk at the leashes and pull them inside the fence. Then he could not get them to move at all, and his face was red as he loosed a vocabulary which contained a number of words that were untranslatable as far as Gwennan was concerned.

"You, Pete!" He looped the ends of two of the leashes over the nearest fence pale, and concentrated on the largest and oldest of the three hounds. "Get on your feet! What in Black Hell is the matter with you, boy? Come on!"

A fierce tug brought the hound perhaps a foot

farther on. Then it flung up its head and the howl it gave was so quavering and wild that Gwennan believed some fear had driven the animal mad. Sam looked down to where it crouched belly flat once more and his expression changed from one of exasperated anger to bewilderment.

He went down on one knee and ran his hand gently along the hound's shaking body.

"All right, boy—it's all right! Take it easy, Pete." He looked up from the dog to Ed.

"It sure ain't right—*somethin'* ain't right. I never saw 'em act this way before. Bear—they know bear—and no bear would make old Pete here turn a hair—he'd sniff up a bear trail as quick as he'd scratch him a flea. But—" He raised his head and turned it a little, drew a deep breath before his face screwed up in disgust. "That there stink ain't bear. Ed, I don't know what was around here, but I'm tellin' you straight—that it weren't no bear!"

"What then?" the deputy challenged him. "Just look over there at that window—the branches all smashed down that way. Something stood up there and looked in at Gwen. It was too dark for her to see much—just red eyes, she said, and something black."

For the first time Sam turned his attention to Gwennan. He stared at her for a long moment as if in some puzzlement of his own.

"Looked at her with red eyes," his voice was lower and had lost its earlier indignation. "That don't sound good. It's been a long time—"

"What has?" Ed wanted to know. Sam was old enough to be his father. Mr. Grimes was close to

Miss Nessa's age if she had lived, as Gwennan knew.

"Since the Black Devil came around," Sam returned. "You young folks probably never heard tell of that. Old times it was and people forget—mostly they want to when it's something bad. Happened when my grandpa was a tad hardly big enough to tote in kindlin' the last time there was any trouble. Two—three times this thing came—usually when there was a big storm with plenty of lightning. It scared one woman clean to death. She had a bad heart and it looked through the window at her. Least that's what they say happened—her daughter heard her screech and came runnin' just in time to see her ma fall and somethin' with red eyes drop down outta sight. The menfolks went huntin'—no good tracks—nothin' they could latch onto. But it weren't no bear then and it ain't no bear now. You ain't goin' get any help from my hounds, Ed. An' if you have the sense the Lord gave a goose you ain't goin' round stirrin' up nothin' as is better left alone."

Sam gathered in the leashes and returned his now subdued and silent dogs to the truck, his determination to be gone made plain in every line of his body. Without another word he jumped the dogs into his vehicle and drove away.

Ed Hawes watched him go, apparently speechless in sheer surprise.

"Now—what made him go on that way?" he demanded perhaps more of the world at large than of Gwennan. "I never heard no story of any Black Devil—an' it ain't like Sam to go makin' up such foolishness. I've got to see the sheriff about this,

Gwen. But I'll wait if you want to close up the house—see you wherever you want to go."

Gwennan shook her head. "I don't think it will be back—at least in daytime, Ed. Give me a chance to think about it—"

He looked undecided.

"Don't like to go off an' leave you here alone this way. I'll stop by the Newtons' anyway. This is a mighty lonely place when you come to think about it. Though we ain't never had reason to worry about that before."

"I'm not worried now," she assured him. "I'll be all right, Ed." She looked at her watch. "This is an early day at the library anyway. I'll get my breakfast and go right in there—plenty to do before I open up. But," she hesitated a moment before she continued, "I don't think Sam was making up any story. I'm going to look through some of the old papers and records—perhaps ask around. If the sheriff knows anything, Ed, do tell me."

"Sure thing, Gwen. At least that stink is kinda fadin' out. Too bad if it hangs around your place. Still I sort of hate to leave you alone—"

"Nonsense!" Her old sense of independence was reviving. "I'm fine now. Maybe it was a cougar, Ed. I've heard some of them are pretty large and a cat's eyes do shine at night."

He shook his head. "That ain't no cat smell either. I'm gettin' the sheriff out here as soon as I can. He had to go to Haversville last night—be back this morning, he thought."

As she watched Ed drive away she wondered if she had been too bold for her own good. But the rising wind was blowing away that noisome stench and the morning light was reassuring. The house looked so much as usual as she went toward the kitchen door that she could hardly understand now what had made her so abjectly afraid. Once more she stopped to look at the flattened brush. The scuff-marks she had sighted earlier were now hidden by wind-carried leaves and she doubted if the unknown could ever be trailed. Certainly not by those hounds.

Black Devil—she frowned as she made toast and brought out a jar of blackberry jam. Black Devil—Black Dog—there were myths and legends of such. She had read collections of folktales about things which appeared and disappeared—which had no earthly counterpart yet were seen by sometimes quite reputable witnesses. Just as the UFO reportings piled up to be puzzled over, so there were these other alien manifestations—strange animals—if they *were* animals—which appeared, trailed, sometimes even attacked human beings—only to vanish completely when a hunt for them was systematically organized.

There was that book suggesting such sightings had been discovered in England to occur most often along the ley lines—that mysterious net of magnetic force channels which was suspected to cover most of the world, though only in England had such been seriously charted. The map at Lyle House showed similar lines to encompass the three stones. Animals—monsters—otherworld beings—who slipped through the gateways the force of the leys might open—It was wild—and yet stranger things had been proven true.

Gwennan set down the coffee pot and started for the phone—to call Lady Lyle, eager to share this new possibility. Then, hand on the dial, she paused. It had been so plain lately that the mistress of Lyle House was not well. Her maid had called Gwennan only last night to put off a planned dinner. No, she must not trouble her friend now.

It was apparent that whatever illness had struck at the mistress of Lyle House had, in just the short time Gwennan had known her, developed swiftly and most seriously. She had dared once to ask Lady Lyle if she had seen a doctor and had been quickly assured that her hostess was under treatment—the statement uttered in such a way as to warn her that any further expression of concern was an intrusion.

Friendly as Lady Lyle had been and as pleasant their relationship, Gwennan was well aware that barriers existed—ones she did not dare to try to pass. She was always in awe of the older woman and she felt too gauche and young to presume.

So now she finished breakfast, put the house to rights, and set out for the center of town as the sun arose to full day. It was colder and she wondered how far away was the first snow of the season. Winter closed in hard at times—tightly if a blizzard came. They might not have to be as self-sufficient as the people on farms or along the coastline where the full force of storms hit, but still winter was to be taken seriously.

She had never considered before that Miss Nessa's house was unduly isolated. In fact Gwennan had enjoyed the sense of space about it.

Now—no, she was not going to let herself be inti-
midated by the events of the past night. And, even
if she wanted to move—there were no quarters
available in town. The motel by the highway
closed at the end of the tourist season and there
were no places to board that she knew of. She had
the phone and, if she felt in any way uneasy, she
could go to the Newtons.

Moving briskly against the wind Gwennan
reached the library, unlocked the door and went
to shed her outer wraps. There was a measure of
warmth already. James Quarles kept a good eye
on the furnace. Returning to the large front room
she stood looking out at the center green of the
village. It was then that she saw Mr. Stevens
come from the white house of the southwestern
corner. It was early for him to be on his way to
his office. No, he was not going in that direction
at all—rather he cut across the open heading
straight for the library.

Why here? He was on the board, of course, but
Gwennan could not account for any emergency to
bring him visiting now.

"Saw you on the way in." He spoke without any
formal greeting, quite unlike his usual way.
"Knew you would want to know. She called me
last night—Lady Lyle that is. Seems she has been
taken worse—they want to see her down at the
hospital in the city—then perhaps fly her west to
some big clinic. There's a doctor there she's gone
to before. She said to tell you goodbye. But I'm
afraid," he looked troubled, "she was very weak
when I saw her yesterday—had a number of
things all docketed and ready for me to take care

of. Looked really bad. But she has a lot of confidence in this man she is going to see."

"Did—did she leave an address?" Why had the maid called Gwennan merely to cancel a visit and not Lady Lyle herself to say goodby? Maybe—maybe this was proof that their relationship had never been as she thought, wanted, that they were real friends—or beginning to be so. There was a feeling of emptiness, of loss, which hurt. "I—might write."

"She gave me none for now, no. Said she would be in touch as soon as she could. But she certainly has taken a liking to you, Gwen—first time she ever showed any interest in any one around here. And she made me promise to tell you as soon as possible." He eyed her now, Gwennan thought, as if he were wondering what the mistress of Lyle House could ever have seen in *her*.

Then he nodded. "That's it. I'll let you know when I hear any more. Or she may get in touch with you when she is settled."

"Yes—" Gwennan agreed, though inwardly she was more than a little dubious about that.

4

Gwennan hurriedly washed her hands. There would be a library story hour in twenty minutes, and she had spent far too much time in the storeroom shifting the contents of dusty boxes in which loose papers, magazines, notebooks and pamphlets—time-browned and fast-disintegrating material—had been mingled. What pertinent information she had managed to dig out of this remnant of the town's past was scrawled on a single notebook page.

Sam Grimes' "Black Devil" tale had sent her here to explore the Crowder bequest. Old Mrs. Bertha Crowder had died five years ago, and, as the last of her family, she had willed their collected papers—four boxes full to the brim—to the library. These had arrived during Miss Nessa's last days, to be simply dumped in storage as there had been no time for sorting. Since then Gwennan had forgotten them until now.

The Crowders had, off and on, for several generations acted as town clerks, keeping meticulous records, according to Miss Nessa. Her judgment had been correct. Here Gwennan had uncovered not only the visit of the "Black Devil" Sam had spoken of, but two hints that it had been known before that time within the valley.

Regretfully she had no more time today to burrow. Instead she hurried upstairs. The library building was really the old Pyron house, one of the first built in the town. Some partitions had been removed when it had once served first as the town meeting house, then as a church when the original had burned down in the 1880s. The rooms remaining were now oddly shaped with alcoves and unexpected corners, and in winter the light was limited. So far, in spite of Gwennan's several petitions to the board, there had been no more lamps added.

Before those shadowed corners had only been an annoyance. Now, to her self-disgust, she found herself glancing at them only too often—listening —especially when there were few patrons and she was alone. This afternoon she was even looking forward gratefully to story hour with its inflow of noise and confusion.

Two mothers, looking harassed, brought up the rear of the children's line today, and Miss Graham herself was frowning. She caught Gwennan at the end of the story time and spoke hesitatingly, as if she did not know quite how to express what she deemed herself duty bound to say.

"We won't be coming on the 30th. There are going to be the new school hours starting that week—"

"New hours?"

"Yes. The parents out on Spring Road and Hardwick Trace are objecting to the early morning hours for the bus—especially now when the mornings *are* dark—also they want the children home as soon as possible in the afternoon. They had a meeting with Mr. Adams and decided best to change the schedule. That will curtail a lot of our extra activities this term."

"Yah—we don't want that old devil to get us—" Thaddy Parker came up behind Miss Graham. "My pop says we gotta be in 'fore dark these days. That old devil—he sure chewed up the Haskins's chickens!"

"That is enough!" Miss Graham possessed the now-nearly out-of-date ability to subdue with a look and tone of voice the near unsubduable. Thaddy withdrew quickly.

"It is only a panther, of course," the teacher said. "But the story has grown so you would think that we are being stalked by a whole pack of bloodthirsty tigers. And I cannot deny that the parents have a right to be upset after what happened at the Haskins's."

"What did happen?" Gwennan had been so wrapped in her own research for the past day and a half that suddenly she felt as if she had been completely shut off from news. In the village rumor and news spread so quickly she could not understand how she had missed this.

"Some animal got into their big chicken house —you know they've gone in for egg production this past season—send most of their eggs on to that new frozen dinner place up at Fremont. It was not pretty what happened. I gather from what I heard that most of the fowl were just wantonly torn apart in a most ghastly way. Also the eldest Haskins boy found a deer at the edge of their largest cornfield treated in the same way. I wonder if the creature responsible is not rabid.

"Oddly enough when they tried to put the hounds on the trail they utterly refused to follow it. And now there's all kinds of stories about—concerning some old legend."

"I know—the Black Devil."

"What *did* you see the night of the storm?" Miss Graham eyed her narrowly. Gwennan was not surprised, undoubtedly the story of how she called Ed was now all over town, perhaps even spread throughout the county—helping to feed this uneasiness.

"Not very much—it was so dark, you know. Just something big and black at my window." There was no use in adding her terror at the sighting.

"And with you living alone!" Miss Graham shook her head. "Don't you question the wisdom of doing that now?"

"Not yet." Gwennan summoned a smile. "But I must admit that my phone line is really hot these days—with all the calls I have been having. As for the Devil—I have no chickens to tempt him. I'm sure that you are right—that it is a panther—maybe a sick one. Sooner or later it will be shot and then everything will settle back to normal again."

Only Gwennan could not banish her thoughts so easily. There was too much in this present situation which paralleled not only material in the books she had read (black dogs, devils, fearsome creatures sighted sometimes in the midst of hard electrical storms) but also in the cryptic notes she had taken earlier this day. The memory of the evil which those red eyes had appeared to project was something she could not even try to explain to anyone else—and that vile odor—.

Could such stench accompany any known animals? Was what she had half seen the same thing which had raided the Haskins's farm? The evidence was too like the accounts in books—though she would not have suggested that to any one in town.

As she closed and locked the library door a little later, Gwennan was startled by a figure stepping abruptly out from behind a big stand of now leafless lilac bushes to join her.

"Miss Daggert—"

Gwennan hoped he had not marked her frightened start. "Mr. Lyle. Oh, have you heard from your aunt?" That was the only reason she could guess for his seeking her out.

"Saris? No, I have not heard from her. Were you expecting a message?" His voice sharpened.

"No. But I had heard that she is ill. Naturally I am concerned—"

"Naturally," once more mockery tinged his tone. "I am not a messenger. Rather—perhaps you might consider me a bodyguard. There is a Black Devil abroad, you know. In fact I believe you already had a personal reason to be able to authenticate its existence. And you do have a lonely walk home. One it might not be too safe to take alone."

"It is one I have made twice daily for most of my life," Gwennan returned, unable to keep a tinge of tartness out of that answer. She had no wish to ever admit to Tor Lyle that she had any fears. Though during the last few moments before she left the library she had been recalling too many dark places along that road as well as the relative distances between one house and the next.

"Ah, but that was before the Devil made his entrance. Tell me, Miss Daggert, what theory do you support—that this is a rabid panther on the loose? Or something else—perhaps out of the past?"

She moved on at a faster pace than usual as he fell into step beside her. Short of manufacturing some errand in the village, she had no way of escaping company she did not want and yet could not refuse without appalling rudeness.

"I have no idea what it might be—"

"Now a panther," he continued, "should, I am sure, have left some more identifiable tracks—at least at your house after the rains. Of course, a Devil, not being of our world could proceed without any tangible traces—should it wish to. For example, soon after the first settlers arrived in this valley there was a blacksmith named Haskins (how these family names do linger on) who lost a particularly valued ox to something which literally tore the unfortunate animal into bits. A day or so later he himself was chased in the woodland for some distance by something he was never afterwards able to describe. Mainly because the poor fellow fell into what was described as a fit and ever after wandered in his wits.

"Again—in 1745 a party of French and Indians coming down on a raid were completely routed and one of the Frenchmen killed with the same type of wounds as the ox had shown. His comrades fled, and no one of the enemy ever ventured in this direction again. But the Devil prowled around for several weeks and killed two cows—as well as drove an old woman into nearly the same state of imbecility as Haskins had suffered. Oh, yes, apparently the Devil does make a habit of visiting this section of the country from time to time."

"It sounds as if you have been researching the subject," Gwennan answered. She had her bits and pieces out of the Crowder papers but it would seem that Tor Lyle also had access to information even more complete.

"Oh, we've kept records of the valley ourselves. I think it amused many of the Lyles to write diaries and such. There are a goodly number of them to hand if one wishes to go legend-seeking. How about you, Miss Daggert, would you like to come up to the house and help me delve into the past? I do not know whether we could uncover anything pertaining to the present case—but it might amuse you. Tomorrow is Saturday, and I believe you close the doors of your library at noon. Will you be my guest for lunch and let me show—"

"No." Her refusal was short and pointed. It was not until she made it that she realized how rude that short answer was. Though inwardly she did not want to qualify it, she made herself add:

"Tomorrow is the monthly meeting of the library board. I have a report to present."

"Then on Sunday—" he began in the same lazy, half teasing voice.

"On Sunday there is church, then I am to have dinner with Miss Graham and her mother."

"Which brings us—"

"Mr. Lyle, I am going to be frank. I have no intention of again visiting Lyle House until I am asked by your aunt."

She seemed to have silenced him. Though there was still a shadow of smile about his lips. Then, after a moment which Gwennan was sure he deliberately prolonged to make her feel more uncomfortable, he said:

"You are running, you know, and you have not a single chance of winning. I can show you things which would surprise you—things to change completely this narrow, tight, dull little world of yours. You will begin to learn them sooner or later anyway but it would be better if you accepted me as a guide—decidedly better—and perhaps—safer—"

That uneasiness she always felt when he was near was fast becoming irritation. "I am not interested. I wish you would understand that—I am just—not interested!" She did not have the courage to blurt out that she did not like him, that he made her uncomfortable, and that the less she saw of him the happier she would be.

"But you will be. Thus when the time comes that you understand just what this is all about—well, just let me know."

Gwennan shook her head stubbornly. Since he made no move to leave her in spite of her open antagonism, she strove to find another topic of conversation—one which would not lead back to devils, history, or anything of the sort. There was an air of self-satisfaction in his manner which jarred, made her feel that perhaps she was handling this situation poorly.

"Where did Lady Lyle go—is she in a hospital? I would like to write to her—"

"You will discover, if you do not already suspect, that Saris is a woman of whims. She has a number of places where she has established retreats in the past, when she felt that the world became too dull. Now she is doubtless basking comfortably in one of them."

"But she is ill!" Gwennan protested. Certainly he was not acting as might any concerned relative.

"Saris is well, or ill, or whatever she pleases, when she pleases. My young friend, you must not ever count on Saris' interest lasting. She has always been one to take a sudden liking to a person, play at being friends, and then drop that acquaintance when she becomes bored. And Saris is, I can testify, most easily bored. A plea of illness is always the perfect unanswerable excuse—do you not agree?"

"I saw her—she looked ill," Gwennan repeated, curbing her irritation—and under that the birth of suspicion—could he possibly be right? She had wondered more than once concerning the reason for her acceptance at Lyle House. Had that really been part of a game? No, she refused to believe him.

"Naturally. Saris is also an actress of skill—"

Gwennan stopped short, half swung around to face him. "I do not know what you want—why you are telling me all this. If you believe that I am no longer welcome at Lyle House as far as your aunt is concerned, then why do you urge me to still come? What is behind this—?"

Though that shadowy smile never left his lips she was certain that there was a glint of what might be annoyance, even anger deep in those gem hard eyes. At their first meeting she had seen them appear unnaturally bright, flashing—but this late afternoon they had dulled close to the shadow of winter ice, and, in their own way, they were as cold.

"You wish a moment of truth. Very well—I have been attempting to spare you distress because I—well, I find you interesting. In this dull town very little is. You have another life—a hidden one, I believe—under that prickly coat you cling to. My dear aunt is a person, as I have stated, of sudden enthusiasms especially concerning people. She becomes quickly bored—especially when she has to camp out in this back-of-beyond family tomb. That's what Lyle House really is, you know, a mausoleum of the Lyles, simply a piece of turgid history in which no one can be remotely interested any more. She found you of aid in reducing her boredom. But you are nothing more than that to her—a matter of passing amusement.

"On the other hand, I—"

Gwennan continued to stare at him. "I am not interested. I have said that before, I say it again and maybe this time you will believe it. You have made *your* offer—do you also need a panacea for boredom at present, Mr. Lyle? I have refused it. Now I think that we have nothing more to say to each other. If you will excuse me—"

She would have started on but he flung out an arm as a barrier.

"You can't—" Here was a breakthrough of something which was on the verge of concern, something she felt was entirely strange in their interview.

"I *what?*" Gwennan's irritation could no longer be contained. "Mr. Lyle, I do not in the least understand why you want to continue this conversation. We simply have nothing more to say to each other."

There was no mockery in his expression now. His lids drooped a little so she could not see the full coldness of his eyes. It was almost as if he were thinking swiftly and forcefully that he needed to find words which had meaning—at least to him.

His other hand had raised to near on a level with her eyes. Now a finger of that moved. She felt a flash of sudden giddiness, nearly as sharp as that which had assaulted her when she had won away from the regard of the eyes during the storm. Her anger blazed and she brought up both her mittened hands, palms out, thrusting away the arm he still held to bar her. At the same time there came a sharp pain in her head—almost as if something had burst there, breaking outward, struggling to be free.

Through a mist which had formed to fog her sight for an instant or two, the girl saw another change in his expression. His eyes snapped wide open, blazed that vivid piercing blue. His lips twisted as if he formed words she could not hear.

Gwennan took a quick step to the left. Her hands met his arm again, pushed with some strength. The barrier fell away as if she had delivered a hard blow. Then she was past him, walking swiftly, firm in her pride that she would not run as every instinct in her urged. She even expected any moment to feel his grip fall on her shoulder or arm, holding her to his will.

This confrontation was so far removed from all she had ever known in her life, that, at first, she could hardly accept it had happened. What were his motives—what did he really want of her? It was plain that in some way he desired no close alignment between her and the mistress of Lyle House—yet he appeared to be urging on her some claim of his own.

Gwennan shook her head. There might have been truth in what he had told her. His version made sense when one thought it over. Save that something within her refused to accept a word of it. She could not—did not believe that Lady Lyle had counterfeited illness and left merely to get rid of her—Gwennan Daggert. There would have been no reason for such an elaborate play—there could merely have been no more invitations. Surely the older woman knew that Gwennan was not one to force any acquaintanceship.

At least he had not followed her. Maybe it was all a matter of jealousy—that he wished to come first with his kinswoman. Gwennan could also believe that. Only, if that were the case, why had he made any move towards Gwennan herself— why the invitation so pressed on her to visit Lyle House as *his* invited guest?

She still kept to the quick pace. However, as she went she found herself unduly aware of the many bushes and hedges which seemed to encroach on the road. Lyle's tales—supposedly culled from family history—together with what she had learned (and had also heard this afternoon) were not the sort to encourage lingering in the speedily growing dusk.

Now she had passed the Harris house, and was skirting the wide frontage which belonged to the Newtons. Their lights were on already in the front room, she noted gratefully. Then came the end of the line hedge with its autumn-dried branches still shedding leaves on either side. Beyond was her own front walk. The Daggert house was small and clung to the earth. Its clapboard walls were gray. Miss Nessa had decided long ago that white paint was an extravagance, and in her final years had kept it repainted a dull tone.

The heavy banking of boughs around the foundation was as usual, leaves formed wind moved dunes across walk and yard. There was something new about the house tonight—or maybe she was just eyeing it as she seldom did. Her normal habit was to head for the front door as quickly as possible and not to note the outside much. She had never been a gardener and had little interest in the yard as a place of display for flowers and shrubs in season.

Now to Gwennan the house looked as if it were crouching, threatened, in fear. Shaking her head against such a fancy, she marched firmly up the walk to set key in the lock, put her hand out for the switch of the wall light, and found herself inside in the radiance of that for some reason drawing a deep breath.

A deep breath—

Gwennan tensed. Just as that miasma of evil had spread from the thing which had peered in her window—so here again was a scent—though far less strong. And—not one which suggested evil.

Miss Nessa's one interest outside the shelves of the library had been an intermittent one in herbs, and she had, as long as she had been able to work in the garden, cultivated as many of the culinary or scented ones which would grow in their harsh climate. She had hoarded spices also which had wafted their strong perfumes through the house at times—cloves, cinnamon, allspice. Even the drudgery of canning and pickling had been redeemed in part for Gwennan by those fragrances.

There was a hint of spice in what she detected now. Yet it was not a cooking odor. Nor was it the more delicate scent of potpourri.

She went down the hall slowly, her head up as if she mimicked one of Sam Grimes' hounds— running to earth a scent hitherto unknown. It grew more and more entrancing. Almost it called

—if any odor could be said to appeal to more than one of the human senses.

It did not lead her to the chill front parlor which she seldom entered these days, except dutifully at intervals to dust. She paused by the door to make sure of that. There was the kitchen. She went on into its warm homeliness, again turned on the light and looked about. All was as she had left it in the morning. Faintly scented with the apples in a small table basket—that was all.

What she sought was not here. There remained her bedroom. Gwennan, flinging her outer garments on the kitchen sofa, went sure-footed now in that direction.

The door was shut. Had she not left it open that morning?

Her hand went to the latch which she did not yet raise. Light—faint—but to be seen through the dusk of this part of the hall. It formed a thin line before her feet where the door didn't quite meet the time-warped boards of the floor. It was too faint really to be from the lamp—still it was there.

Gwennan swallowed. Her mouth was dry, yet the palms of her hands were damp. She must—Her hand tightened with determination on the latch, she jerked open the door with more force than she had planned. Nor did she this time reach for the light switch. There was already a wan radiance, glowing, not steady, but pulsating as if timed to the breathing of some creature.

On the sea chest at the foot of the bed rested a ball of what looked to be yellowish crystal—from the heart of which radiated that glow. The ball rested on a carved base about the size of her hand, centering a tray fashioned like a miniature platter or wide dish. From that dish small tails of blueish smoke curled up—to dissipate quickly in the air. Those provided the scent which was thick in this room.

Gwennan advanced one bemused step at a time. It seemed to her that since she had first sighted it the pulsations of the globe had become faster and stronger. Now she felt again that sharp, outward spinning pain above her eyes, so strongly that she fell to her knees, her hands supporting her head, knowing that something was happening to her as she began to shake with a fear of the unknown and of what lay ahead. This was a beginning, only of that fact was she clearly aware.

A haze began to envelope the globe. Whether it was born of the light, or came as a reaction of her own eyes, she could not have said. Gwennan only realized that she was now captive to something she did not understand, as unable to move as if she had been physically bound.

There were things shifting just under the surface of the globe. Shadows came and went—and with a definite purpose—of that Gwennan was convinced. They became clearer—more distinct. For a flash of moment she was sure she glimpsed that statue from the hall of Lyle House —the woman who was also a tree. Save now it was alive—wind tossed the leaf-strung hair, the branch arms were flung high in exultation, as if the dryad welcomed the coming of a storm.

There passed another who strode with purpose. Gwennan thought she saw armor or a gar-

ment which carried a sheen of metal. The tree
woman looped down a branch, her leafed fingers
ran across the traveler's head. She laughed as the
other jerked away—her lips rounding into a circle—puffing out—sending loose leaves whirling.

Both were gone. Instead Gwennan looked upon
a seashore where waves hurled their way landward to spread foam lace upon sand. In those
waves hopped and skipped small dark things
Gwennan never plainly saw but which she believed were neither fish nor wading birds—but
some form of life quite outside her knowledge of
what was normal and right.

Always the smoke curled lazily and she felt
more and more heavy eyed, almost drowsy—and
as if nothing outside the globe had importance.

Once more the scene changed. This time she
recognized the mound. There stood the three
stones, tall, challenging the sky, suggesting a
strength harder than their own rocky surfaces. In
a way they represented—

Door—or anchor? Gwennan's dulled thoughts
caught and lost, caught and lost.

Her hands were resting on the edge of the
chest, one palm down, on either side of the tray-
plate. On the surface of that drifted bits of a blue
gravel—or so the smoke-producing substance
looked to her—and among them was no hint of
coals or flame. The girl breathed slowly, deeply,
in rhythm now with the pulsation of the globe.
There were no longer any figures moving through
that—instead the light appeared to be ebbing,
fading, even as the smoke itself thinned and was
at last gone.

5

The smoke drifted into nothingness, the light dimmed, vanished from the globe. Gwennan raised her hand—a faint hint of warmth lingered against her fingertips. She picked up the tray on which that strange lamp balanced, holding to it firmly as she got to her feet, turned to carry it into the real world of the kitchen.

When her burden rested on the well scrubbed surface of the large table there it did not vanish— it was real enough. A ball of glass or perhaps crystal, perfectly shaped, polished, but now clear and empty. The girl touched it again warily. It shifted a fraction, then rolled from its base to drop into the tray, crunching on what was left of the blue sand-gravel there. Now was revealed what had been lying beneath it. The pedestal on which it had rested was a dark green glistening stone—carved like the curling upward of breaking sea waves—in the midst of which—

Gwennan stared unbelievingly. She had seen it before—many times—as many as she had seen Lady Lyle. That chain of intricate, intermingled and oddly shaped bits of metal had been silver, overcast with a green which caught and held the eye. The pendant itself was of silver—an orb surrounded with horns, full moon—half moon wedded together.

The side which lay uppermost now was not blank as the other she had always seen before. Peering closely Gwennan detected the disc portion patterned by a circling of symbols as might appear on the face of a watch. Save these, glowing green as they now appeared, were not numerals at all. Small as they were they had been so clearly wrought that they were perfectly visible. These were the signs of the zodiac. Also there existed no hands to mark hour and minutes, but from the mid-point of that disc, shone a bar of light apparently within the surface itself—a triangle which touched, with either end, one of those symbols.

How this treasure had come here—or why—Gwennan could not guess. Only somehow she knew that it was hers, that she was meant to take it, as much as if Lady Lyle had openly put it in her hands at their last meeting.

She was reluctant to touch it. This was like standing before a door—if one opened it, would there ensue a vast change in her life? She was certain of that, as if a promise had so accompanied with this treasure. Was she prepared to open the door—step forward—enter—what?

Gwennan dropped into a chair, leaned her elbows on the table surface and supported her chin in her hands, studying what lay there. She had a choice, a fair and open choice. Yet a part of her knew that though she had not taken any action she had already made the choice. She licked her lips, reached out and picked up the pendant. Its chain swung, curled about her wrist as if it so anchored itself to her of its own volition. Across the dial that bar of light moved also, swinging as might the hands of a watch to point new units of time—so touching with new symbols.

On her palm the metal felt warm, like a living thing. Gwennan knew that she could not have put it from her now even if she wished. Instead she straightened out the chain, found the clasp, so that in a moment the pendant rested on her own breast as Lady Lyle had always worn it, the symboled dial hidden, the blank outer silver surface turned to the world.

The girl sat up straighter, shook her head. This was like waking from a bemusing dream. She was a little puzzled. Save that also there was a growing feeling that this was right, that she had done what was best. Best—for whom? That small doubt she pushed away.

Arising she went about the house, inspecting locks on doors and windows as she had done ever since the night of the storm. She came to the front door last of all, using her torch to inspect the lock outside. No marks, no indication that it had been forced. And the only key was in her possession. Then—how—?

Someone had entered. The weight of the pendant she now wore, the globe which still rested on the table when she returned to the kitchen—those were proof, solid uncomfortable truth. Tor Lyle?

Picking up the ball of crystal she set it back on
its wave base. Was this all some elaborate trick
of his devising? Yet the pendant was Lady Lyle's
—not Tor's. And the mistress of Lyle House was
gone.

Those dark, silent servants of hers—had one of
them the skill to invade Gwennan's house without leaving a trace, to bring this gift? Was it
really a gift? Uneasiness fairly stirred in her—
fleeting and swiftly gone.

Gwennan turned to a cupboard, moved canned
goods on the wide lowest shelf to leave space
there enough to store the tray with its crystal.
Pushing back the cans to hide it, she slammed
shut the door, stood breathing a little faster. Perhaps if she hid the pendant, too, her hands moved
towards that and then fell to her sides. No—this
she must keep with her.

If Tor was playing games she must be forewarned. Lady Lyle was the key—Gwennan believed that now if she believed nothing else. Perhaps the incense or smoke had been drugged. Yet
she knew that Lady Lyle had prized this pendant.
If she herself only knew more! Her head was beginning to ache.

Tor's approaching her this evening—wanting
her to go to Lyle House. Her hands balled into
fists, she slammed them down on the table with
near bruising force. She was caught now—tightly
—in something she could not understand. Her
only hope was to keep a sensible rein on her
imagination, to live as she always had. She went
to pry the notebook out of her coat pocket, refusing to glance at her research from the old

documents. No more of this either—no more of anything which had to do with "devils", standing stones—or the people in Lyle House!

Gwennan was ready to stuff the notebook into the old stove and drop a match on it, but she could not quite bring herself to do that. Instead she jammed it into the drawer of the desk in the corner next to the lumpy sofa. Then she set about preparing supper, determined to keep her mind firmly on the facts and figures of the report which she must put into final shape tonight.

The dark was already thick outside and she could hear the wind rising. Though it was very late in the year for such a storm, she listened to the distant mutter of thunder. Without being conscious of what she did until she moved, Gwennan kept glancing at the windows. All she could see was the glass reflecting the lighted kitchen. For a moment she wished she had curtains which could be twitched across to cover the whole of those openings on the outside world. But the gingham ones hanging there were not meant to meet so. There was NOTHING outside but the night and the wind, raising clouds of leaves. Nothing!

She ate slowly, one forkful after another, but she found the food tasteless, and her mouth seemed so dry she constantly sipped from the mug of chocolate she had prepared. The food lay heavy in her middle, and she was afraid of one of those bouts of stomach disorder of which she had been so much the victim during the last months of nursing Miss Nessa—when she had always been listening for a voice calling from the other room. Now she listened again, actually, with all her body it seemed, to the wind and to what must be distant thunder. So far there had been no flashes of lightning.

Gwennan washed the few dishes. She had never felt so starkly lonely before. Perhaps if she got a kitten—the Newtons' cat was always producing litters. She had thought vaguely before of asking for one. Miss Nessa had never welcomed pets which, she had stated firmly, were far more trouble than they were worth. But to have something alive beside her in this house now would be comforting.

Comforting? What *was* the matter with her? She had never needed anyone before. Miss Nessa had been a duty, never a companion. Gwennan had learned long ago to live inside herself, needing, as she had so often thought rather smugly, no outsider to complicate her life, dull as that might appear to others. She had been entirely content.

Resolutely she got out her papers, laid them on the table, began with a trace of frown to concentrate. To deal with figures was an occupation never easy for her and she had had to train herself rigidly for such a struggle.

The sums scrawled in uneven pyramids as she added, and then subtracted, checked, and rechecked wearily. They were no longer figures— they were solid blocks—towers—fingers of sky-reaching stone! Gwennan gave a little cry, her pen flicking out from between her fingers to roll across the top sheet.

She was looking at the standing stones, first appearing as only sketchy outlines. Then, as if they grew out of the table, they took on substance so she stared at a three dimensional scene—the standing stones on the mound under a night sky. Clouds hung in that sky, still the stones could be clearly seen, for they glowed, pulsated with life, even as had the globe. Gwennan snatched up the top sheet of paper, crumpled it to throw to the floor. On the next piece lying below the stones were again taking shape—

"No!" The girl pushed back from the table. She would not be subjected to this! She was Gwennan Daggert—in her own home. She was herself—she was!

On her feet now she moved to the sofa. Her hands were not obeying her will. Instead they had caught up her coat, were tugging it around her. There was another force in command.

She reached for her scarf and cap—

"No!" She heard her voice echo through the house, hollowly. There was a note in it which frightened her. Was she drugged still—or two people? One Gwennan imprisoned in her own body by another—?

Stiffly, fighting a hopeless inward battle, she put one foot before the other. Frantic to remain where she was, Gwennan left the kitchen, went down the hall. Her hands—those treacherous hands—were now loosing the bolt on the door.

Thunder rolled. She was out in the night while the wind tore the door loose from her last attempt to hold to reality, slammed it shut behind her. There was a swirl of leaves about her. In the distance she did see a flash of lightning though as yet no rain had fallen.

"No—!" Despairingly she still denied what she

was doing. Only there was no escape, no turning back. This was a nightmare in which she was caught and from which no effort of mind could awake her.

That which governed her body was in full control. She did not stumble, but walked swiftly and then broke into a trot. Into the lane—yes, she knew where she was going—to the standing stones!

Her panic was worse than any physical pain—it filled her, made her want to scream, to throw herself to the ground, to snatch for a hold on every bush and tree she passed. Yet she could do nothing but go ahead, answering this compulsion. She began to believe that, even though she might not save herself now, she must conserve any energy remaining to her for a last effort if a chance were given her to fight back.

A wall stretched before her, marking the boundary of the Lyle land. Gwennan scrambled over, knocking her knee painfully. Here was the edge of the wood. The wood—no, not in there! Yes, she would go to the stones, she argued with what compelled her, but not through the wood!

Apparently that small victory she was allowed. For she did not rush headlong under the trees but was permitted to skirt that growth into the open meadow.

As in that scene which had come to her in the kitchen the stones were luminous in the night. They gave off a grey-white glow, while from the crest of the tallest spun a thin streamer pointing skyward as the lighted wick of a candle might stand, unmoved by the wind which buffeted Gwennan herself.

On the girl came to the foot of the mound.
Along the sides of the tallest stone were now
visible those symbols which she had heretofore
seen only as faint lines. These were harshly
strong, dark against the light. Also they appeared
to move, although when she stared straight at any
one it was fixed, solid. Then that above and below
the one she so watched flowed and surged. Step
by step she began to climb to the three rocks.

There was warmth against her breast.

The pendant! She had forgotten the pendant.
There flashed into her mind a sharp picture of
that dial with its ray of light, light which moved
again, touching first this and then that of the
symbols. As if it were busily weaving a pattern—
building a force. In her warmth grew, the panic
shriveled away. She was strengthened, encouraged.

Gwennan reached the twin stones just as there
came a great crack of thunder. The sky itself
might have been riven in two just above her head.
Lightning struck into the wood, releasing a blinding flash which dazzled the eyes for an instant.

She staggered. That had struck something.
There was an echo following. Then she heard, not
another rumble of thunder, but a cry—low yet
carrying—a growl. Movement flowed along the
edge of the wood which hid Lyle House. There
seemed to be a glow, very faint, still discernible.

A torch—Tor? Had he been in wait for her?
Had this compulsion been some trick of his devising? She could not have put into words any firm
belief, still the feeling that he could indeed command something she did not understand grew
stronger in her.

The glow advanced steadily from the underhanging shadow of the trees. It was no torch, rather it outlined some kind of moving figure, one still too dim for her to recognize. The figure itself exuded the light.

Then the wind carried to her the sickening stench she had smelled twice before. Though this certainly was no black monster indistinguishable in the night's gloom. It was alien, however, frighteningly alien.

Gwennan dared not try to retreat from the mound, to attempt to cross the open field behind. This was a hunter. Her knowledge of that came as if it were emitted along with the stench of its body. There was a sense of avid hunger, of also the need to pursue—to cut down—

Gwennan's hand slipped within the front of her coat, caught the pendant as one would desperately clasp a talisman. Such a small defense against that which prowled towards her. She took a step closer to the twin rocks, her shoulders brushed both stones as she edged between them. Though what protection they could afford—

Was it thunder which rent open the world—or another and greater, more tangible power? One Gwennan could not recognize? She was blinded— not by any answering lightning flash, but rather because dark, intense and thick, closed her in— held her. Dark and cold—and a sickening feeling that there existed no stability—that she was being whirled out of all which was right and normal for her kind.

The dark fell away—not being lifted or dispersed evenly, but as if rents slit in a bag, tore

and twisted to give her freedom. There was no
night now. Rather light was all about her. She
crouched on the ground, her shoulders against
solid rock and before her stretched a countryside
—no field or meadow of her own knowing—another place.

She cried out, flinging up one arm to hide her
eyes. What had happened back at the standing
stones she knew? Had she fallen, been injured so
that what she saw now was hallucination? Only it
was unchanging. Instead of any sun there was a
green glow. The watch which she held in her
other hand warmed a little more. There was security somehow in the touch of it—as if the
medallion were an anchor holding her to a point
of precarious safety. She fought a small battle
with her fear and lowered her arm, forcing herself to look about.

Before and below her stretched open land—
though, as she turned her head slowly, first right
and then left—she sighted a dense shadow which
she believed marked a forest, taller, thicker,
more of a barrier than any wood she knew. The
open land possessed a covering of short, thick
vegetation akin to moss. That was broken here
and there by circular patches of what appeared
either to be bare sand of a dull golden color, or
others formed of low-growing, profusely blooming flowers, a grey-white in color.

There was something odd about those patches.
The ones formed of sand appeared, in a way,
wholesome, attractive while the flowers repelled.
Gwennan lifted her head higher to view the sky.
There was no sign of any sun—no source for the

green light. Only when she looked earthward
again, she believed she could detect shimmering
flecks of gold above the sand, wan wisps of
leaden-grey over the flowers.

Nothing moved, there was no wind. The far
reaches where stood the forest, dark walls be-
trayed no trembling leaf, no sway of branch. It
was as if this was a painted landscape, set in
place as one might lower the backdrop of a
theater's stage.

Gwennan had somehow lost all surprise; her
bewilderment was blunted. Holding the pendant
had given her respite from fear. Instead curiosity
began to stir. Though as yet she had no intention
of venturing from her place by the rocks. Now
she slipped her hand along that nearest one, proving by its rough touch that more than one of her
senses testified that she was really here.

No wind—no sound—

Then—breaking the silence as a tap might
shatter a thin panel of glass, there came the trill
of a high-noted horn. Gwennan's head swung
right. Movement at last in that wall of the wood.
From its verge streaked light shapes, skimming
close to the ground. As they came they gave
tongue, belling like hounds hot on the scent of a
quarry they coursed, one which they were fast
running to bay. She could see them cross the
golden sand, but they leapt high to avoid those
patches where grew the flowers. They were no
hounds of earth. Their coats were largely white
but they were marked on feet, tails, and ears with
gold. While their eyes glowed brilliant green—
too large in size to match their long, narrow
heads.

Again the horn sounded. Now, out of the
woods, came, at a steady canter, a huge deer—or
was it a deer? Gwennan could only apply the
terms she knew and that did not quite fit. The
creature was as large as any horse, and its
branched antlers were also golden, as were its
hooves. On its back was a rider, though there was
no saddle nor bridle.

A woman rode so. Her golden hair was fastened
at the nape of her neck, but its long strands blew
forward and about her as if she had brought with
her some tamed breeze of her own as a servant.
She was dressed in breeches of a color both blue
and green, shifting from shade to shade as might
the waves of the sea. A jerkin of the same color
left her arms bare to the shoulders save for broad
wristlets of green-gemmed gold which extended
well up her forearms. One of her hands cradled
the curved horn, and in the other she carried a
short spear of gold, the point of which gave off
flashing light.

As she drew nearer, following the questing
pack of her hounds, her head was held high and
Gwennan could see her features clearly. The girl
shivered. This was not her world—yet there rode
Lady Lyle—or a younger copy of her, the years
banished and strength and beauty fully hers once
more.

The deer came to a halt, but it seemed restive,
moving its feet from side to side, raising its
hooves, to replace them with an impatient stamp,
while the hounds, as they drew level with the
higher spur of ground where Gwennan still knelt
by the stone, appeared to have lost whatever trail
they had been coursing. They scattered, questing

here and there, sniffing warily a goodly distance from each clump of flowers, giving tongue, when near those, to low growls.

None of the pack appeared to notice nor scent Gwennan, for which she was thankful. Nor did the woman look in her direction. Rather she stared at that arm of the wood which lay to the left, as if she expected something or someone to soon emerge from that direction.

There sounded no peal of horn—rather a brazen bellow, harsh, grating on the ear. The hounds pulled together into a pack, fell back to surround the rider and her beast. She slung her horn by its golden cord across her shoulder, took the spear, which looked to Gwennan to be too small and frail to be of much use, in both hands.

The girl stared toward that other strip of woods. Again movement among the outer run of trees. What padded out of that shadow were no clean-limbed hounds. Rather there shambled from concealment under the low branched trees humped figures, shuffling yet covering the ground with deceptive speed. Some stood or moved on two legs as if humanoid, several padded on four paws. All were the misshapen things of men's darkest nightmares. There was a thing with wings and an owl-like head. Yet, though the wings quivered ceaselessly, it did not take to the air—perhaps those wings could not support it there.

Another was a stumbling caricature of a man, its body completely haired. It swung heavy arms which ended in hands equipped with long curved claws. A third ran four-footed. Its forequarters were those of a wolf-like beast, the bare hind legs were human, and it possessed no tail. There were others—all grotesque, twisted. From some Gwennan quickly looked away, feeling a little sick.

They, too, had their master and he was also mounted. A huge reptilian thing slithered in the wake of that pack. Its scaled back was fringed with upstanding plates of bone. Between two of the largest of those a man balanced. His head was also bare, and those tight curls of golden hair were as familiar to Gwennan as the other rider's features had been—he wore Tor's face.

Like the woman, he was dressed in breeches, boots and jerkin, but his were of ashen grey, much akin to the shadowy color of his beast's hide. And he carried, balanced across his thighs, a black rod which lacked any point, yet still must be, Gwennan guessed, a weapon.

The monster band loped or shuffled on, coming to a halt still some distance from the woman and her hounds. Thus the two parties confronted each other. There was no speech, both hounds and monsters were also utterly silent now—though they eyed each other with a hot hatred plain to read in every line of their tense bodies.

Were the two riders communicating in some wordless fashion? Gwennan thought that perhaps they were. This was, without a doubt, the meeting of long-time enemies, yet it seemed they were not about to openly enter into battle.

She shifted her own weight a fraction and—

In her hand the pendant seemed to move, pushing against her palm. Its once-gentle warmth became a blazing coal. She was startled, not only

into a low cry of pain, but into dropping it to swing at the end of its chain. The dialed face was up, the symbols on it afire. She was sure her fingers had been seared—still there were no burn marks on her flesh.

That cry, short and low as it had been, drew the attention of those two below. Their heads turned sharply, their eyes sought her. She felt rather than saw their mutual surprise, for their features remained nearly expressionless. Now the deer and the dragon thing turned, pacing evenly in line but well apart, bringing the riders to her hillock. Gwennan pulled herself up to stand. She could not guess what form of danger she was about to face, but she had pride enough to determine not to meet it on her knees—as if she were some frightened animal pursued to eventual extinction.

Tor—Lady Lyle—she could only see them so in spite of their strange dress and the weird companies they now headed. Their brilliant eyes rested on her and she thought she saw something other than just a faint shade of what might be recognition. It was the lady who spoke first.

"Farfarer—you are welcome for what you bring—"

He who was Tor laughed. "That is the full truth, kinswoman. Only do you think to snare this other to your aid in our battle? I believe you have built too high on far too little. None of the others can now come to your calling—no matter how sweetly rings that horn of yours. Is that not so, outworlder?"

Now he demanded an answer from Gwennan.

"My blood kin here believes that you will serve as a battlemaid in her train. I do not doubt that she has schemed mightily towards that end. But what has our war to do with you? You are one of the others — the short-lived — the unmemoried. Nothing lies in this world for you except—"

He snapped his fingers and the creature with the owl head turned that fully towards the girl, showing red pits of fire where its eyes might rightfully be set.

"Except perhaps a closer meeting with such as this one, my faithful and obedient servant." His voice was low, like the purring of a giant cat, assured of its prey. "You are mortal and the beasts always hunger for rich blood. Is that not so, my followers?"

From the nightmares that had drifted along behind him as he had approached the hillock came grunts, slavering sounds, growls, and a full-throated howl from the wolf-man.

6

Gwennan tried to shape words of protest—even to scream—but she might have been struck dumb. It was that woman who was, and yet was not, Lady Lyle who spoke:

"It is true you have a choice. This is a very old struggle. Yet it is always new born within each of us—and each of you who are of the other blood also. Though you do not understand, feeling perhaps only the lightest touch of it in some dream. You—"

Tor's laughter cut through her speech, drowned it out. One of the beasts (that which was a vile caricature of a man, haired and utterly terrifying to Gwennan) now strode past its master, clawed paws outstretched as if it sought to reach up and pull the girl down.

"You have no choice!" The man denied what the woman had said, crying that out to the girl with arrogant assurance. "You shall join this struggle—whether it is your will or not. There must be some measure of the old blood in you, outworld woman, or you would not have found your way this far. Now that strength one of us can claim to our own purposes!"

The rock held her steady, as if it walled her about. In a way that rough textured stone remained for Gwennan a touch of reality. But it was the pendant which she really clung to, cupped in one hand, the other folded fast over it. The metal pulsed with growing heat. Still she set her teeth and held on as she would cling to a weapon. She did not know how she had come here, and she trusted nothing in this green-lit country. That mounted woman might wear Lady Lyle's face (or rather a youthful semblance of that) but sight of those features carried no reassurance. There was an alien aura about all these lifeforms. Gwennan would willingly ally herself with neither. Now the ape-like monster was at the very foot of the hillock.

Gwennan pressed the watch more firmly. Within her she cried out for escape. Back! Just let her get back where she belonged—into her world where no nightmare would last, and no shaggy beast stump across the land!

And—

As if the very strength of her horror and terror had been enough to turn an unknown key, she once more plunged into that dark—into the place where she had no being, nor any right to travel. There was a whirling within her head, a thrust of pain, striking more at the essence of her identity than her body. Cold—and—pain—then once more light.

Here was not the half sight of a storm-ridden night. Nor did she front the green of that world in

which the hunters rode. Instead rich radiance
shone about her. She blinked, half-blinded—still
so shaken from her journey through the other-
where that it was difficult to understand, to feel
even truly alive.

Herself—who? This present uncertainty of
identity fostered a continuation of the pain which
had struck in the dark. Her thoughts could not be
wholly formed, they were shattered— Who—and
where? Color—masses of color against high
walls. Sound rose and fell—the intoning of a
solemn chant. She knew all this aided one part
of her, drawing together shattered shards of
identity—but into a new pattern. Gwennan, that
other Gwennan, was lost. Realization came as a
forlorn cry from deep within her—a fading cry
for help she could not answer.

She was—Ortha—Seer of the Great Temple.
Did she not sit now on her accustomed place on
the tripod seat of the Seer, before her the murky
surface of the Future Mirror? The waves of color
the Ortha part of her identified easily— Those
were the robes of the Noble Blood permitted to
gather here during a time of Farseeing. She need
only turn her head and before her there would be
the High Thrones, on them the Voice of the Past
and the Future, and the Arm of Purpose, the
Chosen in this generation.

Yes! Her back straightened proudly as the
familiar cadences of the Calling Hymn sent
energy flowing into her, preparing her for what
she must do. Though, she was remembering far
more clearly now, this was not one of the
appointed seeing times—rather an emergency

meeting to which she had been summoned out of Pattern. There was danger and upon her would fall the full responsibility for any warning.

The Mirror—concentrate wholly on the Mirror —push back into the furthest corner of her mind that uneasiness, that feeling that she was another housed in this body—someone very different from Ortha, channel through which the Farseeing might rise and flow.

Under her steady gaze the dusky surface of the mirror changed. First came a clouding, as mist might gather, in its center, spreading outward in rolling waves towards the frame which held the full plate firm. Thicker grew the mist, stronger. Here and there one portion of it began to darken more than the rest.

Those shadow spots deepened, drew into them substance so they were no longer drifting, but stood sharp apart from the veiling which had given them being. She saw people now—small, distinct, if lacking in color—for all the Mirror revealed was not the outward seeming of any person, rather the life force which was the innermost spark.

Behind those sparks of life arose towers and walls—a city. Therein those building cores of spirit went about their affairs, even as did the men and women they represented in life. Swiftly the scene changed, one bit melting into the next. It was as if she were suspended above the rise of walls—those avenues filled with crowds—gazing down upon the far spread of the community from a bird's winging height.

Yet that from which she so arose was a mighty

city—fast shrinking as she watched. From this place all the world was ruled. Its buildings in their splendor spread across leagues to form the mightiest monument the human kind knew. Now all dwindled away swiftly permitting her to see more and more of the land lying beyond its walls.

From where she flew—or floated—Ortha could no longer detect those life sparks. Such were too small, too lost in the wide land. Yet even higher her vision carried her. There was a bright thread of river—flowing to empty into the sea. Tiny splinters coasted on the surface of the waters—ships, the work of men in their pride—tying thus one portion of the world's land to another. Higher still—she could no longer sight the splinters lost in the immensity of the sea.

Then—

Out of the heaven, through which she spun, burst light—a ball so brilliant that it banished the somberness of the mirrored world. The blaze was blinding—yet the eyes by which she viewed it were not so bedazzled that she could not see clearly the horror which it brought.

It fell—that orb of fire, now it was accompanied by an army of lesser flares. Down these plunged, into the sea. As they struck, so the world she looked upon went mad.

Out of the water arose steam, and, following that, the very stuff of the earth itself appeared in ragged, uplifted ridges, spewing forth more fire. While the rest of the water (such as was not boiled away by the fires) rose, to roll towards the shores—mountain-high grew those masses of raging water. She saw the first frantic wave

strike at the land furiously, spitting into tongues
of moving destruction which swept all away—
angry and tormented water against which no
man nor anything of his handiwork might stand.

Inward raged the first of those great waves.
Now Ortha was closer so she could clearly watch
the sea take over and doom a world to destruction. A port city vanished as if it had never been.
Yet the fury of the wave was in no way diminished. Rather it seemed somehow to be fed,
energized by the very destruction it so wrought.
On it went, covering leagues faster than any air-
boat could flee, even with a storm wind behind it.

Now rings of fires showed to the north, burst-
ing forth from the ground even as they had first
arisen from the sea. Raw upthrusts of land
belched forth molten rock and clouds of ash,
tossing that in great masses towards the sky.

The waves washed on. Now she saw the tips of
them loom up and up—and below lay the city
which was like a hill of ants when an unheeding
bootsole came crushing down. The water seemed
to pause for a long instant of agony before it fell,
to leave nothing but the swirling force of it.

She saw towers she had known all her life
topple—among them that tallest one from which
the star readers searched the heavens. There
came a rocking of the land—water—fire— The
wrath of powers which had slept since the forming of the world was being shaken into wakefulness. Man—man could not exist amid such fury.
It was the end of the world which the Mirror was
showing her. She wailed, a thin keening cry.

"Death," she cried with stiff lips. "Death—

that which rides the heavens brings with it death
—by water—by fire, by the torture of the earth
itself. So does death come now upon us!"

She swayed from side to side on her Seer's seat.
Her voice raised into a higher wail:

"There shall be a new moon in our heavens to
move above, hiding that one which is known now
to us. With it comes that which shall fall and kill
—showers of death. Out of the earth shall there
be an answer, raised from grievous wounds, both
fire and poison winds. Against that which comes
even the Power which flows cannot save lives.
There shall be nothing left but the water, fire and
the raw wounds of the earth—"

"You lie!"

The words came cold and clear, cutting
through her terror as a keen-edged knife might
sever a cord. She was so jerked from her Seer's
trance, shaking, sick with what she had seen, also
by the too quick severance of her vision.

Ortha's arms were rigid on either side of her
body, her fingers achingly curled about the edges
of the tripod stool. Only that grip kept her in
place. Now she turned her head to look toward
the High Throne, feeling spittle seep from between her lips and trickle down her chin.

She who was the Voice of the Power leaned forward, her eyes like spear points seeking to impale
Ortha with their hard, gemlike glitter. The blue of
them was ice as they accused.

Now the Voice arose, her perfect body only
lightly veiled by the gold gauze of her robe-of-
presence, the gems of her girdle as hard and cold
as her eyes. Over her shoulders flowed the long

waves of her sun-fair hair, so like unto the gold of her robe that it was hard to tell which was wispy fabric, and which was her natural veil.

"You lie—or else you have been touched by the Dark—" She gave judgment slowly and distinctly.

A murmur rippled among those gathered along the walls.

"It would seem," the Voice continued, "that you do not see the truth, Seer. Thus it is time you be judged and the Power finds elsewhere a new servant."

Ortha shook her head from side to side. That which she had seen still enwrapped her. She could not believe that the truth of her seeing was being questioned. Surely it was known that no Seer could falsify what the Mirror showed. Why should the Voice deny it—and her?

She looked now to the other, who shared the High Throne as the Arm of Purpose. He glanced first at Ortha and then to the Voice, but he made no move, spoke no word. It was the Voice who raised her hand in a small, commanding gesture.

Two came to stand on either side of Ortha. Hands clamped down with cruel strength upon her shoulders, exerting pressure to draw her up. The sacrilege of that profane touch broke through the spell the horror of Full Seeing had laid upon her. No man, be he priest, or guard, had the right to handle a Seer. She felt now the flame of anger rising in her. It was underpriests who were forcing her up and away from her seat— servants of the Arm—still *he* had given no order by word or gesture.

They swung her around now, away from the

Mirror, to fully face her accuser. The Voice continued to stare at her coldly, as if silently daring the girl to raise some protest, to call upon the Power in this, its own place of manifestation.

"You—" Ortha began, but it would seem that the Voice was not going to allow any further word from a Seer she had declared discredited. One of the priests clapped his hand over the girl's lips with force enough to bruise her skin against her teeth.

The Voice turned a little away, looked to those who had Power right, standing uneasy in their ranks, murmuring among themselves.

"This one is clearly forsworn. The heavens have been read for twenty months—there hangs nothing there to trouble us. It may be that the Dark One has found a weakness in our guardianship and so seeks to cause trouble. Or it may be that this one has looked too long. She shall spread no further lies."

The Voice flung wide her arms and now came the manifestation of the Power which was housed in her and used her for its speaking tongue. From the tips of her outstretched fingers arose ribbons of light, weaving out and out. In all colors played that radiance, the green-blue of the sea, the rose-gold of the dawn, the pure white which was always the full Presence. Those rays pulsed into the air, streaming out, to hang above the heads of those present, bringing to them the peace and joy which was the gift of the Power.

In Ortha there was no peace nor joy—only anger and the beginning of a new fear, for she knew that the Power had used her truly, and that

what the Mirror had shown would come to pass—
though the hour of that coming she did not know.
How then could the Voice use the Power to deny
its own truth? This kept Ortha in a state of bewilderment as the two who were now her captors
marched her forth from the hall—those gathered
there falling back as if they feared any close contact with one the Voice had declared to be of the
Dark.

The confusion grew in the Seer as she went. For
she had never before heard of such an act. Her
kind used the mirror and what was seen was
clearly foresight granted by the Power—why then
could it be denied? Nor by custom could the
Voice lie either—for had she not, just after con-
demning Ortha, drawn upon the Power herself?
Such a paradox was something which the Dark
One could well have devised for the bafflement of
the just.

She was hardly aware of where they were taking her, for her bewilderment added to the weariness which always followed a foreseeing. This
time it was not Thrasa, her own attendant who
supported her, nor would there be waiting for her
the cooling, refreshing drink, the long rest on her
own sleeping cushions. Instead she roused from a
half daze sitting on a rough stone niche in a cell
which had been only half carved out of the earth
—the rest of it being a natural cave. She felt
damp, heard the drip of water. Ortha had never
been in this place of Holding for Judgment, but
she could guess that she was indeed a prisoner
until the Voice and the Arm chose to deal with
her.

Leaning back against the chill stone of the wall which she felt keenly through the light tunic she wore, Ortha struggled for a measure of understanding. Go back—go back to that being she had half knowledge of, her sense urged her. See where the roots of the war within the Power truly lay.

The beginning—a memory broke through. She —not the Power—but she herself was two—two now locked in battle, one against the other. All living things knew that the Power was the center of all life, that one was born to hold an infinitesimal spark of it, served it on this tangible world, returned to it, bearing such lessons as one had learned, only after a time to be again reborn. She had touched on other lives of her own during the deep dreaming when she had entered seer training. Some she had been allowed to remember in part because what had been learned therein was important to her present existence.

She had been a fisherman's daughter who had the company of sea animals and had learned to communicate with them in the days when such knowledge was feared. Then she had died upon the harpoon of her own brother when she had broken his nets to let out of captivity one of the friendly creatures who had swam and played with her in the waves, upon whose back she had ridden, filled with the joy of living.

In another life she had been a man who had a talent for the forging of metal and who had chanced upon a secret of tempering that to such hardness that the rulers of nations had come to bargain for what he wrought. And he had been proud of his craft—until a lord so jealous and cunning that he wished to keep such secrets for himself alone had had that secret plucked from the smith's mind and then had slain him.

Only—this memory struggling for freedom now in her was none of those. It had not emerged during seer training, rather it was new born and very vigorous—as if it were no life memory at all but something tied to the here and now.

Because this other identity which she could not recognize might have in it the cause of the trouble, Ortha set herself to welcome it—to allow it to build, setting one fragment against another, hoping to see eventually it as a whole.

Gwennan— Out of those swarming fragments emerged a name—as clearly as if it had been written on the dank air before her. Not of the past —then—when?

Ortha spoke the name aloud, as she might a word of ritual used in control of talent—meant to render memory the clearer. Closing her eyes upon the cell, the dusk, she thought "Gwennan" with all the energy she could summon by her training.

Though she had been taught to be a Seer, she had always been aware of other latent talents. Because of obedience to the demands of her calling she had never tried to explore along those other lines of energy. The Temple of Light was itself erected over a multitudinous crossing of paths of that force which was the natural life blood of the planet. That those arteries centered here had been sensed centuries ago.

Therefore, in this place, the earth's own vibrations were very strong. The Voice and the Arm had been trained to call upon those, tap them for the good of all just as a Seer tapped them in another fashion. Ortha was only a vessel through which Farseeing poured when she faced the Mirror. Never had she attempted to draw upon the Power for her own use.

It was only now in her bewilderment, her sense that something was very wrong with what she had accepted as the very foundation of her world, that she dared this thing. If she sinned, if she were only a fraction from control, then she would be consumed by that which she presumed to use.

Ortha's hands clenched into fists, she willed with her whole mind, all the strength in her slight body, to this task. She set in her mind the scheme of force lines, running like bright gold in the sun —veining the earth to insure that life on it could prosper and survive. Those lines formed a network and there was a center under her—that she must hold in mind.

So—who was Gwennan? What was this other part of her which struggled now for its freedom? And what had it to do with the here and now?

"Gwennan?" she did not repeat that name as an order, no, she called in a low, soft voice as one who coaxed a timid animal, a shy child, to come out of hiding, to make itself visible.

The lines— Feed me! Her prayer was close to a demand because of her driving need.

"Gwennan!" Now it *was* an order—one into which Ortha put the full force of what was rising in her.

She saw—as if her eyes were not closed, but open and fixed upon the Mirror once again. Only now there was no sight of ominous world disaster—rather she viewed a field, a hill, and on that set three stones. There was power in those stones—that which moved within her recognized that. It had been very long since it had been called upon, tended. It was faint, nearly flickering into extinction—no one had used it who knew how to tap and draw.

A woman stood by those stones. The hour was one of night and there were clouds across the sky. But the power in the stones lit her face so Ortha could see her. Only—she had not expected to see that other wearing *her* face! Never before had identification from one life to another followed such a pattern. This must indeed be an undying part of her encased in another shell. Only the stranger was unknowing, stifled, the door to *her* far memory firmly closed. What a spiritual darkness had fallen on her!

Dark—the Dark One! No, there was no evil cloud about this stranger—only a sense of length of time, of ignorance and forgetfulness—as if memory itself had worn away. For this Gwennan who had once been Ortha was not of the past—she stood in the future!

In the future! Ortha drew a deep breath. Had she indeed seen falsely—had she cracked under the continued stress of farseeing? Certainly the world she had watched go down to destruction could have no future. How might there have been any survivors? Mankind was too frail to withstand the horrors of a world tearing itself apart.

Still—there was talent within her, enough to recognize that other who stood by the stones in the night. Even those were not from Ortha's time. She believed them a much cruder way of tapping the lines—perhaps set so by some who had merely a vague memory of what could once be drawn upon. Though, rough and crude as those devices were, they were akin to that which abode here. If the temple she knew had gone as she had watched it, wiped from the face of the earth, what it had housed had not been entirely forgotten.

She strove to push speculation concerning the stones out of her mind, center her full concentration upon the woman—somehow learn from her what had happened between their times of birth/life, and return/death.

Still—she would come to be that Gwennan—in some far time. Therefore—there must be survival. Ortha sighed with regret that her talent was so limited she could not use it to force that other's mind doors. Nor was there anything in what she had learned to solve her own paradox— why she had been branded a false Seer?

However she was aware of a change within herself. That struggle to read the other's identity had, in some manner, altered her. She had been narrowly trained, fitted into a single role to best serve the temple needs. By rights she should never have attempted to step beyond her duties, to go questing. But, because she had done so, now her horizons had been pushed back. She sensed a new rise in her spirit. Of course she was no Voice, she could not control such forces, use the Power as a garment, a tool— Yet she *had* drawn upon it outside her own prescribed pattern and it had answered her.

She was so tired, her body was trembling—she was emptied, weak, as that which she had held within her for moments seeped away—so blood might drain from an unclosed and danger-ous wound. It could be that indeed death was the answer to her audacity—she would be emptied, not only of what she had now drawn in, but also of all else she had had. She would end an empty husk. Such might prove in part the truth of the Voice's denunciation of her.

Be that so—Ortha felt no fear—only disap-pointment. Even that became too wearying to consider. She drifted into a state which was neither sleep nor forgetfulness—only weary un-caring.

Hours might pass in this cell and she would not know it. She was hungry—that required suste-nance which was normally hers as a foreseer had been too long denied. Hunger and thirst—they slowly became pain of body as her weakness increased. Sometimes it seemed she was no longer here, rather that she stood between two tall stones, holding in her hands an object which beat like a heart—and that same beat was all which kept life within her.

She did not even hear the opening of the cell door. The light of a hand lamp roused her. The girl's head turned a fraction where it rested against the wall as she looked to him who carried that. As far as she could tell he had come alone. But this was no warrior priest come to take her to judgment.

He had tossed back the hood of a night cloak, as if he wanted to make very sure that she would see and recognize him. The light caught it in the tight curls on his high held head, turned those into a halo of gold—showing the Power he held in him always.

No priest—this was the Arm himself who had so sought her out. Ortha watched him passively, wondering if her crime (though she was still not aware of the nature of that) was such that he must come to her thus secretly and alone to slay.

And how was she to die? By a bolt of the full force of that fire which he could use at will, even as an untalented man might use a beamer or a knife? Perhaps in an instant more she would be gone—her body ashed into nothingness.

7

He did not break the silence, nor did he threaten by even the raising of a hand. Rather he studied her as if he had a question which he chose not yet to put into words, while in Ortha the first surge of fear ebbed, and there arose a defiance—a determination that he must speak—condemn her without defense as the Voice had done. Nor would he afterward hear her beg for mercy.

The Arm advanced one step and then another, before he smiled, slowly, almost lazily, as if this was nothing more than a meeting on some sunny afternoon in the water gardens where the temple peace lay refreshingly on all.

"So—little sister—" His voice was very low, hardly more than the murmur of a whisper. "You have now discovered that there are truths and truths, some being less palatable and acceptable than others."

Ortha continued stubbornly silent. He was using the terms of a near untrained farspeaker whose vague messages could be turned or twisted to serve as fair answers to several questions at once. Such were not welcome in the temple. They were, or so she had been taught, so lacking in true force of power that much of what they prophesied was as false as the lies which the Dark deliberately used to deceive men. And for him to use such speech here to her—!

"Yes," he nodded as if her thoughts laid open before him. "It is true, little sister, that you have been long sheltered from the world as it is, from men as they are, from even the times now upon us. It is a pity that you were left so ignorant, more that you were allowed to function today without being told the need for concealment, for temporizing—"

Now Ortha did find her voice. "I do not understand you. I looked upon the Mirror—and what I saw therein were not lies. There was death— death of a world—" Shudders ran through her, she was cold with more than the chill of this cell. There was no mistaking true sight, just as she was certain that she had never given the Dark a chance to work through her—no matter what the Voice accused her of doing.

"Yes, you saw the truth." He was not mocking her as she had first believed—no, he was agreeing. But if that was so—then why had the Voice, who shared the supreme power with him, turned so against her? She had delivered a true warning that there was coming peril which no one would escape.

"Oh, but there *is* an escape, little sister." Again he moved even closer. She could smell, through the musty, fungoid scent of this place, the spicy odor of his incensed cloak, the fragrant oils which had been rubbed into his skin.

Ortha shook her head. "I saw. The sea ate the land, the earth opened, and fire boiled from the wounds of that opening. The ground rose and fell, this city itself was wiped away. Who could live through such as that?"

"Those who have been forewarned, who had foreseen, who have prepared," he returned promptly. "The watchers of the sky have suspected for years that there was a chance of that wanderer in space approaching to wrack our system. In the time of Aiden, the first such warning was voiced. Then the secret preparation began—"

"Aiden? But that was more than five lifetimes ago."

"Just so. Our present Moon Lilith came into our sky in just such a way—or so the very ancient records tell us. Now it seems a second far traveler strikes into the heavens we see. With it companies a shower of meteors. Where those fall the earth we know shall be blasted, both land and sea. Now our time grows short. Listen, little sister." He stood directly before her, lifting his hand to cup her chin within his palm. Their eyes met and she felt the impact of the forces gathered in him. Still his power did not flow forth to consume her—it waited. "You have a gift. I have watched you for long, though you were not aware of me."

"I am a Seer. Until this day no one ever denied that mine was not a true seeing," she retorted stubbornly.

"You are the best of your kind," he answered deliberately. "In our records lies the answer—

you have spent other lives in which you also were a Watcher of the Mirror, little sister. And in each such life the power within you grew. Just as one who once worked with his hands to produce beautiful things, shall be born again owning similar skills—heightened because of that earlier knowledge—so does the inner talent grow from incarnation to incarnation.

"Yes, you are now a Seer, but, I believe, one who does not really need the Mirror to which custom has wedded you. You have never been taught to use your full powers. What you may control if you have the proper doors opened will surprise you—and others." He smiled—not at her, Ortha was certain, but at some private thought of his own.

"Why then did the Voice name me liar, a thing of the Dark?" she burst out. "If you, the Arm, know this concerning me—can it be hidden to the Voice?"

"It is not hidden. She would have kept you from the Mirror had she been able. But custom and law ruled against her. Yes, she well knows that you speak the truth—also that you—"

"Then why?" Ortha interrupted.

"Because sometimes the truth can be Dark. What do you think would happen across the world if all now living knew such death was coming?"

Ortha drew a deep breath. For the first time that thought broke through the narrow range of her concentration upon her own plight.

"She tried hard not to have you called to the Mirror—" he was continuing, "but the Coun-

cillors from Vahal insisted as they had the right.
Now we must make it seem that you are mind-
twisted or a creature who has been seduced by
the Dark. Do not mistake that those about the
Voice shall not be ruthless about this. The first
result will be your own death, seemingly brought
about by power you misused. Do you now understand, little sister—you shall be the first to die in
order to hide what they will do—are doing—"

"And what is that?"

"Planning what escape they can—from the
world to be overwhelmed, rent, burnt, even as
you saw. Out of the millions of life forms gathered here, there may be escape for a handful—
perhaps. That is the goal towards which they
work. Publish abroad that the end is coming, yet
a handful may possibly be saved, and you shall
have blood and death and madness. This is what
they are prepared to fight against. So you remain
a Seer who lies, and thus the Voice wins her
battle—or the first skirmish."

"*Her* battle? But surely the Arm and the Voice
cannot be divided?"

His lips tightened. "There have been two ways
of thought for many years now. There is some
merit in what they propose, yes. We cannot save
many of the life sparks on this world. But neither
do all of us accept that the disaster will be as
widespread as it now threatens. If any survive,
then we shall need those who are trained, who
have Talent—such as you. You have strengths
you have never realized. Power is mine by both
heritage and training. But one kind of power
linked with another—who knows what can then

be accomplished? I come to you, for it is only through free will, as you also know, that one talent may be drawn upon by another. I would try this in my own way for survival.

"We had sought through all the knowledge available to us to select places on the planet where the full fury of what is to come shall not rend nor destroy too much. Such a place has been prepared near here. I would have you find me this refuge—"

"Find it?" Ortha was puzzled. "But being who you are you must know of it already."

He frowned. "I do not! I have stood in opposition to certain plans. This handful to be so saved, we are not agreed as to whom should be so selected. In the past toll of Named Days I have discovered that the site I have been led to believe was a refuge is only a counterfeit—that the Voice has won with her pleas for certain modifications of plans. But with such a Seer as you—one who can range time both forward and backward—the real refuge can be discovered. You can go forward—see those who will withdraw there and where they go. Then I and those who stand with me can be among them. It is true that nothing we know at present will continue to exist. So then is it not proper that those who know how to control the Power should transmit their knowledge on to the next age?"

She thought he was speaking the truth as he saw it—that this was a matter of highest importance to him. Also she could understand why he believed her to be the key. But that there was dissension here in the very heart of the Power, was

something so alien, so wrong. Ortha shrank from
that thought, as she would shrink from one of
those staying monsters who emerged from the
Dark when the barriers grew weak along some
line of earth-force.

"Safety," he said winningly, softly. "Not only
for you, little sister, but for others, many others.
Among them those who have great gifts and
talents. Do you not see that if the world goes into
the darkness you saw in the Mirror—there must
continue to abide those to lead survivors when
the tumult and the death are past?"

"But I saw—" Ortha shook her head slowly.
"Surely from what I saw there can be no survivors."

"That is *not* certain." If *he* felt any uncertainty
the Arm did not display any signs of it. Again his
lips tightened while in his eyes smoldered the
flame of his own talent. "There will rise a new
earth, and who are better fitted then to rule than
those who have the summoning of the Power—
can draw upon it with their inborn strength?
There has already been a foreseeing as to that—"

Ortha tensed—a foreseeing other than her own
—here in the temple? Why had she not known?
Her own talent, even if she had not been present
at the Mirror, would have come instantly alive in
answer to any effort by another following the
same path. While the Mirror—who could use the
Mirror save herself? For it was well known that
each Seer became one with her Mirror through
all the length of her days. When she passed beyond, that Mirror shattered of itself—it being her
will which had bound it. Then another virgin one

must be wrought and fitted to the next to occupy the tripod seat.

"Who saw this?" she demanded sharply, aroused from her own misery by the need to know.

The Arm laughed very softly. "*That* touches you, little one? Yes, it is true that no matter how uncertain we may be, how weighed down in spirit, we can be roused by the thought that somewhere there is a rival. No one here spoke—but there is a Seer on the southern continent who has foreseen several times—both for the Voice and for me—secretly. There will be survivors. We are a species which can endure much. There will be some ships able to outrun the storms, even if those in them lose all control and lie at the mercy of sea and wind. There will be some who enter into caves. Thus a handful of our kind shall issue forth once more into a world so strange that madness shall fasten upon many and they will descend until they are more akin to the beasts of the field. Also there will be those of us who shall emerge prepared, knowing, able to stand as men, and once more prove that we can master time, land, sea— Those are the ones who shall rule, little sister. They shall be mightier than any man was ever dared to believe when they venture forth from their refuge.

"You can be among them—as shall I. But only if you will uncover this place now readied to enclose and protect them."

His head jerked suddenly, he looked over his shoulder at the barred door of the cell. All softness was wiped from his face, there was rather a harshness to mouth and jaw, a coldness of eye. He glanced back to Ortha, his hand falling heavy on her hunched shoulder, the fingers clawing painfully through her light robe into the flesh.

"We have but little time—" he did not murmur, rather he hissed that as might a snake prepared to do battle. "You *shall* serve me—I will it. Go!"

Once more he glanced to the door. Then he loosed his hold on her so suddenly that it was almost as if he had hurled her away. She fell back bruisingly against the rock. "You—shall—do—as —I—command—" His words were spaced, uttered with emphasis of one summoning power. Light blazed from his eyes, bored in, to press against her will, her mind—

For a moment he stood so, building his power, ready to beat down any defense she might try to raise. And, Ortha discovered, she did have a defense, frail and wavering as that might be— wavering as might a curtain against the shock of the wind.

"Gwennan—" Had she uttered that strange name aloud, or merely in thought? That other was growing stronger within her—the one which was free of the Arm's world—of familiarity with and fear of his power—one who fought this compulsion, even as she had earlier fought Ortha herself for identity and freedom. From the far future came that one who was different, who knew not the Power, had her own and alien safeguards.

Undoubtedly the Arm could have beaten her in time, but he was to have no time. Once more he listened. Then, with a grimace, he turned swiftly to the door, slipped through it. Ortha heard the

thud of the locking bar falling into place on the other side. She was a prisoner once more. Perhaps she had indeed thrown away her one chance for freedom. Though what the Arm had admitted was too different from all she had been led to believe for her to accept easily.

She wrapped her arms around herself, clutching her shoulders with her hands, leaning a little forward as if she would roll her slight body into a ball.

To the musty odor of the cell something else had been insidiously added—growing stronger in her nostrils with every reluctant breath she drew. The Seer needed no one to tell her what was happening now. Those creatures which haunted the power lines (not in this world but on another plane which touched such a center of energy as this temple), they were here! Monsters, dark things—only twisted minds could command their allegiance—though the Voice, the Arm, a few others could blast them away. She had seen such materialize on occasion during her training. Then there had always stood ready one quick to guard—permitting her to see yet be safe from those terrors which awaited those who were not armed by ritual that used that talent.

The stench grew stronger. Ortha stared fearfully at the door. Her imagination suggested what prowled without. There could even be a number of the creatures. Once within this world, on this plane, they killed, maimed, wrought such vengeance upon her kind as made her sick to remember.

Had she been abandoned, left in this lowest

part of the temple to be their prey, was that to be her punishment? Far better a clean death by the Power! Surely the Voice could not have ordered this!

Ortha could not delude herself any longer, there was a fumbling at the door—even through the bulk of that she could hear. Something seeking prey— Her own fingers now dug into her flesh, as those of the Arm had earlier bitten. Why had he gone and left her to—to this—if she was as important to him as he would have her believe? The creatures from without held no terrors for him.

Vainly the girl tried to remember the ritual—the Words of Sending. She was not attuned to such force directly, but here it was enshrined and she could not believe that this thing from the Dark might break through with impunity.

Unless the death of the world had already begun. Perhaps the lines and pathways of the power were being disrupted, so there was no longer an even flow. It was well known that the creatures were always attracted by the energy of the world, that only a set of rigidly maintained safeguards kept them from, in turn, drawing on that raw power. They sometimes came into being when there were storms and the lightning struck with force—opening for an instant gates—

There came a pounding, a battering at the door. The thing, or things, without had not mastered the simple locking of the bar, but were rather striving to force a way in by brute strength alone. It was true that many of the creatures were near mindless, unless they were ensorcelled by a Dark talent who thus inserted desires and needs within skulls misshapen and totally unlike the human kind.

Ortha fought against her own benumbing fears and the weakness those brought. She drew upon all which she knew—began to recite in a voice, which first wavered and broke each time there sounded a blow at the door, the formula of exorcism. Not for her the easy way of opening her body to the flow of the Power so she could level a hand as might the Voice or the Arm to send from her fingers a bolt of cleansing fire. No, what she could do was little—only strive to enwrap herself within an invisible wall.

How well she was doing that she had no way of knowing. The door shuddered, while the stench continued to gag her with its foulness so that she must breathe in small gasps. She had no chance of holding long, yet her stubborn will kept her fighting.

A crack ran down the surface of the door. Even in this dusk she saw that clearly. Then—there sounded a cry—not from any human throat— rather a howling as some demented wolf might voice when the animal writhed in torment. The stench was overlaid by another—a sharp scent of ozone—as well as a disgusting odor of burning hair and flesh. Once more that howl—cut off in mid-note—as she heard a crackling.

Ortha's own skin tingled, her hair lifted from her head. She twisted in what was not so much pain as an answer to force which struck too near. Once more she heard the lifting of the bar and the door opened.

The Arm? Ortha fully expected to see him again, triumphant from the defeat of an Outer One. But this figure was heavily cloaked, the head hooded, as it slipped silently within, shutting the door quickly, setting shoulders against the barrier as if to add its own body to a defense.

An aura of rising force seeped from the visitor, touched the girl. Only one who had complete command over the Power and had recently used it could project so strongly. Then that hood shrouded head gave an impatient shake and the covering fell away.

First the Arm—now the Voice!

Ortha arose with an effort. She felt as weak as she always did when she came from a prolonged session at the Mirror. Yet she refused to allow her visitor to see her tremble, not as long as she could hold herself erect. She even managed to raise her right hand in salute of reverence to the woman who stood there, breathing fast, harshly, the fatigue of her Power calling still upon her.

"High stands our Mother the Sun," Ortha said. "Blessed be Her Voice. Against the Dark shall the Light come forth to victory."

The Voice inclined her head a fraction. "Blessed be—"

From somewhere Ortha found strength, perhaps it was born of her own sense of outrage and anger—perhaps it belonged rightfully to that Gwennan-to-come.

"Blessed be, oh Voice? That is no greeting for one who walks the path of the Dark. Did you not meet without one whom you must believe was my servant—summoned to loose me from—"

The Voice drew a last panting breath. Her own hand came up before her—not in any salute but rather as if she waved away some buzzing, annoying insect.

"There are times when one must be sacrificed for the good of many." She stood away from the door, moved forward purposefully. "What you foresaw—was indeed the truth."

"And because I saw it I now await the death of a Dark One here—is that the proper award for seeing truth, oh Voice, who is named True Daughter of the Mother, vassal of all Power?" Moments earlier Ortha would never have believed that she could summon from some inner source the ability to answer so, with all the outrage of her spirit.

"What you saw was the death of the world. How many of those listening to you—and those were initiates with training and knowledge, the courage and talent to use it—how many think you even of them could face what you saw and remain firm leaders for these last days? There is a flaw in most of our kind. We still fear death in spite of all our beliefs, our strengths, the signs we have been granted that death is not absolute but only another stage on the road of life. We may know and accept that in our minds, even hold it warm in our hearts, still there is a last fearful portion of us which remains unconvinced—and that portion can be awakened into such fierce life that it will wrest a man's spirit and a woman's talent, twist, eat them up, leaving them mad.

"The Councillors of Vahal have among them one who is Power touched, who speaks with the

Tongue—though she sees not with the Mirror, but has a talent of another kind. She has prophesied much lately. Therefore they came to learn whether she spoke of the past or the future. It was their right to demand a seeing and it could not be refused them. It was hoped by us that so fragmentary was the speech of the Vahalian that they could be satisfied—but there is no way of changing a message of the Mirror."

"Except to vilify me—claim I was Dark-led or broken of mind!" Ortha interrupted. "For that I cannot and will not forgive even one who is the full channel of Power!" Anger filled her at last, all bewilderment burned away. They were indeed playing games, these she had always believed in, had held in high reverence—who she thought never spoke except with the truth (or their own Power would turn on them leaving them sterile and sour). *Her* power had not done that—even though they might have desired it so.

"Why not slay me now with your flame? Or might that arouse questions in others which you cannot answer glibly enough? Do you intend rather to force me into false words—parade me before all who heard to prove me mind-broken, a thing at fault? We have been taught that do we turn the Power to any purpose of our own it shall eat us up. Slay me then, Voice— Or will you suffer for such a deed hereafter— Is that teaching also another lie? What *is* truth now?"

She had fully expected to see some sign of anger on the other's fair face. No one spoke so to the Voice. She was above all the people of the world—even as her Mother the Sun was above

the earth. Yet Ortha dared to accuse her. Instant
death should have been the Seer's portion. Perhaps that final fear, of which the Voice had
spoken, no longer dwelt in her. She had known
death before—she remembered those deaths.
Some had been hard—but the pain and horror of
them had not lasted.

"What has he told you?" The Voice startled her
out of her own thoughts by the quick demand.
Ortha knew that this woman spoke now of the
Arm.

"That," the girl answered deliberately, "there
are places of refuge—one near here—in which a
selected few shall ride out the end of our world—
to come forth again into a new one."

"That is so," the Voice acknowledged in a
monotone. "But it was not to tell you only that
which brought him here."

"No, it was something else—his belief that he
did not share the knowledge of the right place of
safety—that there were two minds about the
needs of those in the future—if there *is* any future
at all."

The Voice pressed both her hands together and
Ortha saw the force of that gesture, yet her
expression did not reveal anything but calm.

"That is also true," she agreed. "It is in the
minds of some of us that the Power is greater
than those who trust in it—that they may use it to
enforce authority in the future. There will survive only a few after the churning of earth and
sea. Many of those will be broken in mind. They
shall, for the very needs of life, force from themselves full memory, wall it away. The Power itself

can well be disrupted, set to flow in other patterns. Those who survive may fear all they once
clung to, they may turn away from all belief.
People shall arise who know nothing of the great-
ness of the past. Perhaps a goodly portion shall
sink to company with beasts, turning to the Dark
eagerly, fleeing from the Light they will believe
failed them.

"Those of us who must carry the burden of full
memory—we shall be the teachers, not the rulers.
We shall not dare move freely, lest they think us
gods above them. We must dwell ever apart,
nursing memory—feeding it bit by bit to any who
have minds which will open enough to admit
precious scraps. There will be a long period of
horror, much sorrow. Some we tutor shall be
hunted down, slain by their own kind, some will
learn and turn to obey their ambitions, strive to
use what they know to enforce over-rule, control
others. There will be many failures, and with
each, a bit of ourselves shall die. Yes, there will
be survivors from out of the Temple—but not
such as shall stride forth to be kings or gods—"

"And this then is the question upon which you
have differed? But what does it matter to me? I
am one disgraced—swept from your path—"

"He came to you—and he is one who would be a
god. He would use your farseeing. He—"

Ortha swayed, not now from any weakness, but
because the floor under her shifted as might the
sand on a river's verge when water washed it
away. She heard a cry so loud that it reached her
even through the thick rock of these walls. The
Voice turned, flung open the door, and ran, drop-

ping her cloak, that she might go the faster, even as a stone thudded from aloft, missing her in that flight by hardly more than a finger's breadth.

8

The cell door stood open. Again the earth moved as Ortha fought to retain her balance. This soon had the end followed her foreseeing? Had the first of the missiles out of space already struck—or had the world, sensing the tumult and death waiting, begun to answer with its own fear some pull from the largest of those wandering visitors?

Yes, the door was open—

Ortha pulled on her reserves of strength and wavered toward that way to her own freedom— her hands out as if she must keep her footing on a narrow bridge which might at any moment give way. She shouldered by the once barred door which swung as if an unseen hand had given it a push.

Another earth tremor brought new falling stones. One struck the girl's shoulder with force enough to wring a cry of pain out of her. Her arm swung limply as she tottered on. There was a maze of corridors down here and she knew none of them. When they had brought her to the

prisoner level she had been too overset with bewilderment to take any heed of how they had
come.

The light bars set into the stone of the walls
were dim, but their current had not failed. Nor
would it as long as the earth lines continued unbroken. At least she was not caught in the dark.
Now she chose a way blindly—for she had no
guide.

The passage curved. Here were other doors,
some also sprung ajar, perhaps by the earth
movements. That shifting continued, each quake
a little stronger, so that once or twice Ortha had
to set her shoulders to the wall, her good arm out-
spread along that, her fingers seeking some ir-
regularity in the stone to which they could cling
for support.

Instinct drove her on—and with it fear— She
would not surrender, allow herself to be trapped
here if she could find any passage out. At last she
came upon a stair and pulled herself from one
step to the next. In all the time since she had left
her cell she had neither seen nor heard another.
She might have been abandoned in these depths.
The quakes subsided for a space—though she
was sure that they might return at any moment.

From above she now heard sounds, cries of
people stricken with mind-rending terror, together with crashes of what could only be falling stones—perhaps even parts of walls. She did
not see now where she went, rather that memory
picture of what the Mirror had foretold. Soon
enough would come that wave—

Her other arm ached, and, if it brushed against

the wall, there followed a thrust of agony strong
enough to bring tears to her eyes, flowing down
her dust-powdered cheeks. If there had ever been
any guards on duty here they had fled at the first
tremors. She took heart from the fact that the
lights remained—therefore the Power still abode.

Thus Ortha climbed from the dungeons of the
temple to an upper hall where she leaned ex-
hausted against the wall, feeling a queer detach-
ment. She might be wandering through some
dream induced by the Mirror, one in which she
had no role save that of an onlooker to play.

Against the far wall lay a body, face down—the
golden yellow of the temple cloak outflung but
not far enough to hide a growing stream of thick
scarlet which curled across once pure white
stone. Leading from that, marked in the same
hideous painting of red were tracks—not of
human feet—but of giant talons, sharp printed
where they first showed by the dead prey,
dwindling then into splotches.

Ortha swallowed the bile which arose in her
throat—then she retched, spewing forth the
meager contents of her stomach, for she had
fasted before the Mirror seeing and had little in
her. That trail made plain that more than one
kind of terror had struck. The earth might be in
uproar—but certain safeguards must have fallen
and those from Outside loosed.

She slipped along the support of the wall, keeping as far as she could from that loathsome set of
tracks. Now she could smell the attacker, that
stench— And she must squeeze past the dead before she could win to the next doorway.

However, she had at last gained corridors which she knew and she turned into that which led to the great hall—to the Mirror. Perhaps from that her talent could pull nourishment. It was her rightful place—perhaps safe—

Safe? Where was there safety to be found now? Yet she saw no more bodies, no one at all. The temple, which had been a small city in itself with a multitude of servants, appeared now deserted. She stumbled on into the Sky Hall.

The golden thrones were vacant, the Mirror—

Ortha cried out and fell to her knees. Her broken arm was afire with pain so sharp that for a moment she could not catch her breath. But what she looked upon was worse than any injury of body. The tripod seat lay on its side, and before that the frame of the Mirror swung back and forth. But the sheen of that surface into which she had so often gazed was gone. All which was left were splinters, shattered dull metal on the floor. The Mirror had been destroyed.

Her heart pounded irregularly as she gasped and tried to form the Words of Departure, of Severance. The Mirror was dead and she—her life was irrevocably bound to it—what remained for her?

It was then that she discovered that what the Voice had said concerning humanity was true, that in her a part still fought for breath, to move, to keep on living. She hauled herself forward, hitching along on her knees, until she could put out her good hand and touch the splintered metal. The edge of one piece pierced a finger, she saw her own blood gather in a full drop to spatter on the floor. It was growing darker—there was a thickening of the clouds overhead. No Mother Sun shone now, still it was not yet night. This was a false darkness drawing in to blanket the death of the world. Then—through that dusk burst an upward fountaining of fire—a distant pillar so vast that its flames lighted the countryside.

Ortha remembered the Mirror vision. Just so had rising mountains of earth broken at their crowns to spew forth the inner fires of the world. One—and now there was another beyond it. A powdery fog settled down about her, bit into her eyes, covered her skin with acrid, stinging ash, clogged her nostrils when she gasped for breath.

Once more she heard screaming from the city beyond. Those there must have gone mad, running to seek shelter where there could be none, hoping for survival. But how could any hope for that when the planet itself died?

She dragged herself away from the shattered Mirror, the symbol of her broken life. How soon would it follow now—that curling wave from the sea—driven forever from the bed once appointed to hold it?

That rumored place of safety—had the Voice reached it? But Ortha doubted if any wisdom of her kind could provide safe refuge. The Voice, the Arm, those they had headed—all were deluded. Ortha laughed as she pulled herself yet farther along. The first step of the throne dais was before her. She mounted that, then the next. The lights on the walls, which had begun to glow after the massing of the clouds, were but sparks—they were falling. So—the Power itself was ebbing. Would it produce some last strong manifestation at the core of those lines crossing which lay below?

Power—she had lived by and for the Power. Her own talent was not enough to control it, she could only call upon it as a source to give birth to the seeing. The Mirror was broken—her talent— dead.

She caught at the arm of the nearest throne, that of the Voice. How often had she stood in the court below during the Hymn of Evening, or that of First Morning Light and watched the Voice, filled with power, weave patterns of blessing over all—filaments of which drifted on, out through the city, making sure that all which was good and right was strengthened, and the Dark held at bay? Ortha got to her feet somehow, half fell, half aimed her body into that seat. She was daring what might remain of the Force, challenging it by doing so. But what did that matter, was she not already dead with her Mirror? Let the Power flame her into nothingness for her boldness, that would be a quicker and better end than to live and see the last horror of all—the rise of that wave above the line of eastern hills.

A third banner of earth fire shot skyward now. The smoke set her to a coughing which tore painfully at her throat and lungs, near blinded her streaming eyes as she wept in torment. She leaned back in the throne and closed those eyes.

The roaring of the earth fires continued steadily. Once more the whole temple rocked. She heard an answering crash of stone. But she

did not look to see if any had fallen near.

"Take me—" she did not realize that she spoke the words until she felt the movement of her lips, for she could not hear through the roar of the earth fires. "Take me now—"

She began slowly to follow the disciplines she had been taught, throwing open her mind as she would have done had she still sat before the Mirror. Opening her eyes, she stared ahead at the swirling dust as if that were some counterfeit of the shining surface she had always known answerable to her talent.

The dust was beginning to form a veil in the air, or so it seemed to her dimmed sight. But what was stronger still, inside her there was rising a new strength which she did not understand. This was not Mirror power—it was rawer, wilder, it pummeled from within against the frailty of her flesh, pressed against the bones which formed her frame, strove to force out parts of her and replace those. She coughed continually from the poisons in the air. Now there was liquid in her mouth which spewed forth as a scarlet lacing through the thick dust. Her head—there was that which had forced its way into her brain—which pushed—pushed— Her eyes were wells of pain.

Ortha's body quivered and shook. She moaned and could not hear her moans. For now the dust flattened out, forming a curtain hung between the dais of the thrones and all else in the world. It was dusky, shadowed—still on it began to move that which was not of its own substance, rather what had been summoned by the new thing in her to display itself.

Again she watched the death of the world, far less clearly than the Mirror had shown it. Nor could she close her eyes—for what she saw came through her and was a part of her.

Death—ever death. Waters which steamed away from flaming islands that arose and sank again. Mountains built themselves up from the land. Forests burnt to ash, rivers dried or changed in their courses as if some great hand plucked up those ribbons of water and whipped them here or there. From the sky above fell the continued bombardment of the lesser wanderers. Then there appeared that master intruder itself lurking—a dead, cratered globe swinging closer and closer to the earth it had come to slay.

There was no sense of time, no day, no night, no hours marked by the ringing of the temple gongs —only dusky death printed on the fog of smoke and ash. While Ortha sat and the Power poured through her to show—

A figure reeled through the curtain—a body wearing only scraps of clothing which had charred away, one who used blackened, twisted fingers to pull itself along. She saw the face turned up to hers, bloodsmeared. Dim memory stirred in her. The Arm—he who had tried to strike a bargain with her to learn a secret which she never knew.

Even as she remembered the secret there came a change of the picture of the smoke curtain. The wide sweep of continued and continuing death rippled—vanished. There grew another vision— that of a stone-walled corridor—ahead a door around which were set bars in a pattern to form symbols on either wall—glowing bars, alive, fresh and strong with Power. She knew that this was the refuge which had been fashioned and which—somewhere—still held safe.

That torn remnant of a man who was the Arm looked up and over his shoulder at the picture on her fog Mirror and then he lunged for her. The wrecks of his hands fell on either side of her body, pinning her fast to the throne. His face was now on a level with hers, and his eyes were as bright with fire as those new mountains beyond the temple.

His lips moved—he might have been shouting —but she could not hear what he said. Did not hear, still she understood. He willed her, would use her, even as she used the Mirror. She was to aid him to reach that place and he would compel her to it.

He was drawing power from her, still that which filled her seemed in very little diminished. More and more his eyes commanded—perhaps he also spoke, uttering some controlling ritual she could not hear. His burned body gleamed, its out-lines now began to fade into the fog through which he had come. He was drawing—command-ing—willing—

More and more tenuous grew his hands. Ortha in turn was losing that strength which had filled her so full. He was trying to accomplish what she would not have believed possible—transport him-self by his will and the energy filtered through her to that place of refuge.

Now he was but a shadow of a man—as worn as an autumn leaf which had lasted too long with a

stubborn hold upon a parent tree branch. Then
he dwindled, fell in upon himself, crumbled as
might a brittle clay figure. He was gone also as
that living, demanding force. Whether he had
reached at the last what he sought, she could not
tell. Nor did the fog curtain show. For that was
aswirl, lacking pictures.

Ortha raised her head a fraction. It would seem
that she was blind now, for there was only a red
haze before her tormented eyes. And she was
alone—utterly alone in a new way. What the Arm
—this throne, the Power had done was accomplished, leaving her drained of all vestige of
talent—a husk emptied of all but the faint spark
of life which would not depart to leave her at
peace. She wept and her tears burnt upon her
cheeks. There was nothing remaining but—

Perhaps it was those tears which cleared her
vision for an instant—of a terror and final agony.
For she saw—the wave was coming—up and up it
reached and then—

She was not overwhelmed by any rush of
water. She was—Ortha—NO! That had been a
dream, a horribly realistic nightmare, perhaps,
but still a dream. Gwennan breathed deeply and
opened her eyes. She was home, of course, safely
home in her own bed, in warmth and sanity—
reality.

Only she saw rocks standing about her.

Gwennan screamed.

Monstrous things crouched at the foot of the
hillock on which she sheltered. There was that
hairy man-shape—also one with an owl's head
and fluttering wings. The latter raised a face

wherein red rimmed pits were the eyes, and that color also marked the opening of a wicked beak— a tooth-edged beak, she noted with added fear. It upheld arms from which the wings appeared to spread, and displaying talons, long, curved, cruel.

In this green light— Green light? It was as if her mind had been shaken again and again by direct, punishing blows. She was not back in the real world—she had returned to that place where the huntress and the hunter feuded. There they were, still watching her as if she had never been away—as if no time had lapsed between the instant when the hunter had loosed his creatures to come at her and this awakening.

Gwennan felt so disoriented that she closed her eyes, opened them again. She had raised her hand to her aching head. Against her cheek the watch-pendant which she held in so unbreakable a grip was warm and somehow soothing. The girl might not understand what had happened to her, but she strove to put Ortha from her firmly, concentrate on what was immediately before her— WHO were before her.

"Farfarer—" that woman who might have been Lady Lyle, who had certainly been the Voice, who might be either friend or enemy, and for whom now Gwennan had little trust, spoke, "you hold the balance." She raised her spear and with it pointed to the pendant.

"The balance," agreed the man. "It must now be tipped—by you—either this way—" a motion of his hand indicated himself and the crew of monsters, "or that." He pointed to the woman.

All the while he smiled as one who expected no

barrier to rise between him and his desires. "My dear kinswoman believes—"

He was interrupted by a single loud yelp from one of the hounds. Gwennan's attention had been so closely engaged by him and his monsters, that she had not witnessed the shifting of the golden-eared pack. They had come between the beds of unwholesome flowers, leaving tracks upon the patches of golden sand, drawing in, to sit in a semi-circle at the foot of the hillock, moving between her own perch and the monsters.

The hunter laughed.

"Would you try such powers then—against me," he asked of the woman. "Is that not just what I have long wanted? Or do you believe that you have already won her to take your side—" He nodded in Gwennan's direction. For the first time since her coming out of that Ortha nightmare she herself spoke:

"I do not know what game you play here—" In her own fears her voice sounded unnaturally loud. The watch pendant she now held cradled directly beneath her chin, the warmth, hot burning heat rising from it, somehow seemed to clear her head, sharpen her thoughts. "I do not know how I came here—or why. But I am friend to neither of you."

She gazed directly at the woman—defiantly. No, she was not going to admit that either of these strangers and this dream—or dreams within dreams—had any hold on her! The pendant—that was what they wanted—that or else her, as long as it answered to her.

Answered to her? The way the Mirror had

answered to Ortha? No—she was not going to think about that. Bury it—bury it deep—keep her mind on what was happening here and now.

"So—" the man made a long drawn out sound of that simple word. "Perhaps you are right, out-worlder. Our games—as you deem them—are not for the faint-hearted. There *is* some purpose to them, I assure you." He clapped his hand to his thigh with a sharp sound.

The owl creature dropped to a half crouch to face the nearest of the hounds. Its beak opened and closed again with a fierce clicking, and it flexed its talons. Behind it the others of that monstrous company edged closer and the green light itself appeared to become more pallid—shading towards grey.

"Your games!" The woman spat. She sat the straighter on her stag and looked to Gwennan.

"You are a farfarer," she said slowly. "Without training and without any foreknowledge to guide you. True enough—how can you judge by the measurements and customs of this world? Very well, think on it now! Think on it—"

She raised the spear and pointed to the hairy humanoid which opened a fang-ringed mouth to snarl back at her.

"There has been an awakening," she continued. "For so long there was only ignorance and forget-fulness—because many of the old race fled, even in their minds, from the terror of the dark days. Some of them sought blood as payment for the aid of false gods. They tore from their own kin the hearts to let that blood flow, believing that this would appease such gods of vengeance as they had imagined out of their terror. They offered their own children to fires in temples, they slew in haste any in whom the true Power kindled and who tried to use that for their good.

"The world cowered in darkness. Power was smothered, slept. Only a handful remembered and sought it—and of those again only a few sought it for the good of all. For one who can summon lightning can also control men with a hard hand. So there was war in the shadows—and sometimes the Dark became very powerful indeed—because of our forgetting—"

"Which," the hunter cut in, his smile gone, the blue of his eyes gem hard, "was because you and your kind willed it so. Had any of you dared to lead during the darkest days there would have been no forgetfulness—"

"No—worse!" She instantly replied. "For the Power itself was then running wild and it could not have been brought under any hand for a good purpose. Rather it would have utterly possessed the one who summoned it, and that one would have lived as a slave to an energy which cared nothing for man. We were left to be guardians, teachers—not rulers and conquerors—"

"For how long?" he challenged. "And to what purpose? Had not the Dark, by our own reckoning, come more nearly the victor because you stayed apart? The lines have mended, they run true again. The Power lies ready for a calling. And the star wheel out of time has also turned. There approaches another period of travail and if we do not use the Power—then this time may be the end for us all."

"Ours the burden, not any victory," she said as one repeating many times an old truth. "We must watch, aid where we can—where it is wise—carry on—"

He shook his head violently. "No, this is the time to come out of hiding, kinswoman! Do you think that the star wheel awaits upon any living thing? It moves on its course and none can stop or slow its turning. Now it rolls into danger and you would burrow once again, and hide, and hope for a dawn which may never come—remaining by choice in a night of nothingness!"

"We do that which is laid upon us."

"Not," he grinned like one of his own monsters, his lips drawing back from his teeth, "I! I did not swear by your oath—remember? You chose that I should not be one of you."

"Even you cannot escape that which lies in your blood, the burden of your birth." She sounded tired, but there was no slumping of her straight back, no change in the keen watch she kept upon him. "The wheel turns, but this time there lies a chance—"

"Even less, I should think, for your purpose," he grinned. "Since this time the change for the world rides upon the will and folly of men, not on the arrival of any wanderer out of space blundering into our skies. And men, while they may be shaped, are all flawed from their birth. They are no sure tools, but turn easily this way and that, even when you believe you have firm grip upon them. Men—only the full use of Power can hold *them*. Have I not said so from the beginning?"

"So—to prove your power you must send such

as these to do your will in the world." There was a shadow of contempt on her face as she once more used the spear to point to the monsters. "Drawing them through to bewilder, frighten, threaten—"

"To amaze also," he added swiftly, "divide, confuse—constrain—even dispose so of some opponent. Oh, there are many uses for my army. A sighting made by a person of influence and reported can discredit at a time when that person's words are most needed. Even an army might be broken should certain of my pets appear among their ranks, freed to do as they wish. While those reporting such an attack would be considered mad and removed from their posts—to further serve my purposes. Men closed their minds to some things long ago. They do not even believe that our time ever existed. They have built up their own legends which are universally accepted —they speak learnedly of ice ages, of men who were once haired and ignorant beasts—like these pets of mine—carrying stones for weapons. They treat the few remains which are left from our days of glory as frauds, and hide them as soon as they can when they are found. Do you deny that this is not so? And part of this hiding of the past is of your doing—so accept the consequences of it.

"I can go to war and make my pawns believe themselves mad, I can rebuild such a world as I wish and perhaps defeat your end of time in another way. But it will be *my* way and to my plan. I do not lie under any oath to see that different. You have called this one—" he gestured to

Gwennan. "Her I once knew, her I used—to such purpose that her own talent grew—a talent which might have led her to a higher plane. But it was burnt out of her and lost because she accepted your teachings. You call upon her because there still moves in her the older blood—an ability to answer—you call upon her—"

"Because," the woman said, and there was a note in her voice which appeared to strike him silent, "the stars have ordained it. Once more they have moved into the places where this one bears again the birthright of their giving, even as she did when you used her. There will come a new reckoning, and she is once more within the circle of Power—even though she does not know it and you have not believed such could be so. She is no weapon, no tool—but shall move freely along the path which that other one would have followed had not the wanderer come. For this is a daughter of the stars born at the proper hour for fulfillment and this time there will be no death from space to deny her her true destiny."

He had lost his mocking, twisted grin now. "You lie!"

"You know that in such matters I cannot. She is the one who was born at the right moment under the proper stars—"

"She will fare no better for that!" He moved his hand. The owl man turned from eyeing the hound. He looked upward and Gwennan knew that he was preparing to spring at her. She crowded back against the stone, the pendant in both hands. At that moment she sent forth what was both a plea for help, and a demand that it be granted her.

9

Gwennan had escaped from one nightmare—surely this must be another. Out—just let her wake and be out of this also! She held the watch pendant tighter, pressed her body against the rock, closed her eyes, centering all her will on the need for waking, for regaining the real world.

Cold—cold whipped in fierce blasts about her, a freezing lash of wind. Then followed a single thrust of fear so deep that it seemed to enter her whole body at one blow. Then she opened her eyes once more.

There was a flash, eye-searingly bright, across the sky, a roll of thunder. Night—clouds—and darkness. She still crouched by stones, between two of them. Flaming mountains—the wave—was she entrapped once more in that world of death?

"Gwennan—"

The thunder rolled into silence. There glowed a light below her—not from earth fire, nor any reflection of the stones. Someone stood there, holding a torch that its gleam might illuminate his own face. For a long moment, so entangled was

155

she in what had happened, the girl could not have named him. Then reality returned.

Tor Lyle—not the Arm—not the hunter—but the man of her own time. Though he had in him both those others. When she stared dazedly down at him it was as if shadows of both of those others came and went, resting on him, fading, appearing again.

"Gwennan—" he called her name a second time. There was no growl from the out of season storm to drown out his voice. Instead, the night had calmed into an odd silence. So quiet it was that the girl felt this man could hear, even from where he now stood, the heavy beating of her own heart. She summoned strength and courage to rise to her feet, though she did not take her eyes from him.

He advanced confidently, as if he believed she expected him to join her, though he came no farther than the foot of the mound. There he halted, the light still turned up at his face.

"You have it—" He spoke in an even tone. They might have parted in good relationship only moments earlier. "Saris made sure of that, didn't she? She—" He shook his head, and smiled. "There was never any trust for me in her. We can hate, we old ones—very bitterly. Have you discovered that much about us yet, Gwennan? No, perhaps it is because in you the old blood has been so diluted—"

The conversation from the green-lit world might have carried on into this one. She did not want to listen. If she had her will she would have thrust her fingers into her ears, but she could not. He would have his way, she found herself unable to escape his voice.

His eyes narrowed a fraction. So clear was his face in the light that she could scan every line of it, believe that never would she be able to forget his features, would instinctively forever know now each reaction or change in his expression.

"So you still do not understand." He was impatient, wearing the mien of one who struggled with a fog of stupidity when time was limited and he had that of importance which she must be brought to believe. "Look upon what you hold then—look with more than just your eyes!"

She obeyed his sharp order, nor could she set her will against his. Gwennan raised the pendant, looked at the dial on which those astrological symbols took the place of hours and minutes, a beam of light the hands. The beam once more moved, also there were other faint filaments of light dividing the dial base—thread fine, still to be seen. Among them stood more symbols she did not recognize. That beam marked time which was not the normal passage of her own world as it swept about, illuminating for an instant first one and then another symbol, imprinting them sharply on her mind. Just as she would never forget Tor Lyle's face, so was Gwennan now convinced she would always remember the sequence of the star time.

"The stars in their courses—" he said. "It takes such time as man can hardly measure for them to make the full circle and return. We are born, we die, we rise again—but there remains always the stars moving in their own stately fashion. When they are aligned aright that which is lost may be regained."

"I don't know what you mean—" Gwennan made her bid for freedom from him and his obscure knowledge.

Tor shrugged. "Perhaps you walk with a closed mind now. But it shall open—" He spoke with determination, a setting of his jaw made her clasp more tightly the watch. It was plain that he had no intention of letting her go until he had from her what he wanted.

"Saris knew—and I know. The old blood cannot be concealed from us who were—are—the Holders of Memory. Now the Power rises—" he threw back his head and laughed, jeeringly. "Ah, how fateful for Saris that her own time had to come upon her just at this crucial moment! Once to her the full choice—this time to me! Perhaps I do have something to thank you for in the past, Gwennan. In spite of yourself you helped me to the refuge. This time—" he threw his arms wide and the beam of his torch flared away from him— raying out across the field to strike at the edge of the wood—"this time I am wholly aware and Saris, being what she is, cannot deny me!"

"I do not know—" Gwennan began for the second time when he interrupted her.

"Do not know!" There was a vicious edge to his voice, his face was hard and closed as once more the torch light held upon it. "Play no games with me! Yes, you are flawed—the Lyle strain in you has been corrupted too many times by interbreeding with lesser blood. Only we two, Saris and I, remain in this generation. I am—" he blinked and his mouth worked as if he tasted bitterness, "I am needful of what you give me—at least for a short space. Some things I can command. The ley lines are near complete again, strong—coursing once more with Power. We have waited here—in this forgotten place for such a length of time as ordinary men cannot begin to conceive—hoping for this very thing—for the coming of the hour when we can call once more upon force and it will answer such summons. But it has taken so long to repair, regrow, heal the ways which were broken, forgotten!"

Ley lines? Yes, so much Gwennan could dimly understand. She fastened on that eagerly, determined to use what small knowledge she had.

"But the leys—they are in Britain—Europe—not mapped here—" Deliberately she repudiated that map Lady Lyle had.

"They form a network across all the world," he returned almost absently, as if, in his mind, he was always busied with another problem. "These stones site mark the crossing of two of great Power, that has strengthened slowly once more into being—just in time—"

The storm had rumbled out, clouds were breaking overhead to reveal a sprinkling of stars. He was silent and Gwennan gathered courage from that. She shrank from the unreal, she must get away from the stones, back to the warmth and safety of her own home. This was not of the world which she knew.

But, even as the girl determined to retreat, he moved a step or so closer to the mound. Now the beam of the torch flashed up, to pin her against the stones where she had sheltered.

"Come! We have much to do—" There was assurance in the order.

"We have nothing to do—together!" She held the watch defiantly against her. "I am going home—"

"You are the one—the key is in your hand. Use it—you must use it!" For the first time he did not sound so confident; rather his words came in a rush as if he must speedily bend her to his will.

"I am myself!" To that belief she held, even as she had held fast in the green-lit world, as Ortha had striven to hold it in that other world which was dying. Now Gwennan must admit that those dreams—somehow, somewhere those dreams had had reality—that she had indeed been elsewhere, elsewhen. However, she was here now, and this was a world which did not acknowledge those other times and places. Therefore he could not so summon her to use that which she did not possess.

It was as if he reached into her mind, knew the defense she strove to raise. Again he laughed.

"Twist and turn, Gwennan, seek as you will to be free. You cannot escape that which has been born a part of you, nor can you flee the future waiting for you. Saris knew—and I agree, now— that you are indeed one of us. Younger in know- ledge, a child among those whom in the past men called 'gods'—as they will again. You will come—you will open—"

Did he sense also that her continued defiance was building? The very stones between which she sheltered fed her the energy she needed to face him down.

"You—will—come—!"

Tor threw back his head, gave a whistling cry painful to her ears. The light of the torch swept away from her, shone full upon the nearest edge of the wood. Out into its beam crept a sinuous body which rose from four feet, when once within the light, to two.

In color it was a dull grey, splotched with patches of black, so that the eyes of those watching it were partially deceived when it moved, unsure of its true form, so well did it seem to blend with the night. As it glided nearer it brought with it that stench which had hung about her home on the night of the storm. Also, as it raised its head, seeking to sight her on the mound above, she saw once again those burning pits of reddish fire.

On its two feet it matched Tor's height and the fact that it could move man-fashion when it desired was somehow as monstrous as its form. Such a beast was a blasphemy.

The lower part of its head formed a muzzle gaping in so wide a jaw that when open it split the skull half apart. Above that was a blot of black covering whatever nose the thing might possess, and around that blot rayed forth a stiff bristle of whiskers standing erect. The same type of long bristly hairs grew above the eyepits and there was very little forehead. Instead the skull sloped swiftly back, deeply furred, with small bare ears tight on either side.

It was narrow-shouldered and very long of

torso, the hind legs ending not in paws but in bird talons, while the fore limbs had the spread of fingered hands. A dark tongue, appearing black even in the full torch light, dangled from between its jaws and dribbled spittle down its narrow chest.

Joining Tor, the thing went into a crouch on the ground, its forepaws doubled into fists which rested against the frost-hardened earth, while its tongue swept back and forth across its nearly lip-less lower jaw. It stared up at the girl with merciless eyes. Gwennan felt sick and weak. Not only did a wave of fear sweep outward from that visible nightmare, but it was so utterly evil, so alien to her species, that the very sight of it was nearly overpowering.

The beam Tor had held on the creature now swept up to once more envelope Gwennan.

"Did I not say that the lines are once more in force? Gates can be opened at a proper summoning and that which abides beyond may so issue forth. Are there not unnumbered dwellings in other times and spaces for even stronger servants than this one? Through centuries men have told tales of devils and monsters only to be jeered at—when they indeed spoke the truth. Just as other men have been swallowed up by the Power and thrown into Outside worlds they did not know.

"Once I offered you the freedom of the Power, the chance to use to the fullest what lay dormant within you. And you would not—until I made you—"

Gwennan managed to control the sickness

which the crouched thing had brought. It was still there—she could mark its burning eyes in the dark. Did he mean to use it as a weapon to force her into obeying him?

"You brought Ortha's death—" Had she said that—or had buried memory?

"Only because I must have what you refused me. There was no time left in which to win you into admitting that I was right." Tor's voice held calm assurance, he must believe that this time he was wholly in control. He had some plan to use her again—how?

"The star wheel turns," now that voice was once more that of the hunter. "We cannot halt its turning—no more than we can stop the stars themselves from their spinning change of pattern —and so manage to alter our destiny. Again the world is about to go down into darkness. However, this time—ah, this time, we do not struggle against forces of nature—rather against the ambitions of men. And what one man can do, so can another alter! Still there must be one to stand forth with the Power—which has been forgotten and discredited—yet it is stronger than any weapon ever known. There shall be no descent into the darkness this time. Rather there shall arise leaders with none of the timid ideas of guardianship to self-limit them in what they must do."

"And such leadership is to be yours?"

"Who better? Once I was forestalled, muzzled, enchained and bound to sterile and self-defeating beliefs of those who deemed they knew best. This time—Ah, this time!" His voice soared like a cry of victory already obtained. "Saris' stars are against her— she brought you out of hiding by her delving, and it is true that you have both the blood and the talent. But you are not strong enough nor knowing enough to rule what must be evoked. And she has had to relinquish her influence over you. They have sometimes also deemed me only half—" he spit forth that last word as if it were filth. "They do not know how I have sought learning—nor what I have learned. Even a half-blood—shut out of their full renewing, is not as short lived as those who fell to the state of beasts and so slowly had to fight their way up again. I have learned much more than Saris credits.

"I would have acted honorably according to the ancient oaths. She cannot deny that I went first to her and told her the truth. However, she turned from me and—" Anger which was no less because it was rigidly controlled harshened his voice, "she would have dealt harshly with me had not the change come upon her too soon for her plans. So—she turned to you—who are even less than you were as Ortha of the Mirror. There are only small remnants of the Power in you. Still that can grow and you can live as no half-blood has done in past time. I offer you a choice—come and join me willingly and you can share. More than you think any person can encompass shall be yours. Stand aside again as you tried to do before and you shall take not only your body into death, but you shall cripple your inner essence which should be turned to light and glory. There is such a war before us now as the world has never known—not even in legends. Though in the far past there were those who, after the great Death, dared to harness weapons they did not understand and, in their madness, again ripped this earth deeper and wider, leaving wounds near past healing.

"That war was fought in the same ignorance as will be the one awaiting us now. Men play with tools they cannot begin to know. But they can be defeated—by using their own fears, their own uncertainties, their very natures. What shall emerge will be a new age in which the Power is supreme and there shall be peace!"

"A peace such as you want?"

"My peace, yes. Can you say that that will be worse than what comes if man is left to himself?"

"Yet your army is such as that—" Gwennan flung out one arm in the general direction of the misshapen thing awaiting his command.

"Man is easiest ruled by fear. If my comrades-in-arms can induce fear as a force of arms—then am I not solving the problem well?"

"These also kill." Gwennan remembered what she had heard in town. "They stink, too, of the Dark—of evil—"

"Evil—Dark—" his old mockery returned. "Words. It is the nature of man to instinctively fear and hate what he cannot understand, that which is alien in shape, or different in mind. I have lived with such fear also, as a threat against me. Yes, my Outworlders slay—for that is their nature, and if they are long tied to this plane they must eat. They live on life forces which must be torn from a living body. Do you hold in horror the cat who kills the mouse—the man who relishes fowl or meat on his table? Look upon your own customs before you question those of these. For in their own time and place they have their rights."

"Words—" Gwennan repeated his own scoffing comment. She was feeling a new strength. Did it come from the watch which had been Saris' gift? Or had it more to do with—she glanced at the dial (the secondary threads of lines showing there were brighter, the symbols they divided one from the other winked as might gems) had it to do with what she herself had passed through—a change inside her she could not grasp. Gwennan felt that new energy. Perhaps, in spite of all his confidence, Tor could not compel her to his will now.

"Words—" the girl said a second time. She stood erect, though her back was set to one of the stones, her hand heart high and close to her breast so that the warmth of the watch reached inward even through her layer of clothing. Had she indeed heard then the far distant ring of a horn?

She did not want to deal with the huntress either, even if the Power of that one could reach across from planes of other worlds. She would be tool for neither!

The girl put out her right hand, laying the bare palm of it against the tallest stone. Almost she jerked away. There had surged into her at the touch, such a thrust of energy as had worked upon Ortha who had dared in the last moments of life to ascend the throne of the Voice. Save that this did not work from within, striving to burst through her flesh and bones, break her because

she could not control it. Rather it entered, to fill a
void opened to it. She was drinking as might one
long athirst drink from a newly found spring.

At that moment Gwennan was no longer aware
of Tor—or the thing which squatted at his feet—
of anything except that feeding—that exultation.
Then—

There came a blast—wind, lightning, a thunder-
bolt from a sky which had begun to clear. She
heard a cry rising to scream, demanding, summoning, such as might be uttered by one in the
forefront of a battle demanding new support. And
that cry was not hers. No, instead her own lips
were shaping other sounds—words—but in no
language which she knew. There was a cadence to
them, like the formula of some ritual utterance.

Gwennan was blinded by the whip of lightning.
Or *was* that skyborn lightning? Did it rather rise
from the earth? Something dark, a black blot of
foul lack of light showed beyond that flash, flung
itself through the air at her. The gleam of the
stones grew brighter, and she was singing, holding Saris' gift to her heart.

Other shapes arose, drew in, to storm the
mound. She could sense that, even if she could
not distinguish them clearly. Nor did she turn her
head to see what might crawl upon her from behind—she must not think of that. This was a
struggle of will against will. Tor had perhaps
awakened more than he realized. Still she felt the
pressure of his concentrated attack, his need to
subdue her.

Gwennan's skin tingled, that which was feeding
into her was making subtle alterations. She

needed time to discover, to explore. Saris—Tor—neither of them mattered. This was a new kind of life—it was—

DARK!

The complete absence of light was an instant of cold, terrible twitching fear. Gwennan was alone, cut off from her source of warmth and life which had so bountifully filled her a breath earlier— She was lost—lost—

Back? Was she being flung back into the dead world of Ortha's struggle? It seemed to her that she breathed again the poisonous dust, knew that ashes choked her lungs. And she could not see! Had she returned to that moment when the wave overhung the temple, about to drown it and her utterly?

No! There was that within her now which could send her back—must send her back! The stones—those stones which were candles of light, pillars of awakened Power. Gwennan fastened her mind upon the stones, fought to see them through the blinding dark, to feel beneath her fingers once again that rough surface which had come alive at her touch.

A wheel—no, it was the dial of the watch! That hung before her in the air, the lines of light on it growing ever sharper, the symbols clearer. So had it once been—and then—so it was again!

She stared at that dial. It was no longer cupped in her hand. Rather it filled a large space before her. The symbols shone with gold brilliance. That band of light which marked the passing of time moved, touching one and then another. It whirled as if time itself speeded forward—was the plaything of unknown energy. Now it was a blur, moving so fast it hid in the haze the symbols it slid across. She felt a beat which was not that of her own heart. Rather it moved another part of her—which was not of her physical body at all.

Now the dial was huge. It was taking over the world—there was nothing but that—

She could see nothing but a ball of light with streamers floating out to weave about her.

Warmth—light—

Gwennan moved — her hand touched rough surface. She was on her knees, leaning forward a little, one hand braced against the tallest stone. The sunshine of early morning lay across the frost rimmed grass of the meadow. There was the edging of trees which marked the wood—the grey line of Lyle House roof.

Tor—?

No one stood at the foot of the mound. No sign of the master nor of the monster he had summoned. She looked down at the watch. It was—

The dial had changed. It was only now the circle of zodiac figures, the single bar of light. It was dead—or sleeping. Gwennan sensed a quality lost. Slowly, tentatively, she tried to reach inside herself. There were no words to describe what she was attempting. What *did* lie newly awakened within her?

She touched something—instantly recoiled. No! She was not prepared, not yet ready for that. Even after her confrontation with Tor she was not ready. Something had been too greatly strained, was sore as from a deep wound, and it had flinched under her slight probe. She must wait and see—wait and see—

Gwennan got to her feet. The stones appeared as they had always done—only rough pillars of rock. She touched the tallest again, held her hand against it for a long moment—but she dared not will any response. That warning—that flinch from impending struggle and pain— Not yet—not yet!

Staggering, for her body was cramped with cold and she felt worn out, she stumbled down towards the place where Tor, in his pride and strength, had stood. The frosty grass held no prints. Had he ever been there at all? Had—yes! She knew that from a stir within her as she stood near where she had seen him last—a stir she did not want to deal with.

Tracks! Gwennan stopped short. There was a blackened spot—a second—a third— They led across the meadow towards the trees. She caught a faint whiff of the stench. That ground had been burnt, the grass charred away, to bare scorched earth. While on that blackened earth there were unmistakable prints—sign of talons deeply set as if a blazing iron had been used to mark the coming and going of a creature who had no place in the sane world at all.

From the woods that line came. She had been wrong—there was no returning trail after all. Rather the night sulker might have vanished into nothingness at the very spot where she had seen it crouching to wait upon Tor's will. Had it retreated to its own place? And what of Tor? The girl stood gazing at the roof of Lyle House. Did he claim that now for his own? If he had what did the future hold for the two of them? That he had been completely defeated she did not believe.

Gwennan hunched a shoulder as she turned away. Far more than she could understand struggled within her. She must have time—and a chance to relax in the everyday world. For it was in this world, of that she was now sure, that Tor must finally be faced and the last decision made.

10

The sun was well up, though its limited warmth had not melted the pattern of the frost. Gwennan pulled her scarf closer about her throat. She wanted nothing but to get back to the warmth of her home—to find there the real world which she had known all her life. Too much had happened—those dreams, encounters, whatever they might be—had left her both wearied and dazed.

As she went she was careful to angle away from those blackened tracks, and she kept as far as she could from the edge of the wood. There were no birds, no sounds, except the thud of her own boots.

Now it became a matter of setting one foot before the other, using her dulled determination to reach the wall, cross that into the lane. No car passed her—she walked numbly through an utterly silent world—nor were there any tracks here.

When she sighted the curl of smoke from the Newton place, she gave a small gasp of relief. That single trail of vapor was an affirmation of reality. She stumbled as quickly as she could towards her own door—only to halt, her mittened hands to her mouth—staring at the walk before her, open lawn on either side.

Black—dead black—as if someone had taken ebony hued paint and, with great deliberation and skill, set out to make a foul trail. The same burnt signature left by the monster she had seen on the land near the standing stones was here. So plain she half expected to see a curl of steam arise from the tracks. Gwennan thought to pick up the familiar stench. But that had not apparently lingered—thus the sulking menace had not been here recently as these stark marks would suggest.

Gwennan did not head for the front door, rather she turned to trace the prints. The splotched marks encircled the whole of the house bringing her again to the front where they ended abruptly. That creature who had prowled here, in threat or warning, might have stepped out of nothingness, then returned again. For beyond that circle of prints there was none marking arrival nor departure. Only this was left to prove what had passed on sentry duty around her own hope of safety.

The girl took a deliberate step forward, crossed that line with fastidious care so that her own booted feet did not touch any print. Only tracks they might be—but still she wanted no close contact with even so little left by that alien being.

Her key—now she could not remember how she had left the house last night. Had she even locked the door? Gwennan hesitated on the worn doorstep studying the thick boards of the door itself. Those had been put together in the old protective pattern—the double cross as a charm against evil, a ward against what might prowl the night. Fragments of which she could no longer be sure, garnered from her own reading (or had they appeared in her mind during her experiences by the stones?) were a jumble in her thoughts. She looked higher—to the frame of the door. There was set that dark painted curve of iron—a horseshoe with ends carefully up to hold luck within the house—the cold iron which, by tradition, was so potent a weapon against the unseen.

For the first time Gwennan noted markings flanking that country symbol of good luck. There were certainly faint indentations in the ancient, weather worn wood of the beam to which the horseshoe had been fastened. So greatly eroded were they that it was like the tracings on the standing stones so that only light striking at a certain angle brought them to notice at all.

She shucked a mitten, lifted her hand to try to trace the inequalities of the wood, to assure herself that her eyes were not deceiving her.

They—

Gwennan dropped her hand and retreated a step, her eyes wide.

She had not used any torch to illuminate that piece of centuries-old wood. Yet now, as if the very approach of her fingers had the power to summon them, the markings glittered into life. Only so for an instant or two, then they faded once more into the grey. In fact there was a dulling cast across the house, the yard, for a cloud had crossed the sun. And with that came a chilling blast of wind.

Still she had seen—a face—a strange face from the mouth of which issued two curls of vines to encircle the head. And the second symbol was one she had long known—an ankh—that looped cross which the ancients considered the key to life eternal. Who had carved such potent signs here? That vine-wreathed face—her memory presented her with an illustration made of carvings from a very old church overseas. The Green Man! He who commanded potent forest rites—

Slowly Gwennan stepped forward. Had she really seen those? Now the wood appeared utterly bare. Perhaps her experience of the night had given her once tightly reined imagination too great freedom.

She plunged at the door and found it indeed unlocked—passing her easily into the gloomy hall to meet the warmth, the familiar smells of home. Her breath coming in what was close to dry sobs, Gwennan fled on to the kitchen, to stand at last in the midst of its homey comfort, striving to draw to her a feeling of safety, even as a child might huddle into a blanket in the midst of a cold, dark night.

Nothing had changed here, there had been no intrusion she could sense. Gwennan threw off her coat, scarf, hood, and hurried to feed wood into the waiting stove. There were still embers which had been banked well enough to bring the fire to life. Mechanically she went about getting breakfast, bringing out eggs, bacon, setting on the coffee pot, cutting bread to toast. Busy at such tasks, she lost some of that feeling of otherness, became again the person she had always believed herself to be, shutting out all else.

A glance at the shelf clock, whose comfortable tick added to the easement of this moment, gave her a start. Ten—and her meeting with the board—! Those papers she had meant to go over so carefully—she had no time for checking them now. Eat, change into the respectable suit Mrs. Abers would expect her to wear—hurry into town.

She ate swiftly and wondered what would happen if she cited her night's adventures as an excuse for any tardiness. The board would immediately set searching for a new librarian, for poor Gwennan Daggert would as speedily be whisked off to some safe rest home where her delusions might serve as a classic case for some psychiatrist. Why, she might even end up in one of those sensational horror novels so much in demand at the present moment.

To cling to the duties which had been so long her whole life, that must be her present anchor. She stacked her dishes, a slovenly trick, Miss Nessa would have termed *that*. The sharp ring of the phone startled a small cry out of her, and her coffee mug fell from her hand, to shatter in the sink, spattering her with the dregs.

For a moment she could not move at all. Then she reached the other side of the kitchen and managed a hoarse "hello."

"Gwennan?" Mr. Stevens sounded surprised, even uncertain.

She pulled her wits together quickly. "Yes. I

think I am coming down with a cold—" That surely would excuse any strangeness another might see in her this morning— "But I will be at the meeting."

"Save me some time after, Gwennan. There is a matter I must discuss with you. Thought I had better let you know ahead of time as this is of the utmost importance. You planning on walking in?"

She thought of those black tracks encircling the house, what they might just threaten. However, she did not want anyone to see those and ask questions—not now!

"Yes, of course, I always do."

"You are pretty much alone so far out there."

"Never bothered us. Miss Nessa liked it that way. I'll be in on time, Mr. Stevens."

"The time—yes, it *is* getting along. Well, just remember I want to see you after the meeting— important or I wouldn't insist—this being Saturday."

She went to change her clothing, leaving what she threw off again in a muddle Miss Nessa would have highly disapproved of after the long years she drilled Gwennan in tidiness. Then she was off, briefcase in hand, hoping that when the proper moment came she could call to mind all the figures she had been so laboriously compiling for the past month. She glanced at the yard, somehow not surprised that the black tracks had disappeared. Perhaps she had reached a point where nothing could really surprise nor astound her again.

The old set pattern of life pushed more and

more of the past hours into the realm of dream, until she began hopefully to doubt her adventure. Gwennan concentrated dazedly on her report, using that skill she had long ago learned as Miss Nessa's assistant and representative, to throw herself entirely into the work at hand, shutting out all else. In the past it had been her own very meager personal life she had so exiled, now it was these wild dreams. She was startled at the end of the meeting when old Mrs. Kitteridge, apparently roused from the semi-doze which of late years enveloped her at their conference, asked:

"What about the Crowder papers? We've never decided what to do with 'em, have we now? Emma took a sight of pride in all those books and letters. Thought once they should go to some college."

Mel Teague, who clung to his status of representing the farmers, usually rallying a negative vote swiftly to any hint of new expenditure, settled his big bulk more firmly in his chair.

"Now there's somethin' else 'bout those there papers. The Crowders—they always took a sight of real interest in this town. It was old Thad Crowder as made the first bond with the Lyles when us Freeport people came up river to settle here. He was a learned man for his time, they say used to go around huntin' up strange things— doing 'em, too—like talkin' to the Indians 'bout their devils and such. He was the one who just up and disappeared—or so they tell. Story was that the devil himself came down and snatched him right out of the meetin' house during a big storm. Now *that* story was one of my family's tellin',

Matt Teague bein' there at the time and never the same afterward. The Crowders—they didn't talk much—but they kept the town papers and records fair and square—very good at that. And everyone knows they were a writin' family—kept their own accounts of what went on here. I heard from my Granddad that in the old days if anyone wanted proof of this or that happenin' in the past —like where was the landmarks of a piece of property or the like—they'd just trot over to the Crowders and ask.

"Then one of them would get down some big old book and look in it. Sure enough there it would be, all wrote out fair and square. They kept an account of everything whatever happened here. Maybe they kept too good an account to suit the Lyles—or Thad might have. The Lyles were livin' like lords, with all them servants waitin' on 'em when the Freeport people came. And they were always mighty friendly with the Indians, too. That devil story—"

"The Lyles," Mrs. Abers spoke with her usual precise diction and that well-known quelling note in her voice, "have never done this community anything but good. When the Indians were raiding everywhere else, they never entered this valley."

"Yeah, those who had a mind to didn't come to no easy end," Mel commented. "I remember *that* story, too. It was one of the Teagues as come across the camp where them French and their Indians met up with something they never bargained for. He always said afterwards that it was a sight worse than any massacre as he ever heard of—that it weren't no human work at all—but the devil must a took a hand in the business."

"Just as," Jim Pyron, editor of the *Weekly Clarion*, looked thoroughly interested, "he seems to be making himself known to us in the here and now—"

Gwennan stopped stuffing her papers back into her case. She did not quite dare at the moment to look straight at any of those old or middle-aged faces. They were all of village founder blood and there were family tales well known to all of them. She knew what she herself had discovered in her own one short search of the Crowder papers. Who could guess what else might lie in the still unopened cartons?

"It's been just about a hundred years now," Mrs. Kitteridge observed, "since the last time. I remember Granny Whatton—" she paused before continuing, "*that* was no made-up story, neither. I don't think any one can deny that there *is* somethin' here in this valley which shows up now and then—somethin' strange—"

"Which does a killin' or two." Mel's emphatic interruption brought a moment of silence.

"It might be well for us to do a little lookin' through those papers," he added. "Or suggestin' it to Bob Baines—as sheriff he might get himself a few helpful ideas—"

"Never knew," remarked Jim Pyron, "that the law would take to hunting down the devil. That usually just deals with his works—not his person. What is making trouble now must be some kind of animal—maybe a big cat. Those are coming down from the north—more of them than people know about."

"Now you've taken to arguin' on both sides, Jim," Mel said.

The editor laughed. "That's what's known as keeping an open mind, Mel. I did a little looking around myself in our files at the Clarion. Of course the paper doesn't go back before 1830, but, yes, I found a few queer stories scattered through back issues. I'll agree that there are a lot more things in this world than people are willing to admit exist. These Crowder papers—they do sound like something worth shifting—not just for devil stories—but for local interest. Might even do to run one of those columns in the paper like 'A hundred years ago today' and quote from them. What about it, Gwen, anything been done with the papers?"

"No. The boxes are in the store room. I did open one with town records in it—the duplicate ones, I mean. They seem to be in good order."

"Mind if I drift over and do some poking around them? I can see a story, maybe more than one, in this." Jim had totally lost that bored glaze of eye which he usually wore during board meetings. Though the Pyrons were an old family, Jim was relatively a newcomer, having inherited the paper from a cousin, coming back to town after college, then a stretch in 'Nam. In this company he ranked near the well-traveled Lyles for worldliness.

Mrs. Abers glanced up from the thick, old-fashioned galoshes she was pulling on.

"Heard that Lady Lyle's gone again. They say she was ailing. Too bad—I didn't take much to that nephew of hers when she introduced him at the store. Suppose if anything does happen to her he'll be the one to take over Lyle House."

"He's young—no tellin' 'bout him," Mel commented. "He's already stayin' up at the house. Saw him goin' down the lane last night. Friendly enough seemin', I guess, but he ain't like the Lady. She was one to keep to herself maybe, still there's never any need she hears of that she doesn't lend a hand in helpin' out. You can ask the Reverend about that. Too bad he couldn't make the meetin' today. Heard tell that Sally Edwards was taken ill so he undertook to drive her to Freeport—"

"What's wrong with Sally?" Mrs. Kitteridge showed even more animation. "Why, I met her in town just two days ago and she looked as good as ever. Said she had nothin' to complain about either. Was it some sort of accident? Why didn't we know?" Her indignation grew with every word.

"No accident," Mel shook his head. "Think the family don't want it talked 'bout—but it'll be all over town sooner or later anyway. Sally was found at the edge of Brink's Woods near clean out of her mind—real hysterical she was. Then her heart took a bad spell. They figured they had to get her to the hospital as soon as they could. We need us a doctor in this town. Ever since old Doc Anderson died, we've needed one. But these here young fellows nowadays—I guess they figure they can make a lot more money in the cities, and there're too few of us to give them that kind of a livin'. Maybe we're just all too healthy for our own good."

"Brink's Woods—" Jim, who was generally

keen on the subject of trying to attract medical aid for the town, was more interested in the other part of Mel's report. "That's on the other side of the Lyle place, isn't it? I was thinking when I drove by there just the other day that it was unusual there hadn't been any logging done there for so long. Lots of dead stuff ought to come out—a dry summer and a lightning strike there—then we might find ourself with a real fire."

"True enough. But you ain't goin' get old Lovey Brink to do anything 'bout it. She couldn't care less, long as she has her garden patch and her check comin' in regular at the bank. Her son ain't been home in ten years or more. Brink's Woods—you know that is a place that devil critter, whatever it is, might well take to hide out in. And were a woman like Sally to maybe be chased, or even see something strange, she could well have a heart attack. I think Baines ought to look a little in the direction and I'm goin' to tell him so. Well, time to be gettin' 'long. We got some things settled anyhow. Gwen, you watch out for the pennies now. They mightn't go far these days—but they aren't to be thrown around carelesslike neither!" He heaved his bulk out of the chair.

For the first time Gwennan realized that Mr. Stevens, though he had been present, had had very little to say. He had even pushed his chair a little away from the table, making only absent-minded comments when he was called upon. There was a briefcase leaning against one of the legs of his seat, but he had never reached for it, though she had expected him to produce something pertinent to library affairs. Instead he had steepled his fingers together and more or less fixed his attention outwardly on them, as if his patience was being strained to wait out the conclusion of the meeting.

She ushered the rest of the board out, assured Jim Pyron he could have ready access to the Crowder papers whenever he wished, and returned to where the lawyer waited for her.

"There is bad news." He greeted her. "Lady Lyle is dead."

Said so bluntly, it shocked her, yet part of her had been prepared. The pendant which she now wore within her blouse—that could not have come to her had its former owner still been alive.

"I—I am sorry. She was kind to me." Gwennan used those words said so often. They did not express the depth of what she really felt, but they were the ones expected from her.

"She knew that she had very little chance of returning when she went—I have since learned. Before she did go she left this with me—to be given to you." He opened the briefcase to bring out a large envelope. "What did Miss Nessa ever tell you about your parents?" His abrupt change of subject surprised her.

"My mother was Miss Nessa's half-sister, but she was much younger. She went to college, working her way. Miss Nessa did not approve. Then she met my father before she had finished her second year, and they were married very suddenly. Miss Nessa disliked that also—she believed in finishing whatever one had once begun. My father—I don't really know what business he was in, but they traveled all the time. I was born abroad, somewhere in South or Central America. I saw the papers once—they are at the bank in Freeport now. But my parents registered me with the nearest American Consul and I am an American citizen. They brought me back here the next summer. After that we went to India and— But I do not remember very much of that.

"When I was old enough for school they returned here again before they went to the southwest and were killed. It was one of those freak accidents you read about when a plane is missing —like the Bermuda Triangle.

"Then I just stayed on with Miss Nessa and as you know I've lived here ever since."

"But you took the name Daggert. What was your true name?"

Gwennan flushed. "I—I don't know. Miss Nessa entered me in school under her name—told me that it was mine now. I always wondered if my mother had not married some distant family connection whom Miss Nesssa had not liked."

"I think that it was a very different name," he pronounced that as if it were a judgment. "Lady Lyle had a distinct interest in you from the first —though she never revealed it to you directly until lately. I know she asked for reports concerning you—sometimes writing from other parts of the world. Though she never explained why she wanted them. You know that the Lyles, though there have never been more than one or two to appear here in a single generation, do have connections elsewhere. When they married it was always away from home, and within the ranks of their widespread family, choosing a branch sometimes from another country. It may be that your father had Lyle blood. That would be an excellent reason for Miss Nessa to keep your relationship, as she thought, secret."

"But why?"

"Miss Nessa was a very proud woman. It could be also, and do not mistake my motive in saying this, Gwennan, that she did not consider, for some reason, that the marriage was a legal one. Miss Nessa, as we both know, clung very closely to the manners and morals of another generation. If your mother was not married openly here in the church, to a man well known to the community, Miss Nessa might deem the union to be a dubious one."

He was right, as Gwennan knew. But one of the Lyles—what had Tor called her in the tempestuous interview—a half-blood! Only his taunt was no evidence. Perhaps the envelope she now held would provide that.

She tore it open. Mr. Stevens was buttoning his coat. He nodded to her.

"If there is anything in there which you believe needs legal handling, do not hesitate to come to me, Gwennan. There are matters now to be settled concerning the estate. I suppose this young man gets everything—he seems to be the heir Lady Lyle acknowledged, to the extent of bringing him here before she left."

He went out as Gwen sat down slowly at the table. What she pulled out of the envelope was a sheet of stiff paper on which was an intricate drawing. With that fluttered a page of much lighter and thinner weight. The larger sheet was, she recognized from her reading, a very detailed astrological chart, but she did not know enough about the subject to interpret it for herself. Only there was a birthdate printed at the top and it was her own. Plainly this must be intended for her—for a reason she could not understand.

She picked up the second page which had accompanied it. The writing was very clear and bold, resembling the printing on the chart, yet possessing the individuality of hand script. It was Lady Lyle's.

> "My time is much shorter than I had hoped it would be. My body functions have been tampered with in an obscure manner, and I believe I know the reason. Therefore I have not the full chance to pass to you what should be part of your knowledge. You will have to learn for yourself, in that learning you shall grow—for doors open when you knock. Within will lie many things you have forgotten or which were purposefully reft from you. What you were meant to be was once changed—"

"Ortha—" Gwennan whispered. "She must be speaking of Ortha!"

> "The old knowledge, the control of power which was your right, was drained from you, so that you come lame into the land of the free. What only can be done is to give you the opportunity to relearn, to strengthen, to so approach the person who you were meant to be. I shall leave you the key—also a certain

other tool. But I am able to extend you no protection.

"What you do you must learn for yourself, choose for yourself—that is the Law of the Power. We are free in that much. There are always choices before us. When we make those we alter our lives, and sometimes the lives of others, one way or another.

"The stars have returned to old courses, for so do the heavens circle with generation upon generation between. Once more they stand as they did when you were born before —to be plundered of what was to be yours. You again may choose.

"This much I lay upon you. At Midwinter Day go to the standing stones and there use the watch of the star hours as instinct moves you. What will thereafter follow will provide your testing choice. I wish you very well— you have that in you which was meant to draw us close. And, the Power willing, it shall again."

Just as there had been no salutation on the letter, so there was no signature. Lady Lyle might have written so that what she had to say would remain a puzzle to hostile eyes. Only the date on the horoscope assured Gwennan that what she held was meant for her alone. But *what* it meant she had yet to learn.

11

Gwennan sat at the kitchen table, the only surface large enough in the house to hold the burden of papers and books she had so carefully been able to assemble. A little of her experience by the standing stones had been time dulled. It was days—weeks—since that night which had made her aware of more than one world—painfully and completely aware. There had been no further sign from the new master at Lyle House. In fact Tor Lyle might have disappeared as completely and finally as his kinswoman as far as Waterbridge was concerned.

Nor had there been any more traces of the "devil." Jim Pyron delved into the Crowder papers and came up with enough odd tales of village history to furnish him with his proposed column. In fact he made a habit at present of dropping in at the library on Saturday mornings for research. Gwennan found his discoveries and opinions concerning them interesting enough, but it was her own private reading which occupied her evenings and as much time as her conscience would allow her to spare from regular duties.

Miss Nessa's house suffered no thorough weekly cleanings these days. If the bed was made and the dishes done, the worst of the dust smacked away in the two rooms which had come to center Gwennan's life, she decided she had spared time enough. The reading was more important.

She longed for intelligent and trained help, and knew nowhere to seek or ask for such. The chart of the stars remained a closed secret to her, no matter how much she sought out explanations in the various astrology books she gathered and pored over. Mathematics had always been a defeating study for her, and these all drew upon an esoteric form of that science.

There remained the stones themselves and the ley lines. She had ordered, through loans, everything possible on the subject. Now the mass of assembled but hardly correlated material engulfed her with piles of notes. There existed all over the world large and small stones, some with holes fashioned in them. Some such were thought to heal; the afflicted person, an ailing child could crawl or be passed through such a hole to be cured. There were other holes which seemed to be sacred places where one swearing an oath set his hand to ensure his loyalty to a bargain. There were cups hollowed in stones in which lay pebbles which needed only to be turned to ensure either good fortune or an efficient cursing. There were stones upon stones upon stones!

Stones which moved, according to old legends,

upon certain days of the year or at night. Stones which were said to be sinners turned forever into rock to suffer for their various crimes, stones which the devil had tossed spitefully at sacred places, only to have his bombardment fall short, or else be turned aside by the equal power of some saint. It would seem from her now feverish reading that England, in fact all of the British Isles, was completely paved with stones possessing one form of "magic" or another. And that was just England!

There were the stones of Brittany and others scattered over Europe, though the legends concerning those had not been so carefully kept or gathered. Then one turned to South America. What of the single mountain there covered with carvings which no modern archeologist or artist could account for or understand—strange beasts —the head of a man which showed as that of a youth in the morning and slowly aged during the day as the light changed and moved across it, a whole mountain which was a monument to a nation or people completely lost—whose work was to be found nowhere else in the world.

Gwennan compiled reams of lists—marked over maps. She became inundated with utter chaos, bewildering more than instructing her. Now and then, looking upon some photo illustration in a book, or coming suddenly on a scrap of legend, she had a flash of thought which might almost be a scrap of memory—but certainly no memory of her own! She knew that theory of folk memory also—of a storage of ancient learning which could be touched and drawn upon by the far descendants of one who had lived or seen—

Many lives? Was that the answer? Did some personal essence travel away from a vast parent identity, incarnate in order to learn—to expand certain attributes—live so as a separate entity, to return eventually to the source? Had she indeed been once a temple seer named Ortha in a civilization so devastated by worldwide disaster that it was totally forgotten?

Those who had passed through, had survived such an overwhelming of the land, the rolling of the sea as she had witnessed before the Mirror— yes, those might emerge with a madness in them walling away the full memory of what had been. Reduced to wanderers—thrown back into a time when stones were tools and man could turn against man for a scrap of food, a place of safety for a night—how long would they hold in mind, except as unbelieved stories, what they had once been?

And there *were* such legends—from India, from many native peoples who trained memories rather than trusted to written documents and scientific forms of retaining knowledge. What of that obscure and primitive tribe in Africa who know well the orbit of Sirius and worshipped it? What of the worldwide tales of survival from a great flood—men, women, a few animals saved— some on ships, rafts, some crawling out from mountain caves, to face an entirely new world? She had them here—those stories as they were now reported, printed, open to the reader who wished to speculate on the strangeness of imagination which stretched worldwide—save what if such were NOT born of imagination at all?

Gwennan's pack of papers grew. She compiled from all she could find those facts which were pertinent to what she had seen, experienced during that single night. And, though she would not have admitted the fact to any, she believed in the truth of Ortha's world, and in the existence of the ley lines.

There had been no more reports of the "Devil." With the disappearance of Tor from sight the night prowling monster seemed also to have taken its departure. The girl no longer doubted that it *was* Tor who had somehow, willingly or even unknowingly, summoned the thing.

There were many tales of such which had appeared and disappeared — either in electrical storms or along the ley lines. If those were indeed sources of a power as strong as any man's efforts had been able to generate and which the stones gathered, or transmitted, why *could* not that unknown power, wrongly used, or uncontrolled, open gates into other places of existence? She had now hundreds of accounts of monsters which had appeared, had devastated and killed, or merely frightened, had been slain, or had simply disappeared. The knight and the dragon in conflict—was that the remainder of a very ancient real happening—outworld things faced down by one who had the Power?

She was feverishly intent on what she tried to learn, what some driving compulsion within her said MUST be learned. Only now and then her Miss Nessa trained good sense clamped down. So far she *had* managed to keep her absorption with all these studies apart from her every day life, and, since she had never been very socially inclined, no one suspected what she so feverishly sought.

Now she leaned back in her chair to survey the pages of notes she had compiled out of all the books and clippings which littered the table, or had littered it and been discarded, during the past weeks. These—she laid her hand firmly down, pressing on the papers—were the only answers she could find in all her searching. And they remained so vague, so few. Even strung together as tightly as she had tried to put them, they were not evidence any other person in this town would consider as meaningful. There were other places in the world—there were all the writers of the books she had consulted—they had in them belief that things were not as they had always been told or they would in turn not have gone seeking. For the first time in her life Gwennan considered the idea of traveling—of trying to make contact with some other of these seekers.

Considered—and knew that it was impossible. She had never had any wish to leave Waterbridge. Now she discovered such a suggestion aroused more than just a tinge of uneasiness in her— she shrank from the thought entirely. It was as if she must remain here waiting—

Lady Lyle's letter—she had read it many times over—had told her to seek and certainly that was just what she had been doing. Yet what concrete facts might she learn from this collection of folk- lore, speculation, guesses—some of them wild enough? Space men who had landed long ago to

father a new race upon half human beings, men
and women whose powers had deified them
among their fellows, lost cities deep in jungles,
vitrified patches in desert lands which might possibly mark ancient atomic disasters, the news
that the moon overhead was far older than man
had believed, that there might be two other
planets always hidden—the dark moon Lilith—
the sun-washed Vulcan—

None of this was of much use to her. Gwennan
was suddenly tired, as if the fatigue gathered
through the hours of her searching settled upon
her all at once. Now she slumped a little forward,
her head in her hands. Her eyes smarting from all
that feverish reading, closed. What *was* the sum
total of what she had learned? Nothing of any
value.

She had not returned to the standing stones
since that morning when she had fled their
mound. Nor would she go—not there! Now she
raised her head and looked to the old desk where
Miss Nessa had kept, in small neat packets (each
fastened with a rubber band or tucked into an
envelope) those few papers which to her had importance. There was the deed to this house, tax
receipts for many years, some receipted bills, the
insurance papers. Nowhere was there anything
pertaining to Gwennan except her own birth
certificate, the paper signed by a consul in a
foreign land proclaiming her American, the child
of American citizens. She had hunted through all
that hoping to uncover a marriage certificate
stating her father's full name, something of her
past. If there ever had been any such Miss Nessa

had deliberately disposed of it.

Until Mr. Stevens had asked her Gwennan had even forgotten that her name was not her own. She had sought for that certificate upon her arrival home that day—

Ketern—certainly an odd name—one bearing no resemblance to any family hereabouts. NOT Lyle. The lawyer's hint of that had been a mistake.

She was so tired. A glance at the watch on her wrist gave her a start. It was after twelve. She would awake stupid and unready for work if this kept on. Mechanically the girl gathered her papers into a pile, put the books into order. However, though she stood up—she did not at once go to bank the stove.

There was a howl of wind tonight. The first snow had fallen three days ago and there was talk she had heard in the library of a bad storm on the way. This evening, before Gwennan had sat down to study she had made sure there was a good supply of wood to hand. And she was wearing three layers of sweaters now. There were storm supplies in the cupboard straight ahead—a prudent laying up of what every householder needed in a season when one could be snowed in.

Tomorrow was Saturday—another half day at the library. But that did not mean that she was excused from opening up, unless a blizzard closed the roads tonight.

Gwennan went to the window and looked out. There should have been a moon, but clouds hung heavy, and there was the steady hiss of falling flakes against the pane on which frost was already building a veil.

She made her preparations for the night slowly, loath to leave this room which was always the warmest of the old house, almost deciding to bring in bedding and spend the night on the sofa as she had done in the past. But at length she hurried through the process of going to bed. Only, tired as she was, sleep did not come.

Instead she found that her eyes were continually drawn to the frost paned window through which that thing of the Dark had watched her on the night of the storm. Would the cold ward off any such which might stray through between the leys? *If* that thing had so come, and now she believed that that much was the truth.

Under the mound of covers she clasped the pendant. That she had kept always with her— even though she hid it beneath her clothing. It was made of a metal she could not name, for, though it had a silver sheen, she did not believe it *was* silver—it was never cold. Rather was a small core of reassuring warmth always to answer her touch.

The watch of the Star Hours, Lady Lyle had named it. However, since Gwennan had left the vicinity of the stones that morning the symbols became so dim they could only be seen in the strongest light. While the bar which had moved about the dial disappeared from sight entirely. To take it to the stones at Midwinter day—almost a month away still. Did she want to go—perhaps to plunge into another series of adventures which would separate her even farther from her own birth world?

Yet to cup the watch as she did now between the palms of her hands and her own breast gave her such a feeling of security as she might have had if some friend stood beside her shoulder to shoulder. She closed her tired eyes upon the dark of the room.

Cold—tight—

Did she walk, run, or was she borne in some fashion above that long ribbon of light? There arose a wall of dark on either side, so thick, in a way so menacing, that she knew only with the light she followed was there safety. Now from that narrow path arose tendrils of mist—some pure white, some tinged with gold. Those close to her were only streamers—yet it seemed that those farther ahead formed tenuous figures and shapes—only to melt as she approached.

There was a pyramid. She might have been viewing the huge structure from a far distance. From its sides streamed tongues of light as those ribbons had once curled from the fingers of the Voice when she wove her peace and harmony spells. Then, as Gwennan floated the nearer, the pyramid vanished. A wheel arose in turn, to stand before her as might a barrier refusing her passage. Within its rim glowed a five-pointed star and where each point touched the outer circle a ball of light gave new source to the floating ribbons of Power.

The wheel faded, was gone. What waited ahead now was a symbol she knew well—part of those same half-effaced markings carved above the doorway of the house which she claimed as her own. This was the ankh—the key—and from loop above, arms below, always the light—

No longer was she cold, for her body, if it was in body that she roamed so, was washed by warmth as well as by a feeling of peace—of power leashed and made servant to the light.

She passed through the mist which had formed the ankh. Now—

Here hung the sign of the pendant—a full orb of moon surmounted by the horns of its birth. From the tips of those horns the light trailed now —not uprising but outward to either side, between her and the wall of the dark. Nor did the moon orb disappear into its mist birth as she came to it. Rather the vast circle of its light formed a doorway through which that which carried her wafted her on.

What was the rest of it? There came those to meet her. Some of them wore faces she knew well from other times and was glad in her heart to see. She had a vague memory of riding—not a horse of her own world—but a creature which carried its head proudly high with a single horn springing heavenward and that horn was purest white, spiraled with a thread of gold. She walked through a great place where gathered men who wore splendid mail under surcoats of the finest silks patterned with gems and threads of pearls, women whose gowns might have been woven of pure sunlight and seafoam.

Only there was not all light. She ran, her body taut with fear, her heart pounding so in her breast that it would seem about to leap from its encasing of bone, down a street where all doors were closed against her, knowing that she sped so

because she was hunted by a dire and terrible danger, from which she must expend her last breath to escape.

She lay in dirty straw, her throat parched with thirst, while a molten hot sun beat in upon her through a ragged break in a tumbling wall. In her nostrils then was the smell of dissolution which she knew to be that of her own mortal body, rotting before the life was free from it, and she cried inwardly for death which was pitiless because it did not come.

There was a wood where the trees were sometimes women and then bark and wood. Those jeered and mocked her as she tried to escape their flailing branch arms and strove to find a way between their trunks which swayed to cut off her path.

Then she stumbled over the stones that a mighty sea had rolled landward—leaving no soft sand of beach—rather a maze of rocks among which it would be very easy to fall and break bones—and which were slimed green and brown. Over her head passed a shadow—something winged which was large enough to pluck her up did it wish. So she crouched among the rocks, her arms across her head with little hope of escaping its notice.

There was sand underfoot now—but not water-washed—endless drifts of it—no marked road. Save here and there the wind had capriciously laid bare a skeleton—some of beasts, some of men in rusted steel—or smaller tumbles of bones in rotting cloth. She might be moving through the remains of some great company who had fled into this waste land to fall and die one by one. She stumbled across the edge of a shield standing near upright in that ever-traveling sand.

No forest, even one formed of women trees, no sea and rocks, no desert now—this was a place of greyness in which grew what looked to be giant fungi, sickly yellow, with here and there a brilliant cap of red on a slender trunk—towering above her head. Here she did not stumble, walk, nor run, but went forward in hops, her body bent, transformed into something she did not want to look upon or imagine.

So it went—as ever she passed from one place to another, always different—some bright and beautiful—some dire and of the Dark. In each, she came to understand, she had a place—had had a place—or would have a place. In each there were some duty or needful action which was hers alone, some choice she must make. Nor did she even learn what those duties or choices might be, for never did she linger long enough.

Finally there was a last time of all, when she stood on a dark hillside. Above the night was clear and cloudless—the stars plain in their light and beauty—seeming closer than she had ever seen them—so that she marked many she believed she had never seen before. The stars were not fixed, rather they moved in a stately parade, across the sky, making a circlet of the heavens, changing their positions time and time again. Until, once more, they reached the same position they had held at her first looking upon them. The wheel had turned completely.

Then she was enveloped by dark—yet it did not

frighten her—rather it enwrapped her warm and welcoming. In it she neither dreamed nor envisioned.

Gwennan awoke, the window near her bed was near frosted over, still that did not shut out the daylight. She looked at her clock—eight! She had overslept and there followed a scramble to dress, eat, get ready for her work. The snow had drifted, but she already heard the clank of the plow. Red Anderson, who kept that in his barn just outside of town, was headed in for duty. She would have a path free for walking.

Her phone rang—the Newtons wanting to know if all was well and she reassured them quickly. Ralph promised to bring in some more wood for her later that day. Gwennan was so quickly caught up in the round of winter living that she half forgot the dreams of the night—in fact many of them faded already, as dreams so often do. She ate breakfast with one hand while she listed those items it would better be added to her emergency store.

The sunlight was very weak and thin as she fought her way through two drifts to the road, her ski pants gathering knots of crusted snow. There were new clouds gathering. If it began to snow again she might be wise to close early and head for home.

A snowmobile swooped in the distance with the laughter of the passengers carrying through the crisp air. Gwennan wondered as she tramped along the cleared road at that touch of another, simpler world. What lay in her mind, what was about her—there was a growing gulf between the

here and now, and herself—could that be true?
She shook her head. No more midnight work on
strange concerns. She did not dare. This morning
she had had flashes during which the familiar
kitchen, all in the house, appeared alien—not
hers. It was dangerous—what was happening to
her. No! This might be the end. She must keep her
feet firmly on the real ground.

Reality *was* this crunch of snow underfoot, the
sting of cold against the very small exposed portion of her face between high tied scarf and
pulled down, knitted cap. She was Gwennan
Daggert, and it was only Gwennan Daggert that
she wanted to be. The rest—

This was a sharp reaction, one of fear—a fear
which grew the stronger as her thoughts suggested what might happen should she allow her
obsession to become visible to others. Most
townspeople already thought of her as odd—she
was well aware of this. And there was a very thin
line of safety between being "odd" and being considered mentally disturbed. She must concentrate on life as it had been before she had been
drawn into this wild series of dreams and speculations.

When Gwennan reached the library, she had
made her decision. Quickly she caught at the
chain of the pendant, pulled that from around her
head with a sharp jerk, feeling that if she did not
free herself from it swiftly she might never do so
again.

It was warm—no, *hot*, in her hand, almost as if
it were heating up with anger or in warning. She
picked up an envelope from her desk, slid the disc

and its chain into that, sealed it. The envelope in turn she pushed to the very back of a drawer. She would gather up all the books, see that they were returned to the institutions from which she had borrowed them. The notes—she would light the fire with those notes—as soon as she went home today. She was through—she had to be for the sake of her own sane outlook on the world.

There were not many patrons today but Jim Pyron dropped in as she was using slack time to straighten shelves and replace books.

"Weather news is none too good." He stamped most of the snow from his thick boots, but he tidily sat down on the chair by the door to rid himself of them, leaving them standing while he crossed the floor in his thick double pairs of sock. "They say there is a regular blaster on the way. You stocked up?"

"I'll get some more today," Gwennan promised. "Brought a list in. Paul Newton is going to pick me up at the store and see about my wood."

"I'm going to take a couple of the Crowder ledgers if you'll trust me with them. Might not be opening up on Monday, and, if I were you, I'd close right about now."

He went with the ledgers and Gwennan did dress once more in her heavy clothing, was heading to lock up, when she paused by her desk. If she were wise she would certainly leave the pendant exactly where it was—it would be safe in the library—and *she* would probably be safer than she might be with it around as a temptation. Only she discovered that, certainly not by either her will or volition, her hand pulled open the drawer and that envelope was transferred into the front of her ski jacket before she zipped it up.

However, to counter the attraction of that arti-fact, she also caught up a book bag she had deliberately filled for herself volume by vol-ume during the morning. No more esoteric reading—she had crammed in three newish mysteries, two biographies suitably dull enough to send anyone into dreamless slumber, and a travel book, beside three of the lightest and most frivolous historical romances one could pick for the lighting of the brain's occupation. These were going to be her home reading! She was Gwennan Daggert, town librarian, and a very ordinary and sane person—

She held firmly to her inner impression of that ordinary and sane person as she visited the store and gave in her order. There was no supermarket in Whitebridge and the homey smells, the com-fortable in-townness, of the old building set another barrier of reality about her.

Then Paul came in with his own list, and they tramped back and forth from the pick-up with their cartons of emergency supplies. Snow was beginning to fall again. The sunlight had dis-appeared and the clouds massed. There was a rising wind which could cut like a knife or take one's breath away. It was clear that the promised bad weather was well on its way, and Gwennan was very glad to be home again. Paul came in to fill, first the wood box in the kitchen, and then make sure that there was a future stack as high as he could cram it in the shed where she could reach by the inner kitchen door.

Gwennan swept the table bare of the book piles, stacking them swiftly into one of the grocery cartons, and pushing that into the frosty cold of the parlor where they could freeze, she decided, as far as she was concerned. But she did not light the fire with her notes. Just as she had been unable to abandon the pendant, so she could not destroy the work of the past few weeks. However, she did push all out of sight into another carton, toss the envelope with the pendant on top, and place that in the parlor also, shutting the door very firmly upon all of it.

12

Gwennan had half expected to be beset by more dreams of visions, put under compulsion to return to her studies, thus she prepared to fight any such subborning of her will. But such an assault did not come. Her sleep was dreamless, as if she had emerged from some illness, free of the shadow on her mind. The promised storm hit hard and for three days she had been prisoner in her home, keeping close to the fire, making only quick raids now and then upon the stacked wood.

She drowsed away hours, curiously tired, thus willing to laze out time. Miss Nessa's training, which had been always a spur to accomplish, to keep busy, had released its hold on her, so that Gwennan was lazy as she had never been in her life, napping, rousing to languidly spoon up a bowl of hot soup—or if ambition were a little stronger, make a stew to bubble on the stove, its pot to be dipped into for more than one meal.

The Newtons phoned twice, checking on her. Then the phone was silent, so when she tried to check with Pyron in town as to the state of the library, she discovered the line was dead. In the past such times of isolation had never been so wasted. Miss Nessa's hands had never been idle, nor had she allowed Gwennan to escape such duties as the darning of thick winter stockings, the careful turning of already well-worn sheets, the cutting and sewing of rags for another rug, even though already balls of such raw material long awaited the braiding.

On the second afternoon when it was growing dark enough in the kitchen for Gwennan to reluctantly bestir herself to flick on the battery-run storm lamp—for the electricity had also failed, ice-burdened lines down in the wilderness of snow—she felt more alert, restless. Those hours of half-sleep had apparently renewed her into wanting action.

While Miss Nessa had always scorned any needlework which was not practical, and she herself had disliked what she did because of her rigid sense of duty, there were at the bottom of an old chest some lengths of cloth, long folded away— fine and unusual pieces of silk and brocade. Some, judging by their shape, must once have been rich garments laboriously picked apart for purposes which had never been afterward accomplished. As a very great favor when Gwennan had been quite young, Miss Nessa had allowed her to take these out—smooth and examine them, marvel at ancient sprays of embroidery so perfect and delicate that they might have been woven into the surfaces which formed their backgrounds. There had been the glint of metallic threads — time dulled — in those sprays — and some of the flowers had been centered by pearls or crystal beads.

Gwennan had no idea why she remembered these now—but she went to that sewing chest, rummaging through the dull scraps and pieces kept for dish cloths, dusting squares, and the like, pulled up the layers of brittle yellow papers which had been always kept to protect the treasures below. Where had these come from? Miss Nessa had always answered firmly that they were old things—belonging to some one far back in family history. She had eyed them with scorn—certainly the Daggerts who had for generations been farmers, had no use for such fripperies. Did some one of those sturdy, unimaginative farmers once marry a woman of another background, bringing her into what had been a bleak outpost?

If so—what then had been her life? Who had unpicked the dresses? There were parts of at least three such, as well as several uncut lengths which were yellowed, ready to tear at the folds from which they had never been shaken forth for any seamstress to lay pattern on. Gwennan gathered up the armload of ancient silks and fraying satins, time-rubbed velvets, to lay them out upon the table.

Here were parts of a bodice. She deduced its shape from the remaining portions, of a sea green brocade. It bore metallic embroidery around a neckline which had been cut quite immodestly low by what must have been the village standards of that day. Silver those threads could have been —they were black now, with dull pearls caught in their webbing. Just the remains of a bodice—no skirt.

There was a rich yellow—perhaps the dye of

that laid away had not faded over much—under-skirt—or two breadths of it—the whole pain-staking embroidered at measured intervals with knots of pansies, strikingly lifelike with their purple and white faces. Then some velvet which Gwennan deduced had been part of a cloak. It had been a cinnamon brown, and to one strip of it still adhered fluttering tatters of lining—as yellow as the skirt.

Last of all were the uncut pieces. One was purple, very dark—a rich shade which made one think of a queen attired for her crowning, a brocade so heavy that a gown made of it might have been fatiguing to wear. Below that was silk which tore, even under the careful handling Gwennan gave it—too old, too frail to even keep its substance when folded.

At the bottom of that pile was a third piece and this Gwennan frowned at. She remembered all the rest. Had she not handled them before? But somehow she had forgotten this. It had none of the tarnish and worn magnificance of the rest. Instead it seemed almost to belong—be better among household discards and scraps which had been piled above it.

The texture was coarse to the touch especially after fingering those silks and satins. In color—Gwennan spread it out closer to the storm lamp —it was dark green. But, oddly enough, as the cloth moved under her careful handling there appeared caught up in it threads of another color, causing a simulation of rippling across the surface.

Under the full light there existed a silvery overcasting. She might be looking down at a pool of water which had been disturbed, on which foam was slowly rising. As she shook it out, what appeared to be a short length of fabric, hardly wider than the panels of the nearly destroyed cloak which had lain above, enlarged into a sweep of material that Gwennan could not have believed had been fitted into so compact a folding. Though it was harsher to touch than silk or velvet, the longer her fingers caressed it, the more it clung to her skin. The girl had the odd feeling that there was something in it of the quality of fur—that this was no warp and woof woven on a loom by a forgotten craftsman, but rather had once been organic—alive—and that a shadow of that life still clung to it.

Unheedingly she swept the other remnants of that battered treasure trove on to the sofa; now she unfolded, twitched, smoothed this find. The oblong of cloth stretched wider and wider. It covered the top of the long table, now it uncreased to hang over the sides—there must be yards of it!

While, under the light, those silvery, foamy streaks were altering, too. From indistinct swirls which had reminded her of an attempt to picture clouds across some sky, they were changing, drawing together into distinct and definite lines. She stopped, jerked away her hands. Those lines —they were indeed patterns—and she had seen their like before—though she could not truly have identified them one by one. These were akin to those misshapen scrawls which were a result of her attempting to reproduce the hidden mark-

ing on the great standing stones. In whatever forgotten language that had been inscribed—its like
had been woven into the fabric she now discovered.

Perhaps the weight of the cloth itself provided
the last revelation. It no longer resembled an un-
sewn, uncut piece fresh from a loom. There was a
last rolling of one edge over the far end of the
table. That displayed intact this as a garment, un-
attacked by time. What she viewed was a long
cloak, not hooded as had been the one Lady Lyle
always favored—for the drawn-in neckline
formed a band on which the lines of weaving
were very closely set, in so intricate a combination of unidentified scroll and hooks as to be
hardly distinguished one from the other. What
was spaced well apart on the rest of the cloth
surface was here concentrated. There was a clasp
also—perhaps it had been the weight of that
which had pulled the collar apart. The metal was
silvery—yet no tarnish dimmed it. Gwennan
thought it akin to the pendant she had discarded.
Its form bore the semblance of an eye—elongated
—inset with a milky stone which had no glitter,
just an opaque surface, that surface divided by a
single green-blue vertical pupil which might have
been a cat's eye nearly closed in the full glare of
the lamp.

Gwennan stepped back warily. That brooch or
clasp—it appeared to center her attention as
might a real eye, one acting independently of any
body. Perhaps her sudden retreat in some way
influenced the cloak as it lay across the board,
for it slipped, falling forward in folds to the floor

where the shadow cast by the table half hid it from view and she could no longer detect those lines of pattern. Only the eye lay in the open, gleaming, and she had a difficult time convincing herself that the pupil line in it had not expanded as it passed into the shadow.

She did not want to touch the thing at all, her curiosity swallowed and dispersed by growing uneasiness, or she was sure that this was no remains of Daggert clothing—kept only because of the ever-abiding need for thrift. No, this was something very different and she could not understand how it ever had come to be included among Miss Nessa's carefully stored scraps and pieces.

Reluctantly Gwennan stooped, caught at the material, crumpling it together in one hand. Though the cloth felt so coarse and heavy to the touch when she had first unrolled and unfolded it, the garment as a whole was much lighter than she had expected it to be, and she had no difficulty in dragging it up from the floor one-handedly.

No wind could have found a way into the carefully close-battened kitchen, yet, as the length of patterned green arose, it fluttered, its edging swinging out to brush against Gwennan's body before she had time to fend it off. Then she had no will to prevent the next happening. Her hands, moved by no orders of hers, speedily brought that green length about her body, settling the cloth straight on her shoulders, letting it trail about her, while the upstanding collar, so stiff that its edge rasped against the underside of her chin, clung in place. By sheer exercise of will she defeated whatever purpose had moved that enfoldment; she did not allow her hands to follow through, to clasp tight the eye brooch.

The green lengths covered her from throat to within an inch or two of the floor, swirling about her so that when she looked down she could see nothing of her body, only the flowing cloak. Nor did it rest easily on her. She moved her shoulders, took firm grip of the edges, strove to shrug off its weight. There was resistance to her efforts. Her fear, flaring higher, led strength to her pull. Thus at last she freed herself from something as entangling as a net might seem to an entrapped fish.

That lore she had promised herself she would not again draw into the forepart of her memory supplied a fragment of old legend—the People of the Hills—those who were said to have their own land under the surface of the earth into which human kind could vanish for a night on invitation, and issue forth to discover that years had passed and all they had once known had long since vanished.

Gwennan managed to drag the garment off her —though it clung with a stubborness which was not that of any woven material she had ever seen or known—almost as if its underside had instantly produced roots to fasten upon her other clothing. The girl pushed it back on the table and flipped over one corner to inspect the lining, see what it was that had seemed to catch.

As her fingers slipped across the edge of that greenish inner surface she snatched them away,

put one tip to her lips to lick off a small spot of blood. Some pin long caught there to scratch the unwary? No, when she leaned closer the lamp light showed her no shine of metal. The inner side of that cloak was—

Scaled skin? The scales set so to inflict a warning cut on the unwary handler?

The skin, if skin it was, appeared very thin, scarcely more than tissue, and the scales remaining fastened to it lay in irregular patches. This lining was a silver gray but the scales (and those were smaller than most beads) were silver with a black rim, overlapping where they still clung.

Perhaps it was the heat of the lamp, or her own actions in pulling the cloak so about, but there now an odor began to rise from the huddle of cloth. Not stench such as she had come to associate with manifestations of the Other World. Rather this was fresh and clear—akin to the scent of pine, or one of the other pungent evergreens. It wafted ever strong as she refolded the cloth as nearly as before as she was able. Her curiosity stirred, but her determination to be free from all which was not of her own time and place, kept Gwennan to that smoothing, turning, lying in folds. Stubbornly it would not return to the narrow band of cloth which it had earlier been. Even when she crushed her weight upon those folds they refused to stay together.

At length, a little out of breath and more than a little uneasy, she gave up the struggle. That eye brooch had fallen to one side in a position which still watched her. Gwennan got up quickly, pushed aside that wretched bundle of the cloak

which refused to be refolded. She stowed away
the rest of the old and disintegrating finery, returned everything she had found, save that swath
of dark green. Since her discovery concerning the
nature of its lining she had the greatest dislike
for handling it. But she could surely not leave it
lying where it was.

At last she made another half-hearted attempt
to reduce it to order. By now the scent thickened
—almost she could see that spiralling up as
incense smoke. She clutched the folds together as
best she could, then made a quick sortie, flashlight in one hand, the roll of the cloak in the
other, to the parlor, dumping this new, upsetting
discovery with all the rest of that of which she
wanted no part.

When she returned to the kitchen she washed
her hands twice over, scrubbing hard, for the
scent permeated her skin until she at last used
strong smelling scouring powder, leaving her
fingers red and wrinkled. Then she turned to the
making of a pot of tea, the leaves drawn from one
of those packets Miss Nessa had been so meticulous about mixing from herbs. These were supposed to quiet the nerves, to allow one to sleep—

Snow still hissed outside, but within, the kitchen was as it had always looked from the first
day she had arrived at Whitebridge. Gwennan set
her mug of tea close to hand, curled up on the
sofa with two blankets pulled about her shoulders, reached for the nearest book. Slowly her
will began to win the battle. She felt herself re-
laxing—all that uneasiness and excitement of
moments earlier eased away.

On the third day the snow stopped. Gwennan, impatient at imprisonment, always a little fearful of being drawn to the parlor and what it held unless she could get free of the house, was glad to hear the snow plow again in action. At least she could get as far as the Newtons and perhaps discover when the light and the phones might again tie them to civilization.

Putting on her warmest and most storm-resistent clothing, she ventured out, though it was necessary to flounder through a drift which had near barricaded her front doorway. The yard was a strange territory with no bushes to be seen, save for mounds here and there. Red Anderson hailed her from the road, waving vigorously. Gwennan answered back, then fought her way out to follow along the path the plow had opened to the Newtons' where Paul was shoveling paths. The snow had really outdone all previous records for several years, she learned from the battery powered radio of the Newtons' which filled their kitchen with bulletins and warnings breaking into one another against a constant crackle of static.

"Town's gone into hibernation like a bear," Paul announced as he stamped in. "They closed school for a week. No use you going in, Gwen. Nobody is going to show up at the library, and that place takes too much to heat it. The furnace always was cranky."

Remembering the suffering of her toes and fingers during past cold waves, she was perfectly willing to agree with him.

"Something queer," Florence remarked as she

reached for the coffee pot to fill a mug for Paul,
"they've been talking about some lights in the sky
last night—thought maybe there was a plane off-
course. Announcer real excited about it, said they
were planning to send up a helicopter as soon as
they could to check it out. There was no answer
to any signals—and no one has reported a crash.
Nobody took off from any field around here
either. All those are closed down by the storm.
They kept calling back and forth, trying to find
out what flight might be missing, but no one
seemed to know."

"Lights—?"

Florence nodded in answer to Gwennan's one
word question. "Red ones—and yellow ones, they
said. Then they got excited because no plane uses
yellow signals—none of ours anyway—"

Paul laughed. "UFOs again—though this isn't
the season for them usually. If the Martians have
any sense they'll keep away from our storms. And
they should have plenty of weather sense, seeing
as how they appear to have been navigating our
skies for a good long time now. Could be northern
lights—"

Florence shook her head. "These were small—
not spread all over the sky, as they told it. And
they moved. Well, if it were some plane, that
could be down, and it may be weeks before we
find out. They said clouds were banking up in the
north to come hard at us again. Gwen," she spoke
earnestly now, "why don't you come on in with
us? No sense you staying over there by yourself,
if we get really locked in. We got plenty of pro-
visions. You aren't trying to keep that whole old

barn of a house warm are you?"

"Moved into the kitchen," Gwennan returned. "I don't know, Florence—" She was greatly tempted. Not only by the fact, that, for the first time in her life, she had felt herself a prisoner during the past three days—but also she could so get away from everything which reminded her of what she wanted most to forget. Over here at the Newtons she would not be tempted to visit the parlor to look again at what she had stored there.

"What Florence says is only good sense, Gwen." Paul nodded. "You go get your things— stay here until tomorrow anyway, then if that second storm doesn't hit us, you can make up your mind about it."

"All right, I will!" Gwennan felt defiant, as if she were answering back against a command from an unseen other, one which she had no intention of obeying. She had clung to her independence for a long time, it had been so much of Miss Nessa's training. However, if the cold built up and there was another bad storm—what the Newtons proposed *was* only good sense.

The second storm did hit and its fury was such that Gwen was glad of company, as it appeared they were about to be caught up in another ice age. She sat in a comfortable rocker with Justinia, the black Newton cat who had accepted her at once, curled in her lap, and listened to the howling of the wind. The radio, which had occupied the center of the table since the beginning of this time of fury gave forth distorted voices between crackles of ear splitting static. Now and then they picked up calls of ham radio operators

—asking for help for someone trapped and ill or without adequate supplies.

Paul stood listening to one such plea, the pile of wood he had brought in still across his arms.

"It's a corker this time," he observed. "Makes me think of that article in the magazine—that one I told you about, Gwen. Seems like one of these fellows got to saying that this was about the time for the world to come to an end—talking about the poles changing around causing tidal waves— earthquakes and such. And we have had a couple of hard winters—this one's worse than last. Maybe that north pole is just moving down our way now."

Florence laughed. "End of the world? I've heard them talk about that ever since I was a kid at home. There was some church once that believed that—sold off all their stuff, the people did, put on white robes, and went up on tops of hills waiting to be pulled right up into heaven. Ma always said that no one knew about the future and there weren't no sense in spending time and trouble worrying about it—that all the worry in the world wasn't going to change things.

"If the north pole is going to move down I don't see how any one is going to go out and say 'Stop' and have it do just that. The world's been bumping along for a good long time. We've always had earthquakes—look at them out in California. My niece Margy—she's been through two that knocked her dishes right out of the cupboard. Broke two of the fine old plates Grandma Henshaw willed her. And there was that volcano out west that blew its top off a couple of years or so ago. We've had a lot of things happen—but the world hasn't come to an end yet."

The world come to an end— Gwen was not looking at the table, the Newton kitchen—the warmth and comfort of this room here and now. She hung suspended in space above a sea filled with burning islands, its water steaming away, or heading towards the land in waves too large for any human being to conceive, she saw the earth break apart and spout fire—she saw—death—

"Gwen, Gwen! What on earth's the matter with you, girl!"

The world died as she watched and there was nothing which could be done to stop that fury—nothing—

"Gwen! You sick?"

She was being shaken. That picture was gone as if the earth's fire had crisped it into ashes, the waves rent it apart. Florence leaned over her, her face full of concern. Before she thought, Gwen answered:

"It happened once—once before—"

"What happened, Gwen? You feel faint—you look awfully white. Something wrong? You have a pain somewhere?" Florence's hands were on the girl's shoulders as if she feared Gwen might slip completely out of the chair.

"The end of the world." Gwen was still dazed, still caught in the horror of the Mirror. "There were tidal waves—and volcanoes—the land—everything was swept away." She blinked then and a measure of common sense returned swiftly. "I guess I read too much sometimes, Florence. There was a book." Quickly she summoned her wits to manufacture what her neighbors might believe. "It described a theory—that the world has gone through a number of catastrophes which ended most all life, then everything had to start over again. The author had some very graphic descriptions—you could read them and almost see it all happening."

"You mean the Flood—like in the Bible," Florence nodded. "Yes, Paul said there was more in that magazine article he was talking about, how people all over the world had stories of a flood and how just a few were saved—people who had never heard about our Bible either. Sounds like they all had the same story. But that writer who did the book you're talking about, Gwen, he sure must have written something really upsetting. You looked there for a moment like it was all coming true right in front of you—"

"Miss Nessa always said I had too much imagination," Gwen strove to cover up her self-betrayal. "I guess I just get carried away sometimes when I read something like that. I don't think that we'll ever know the truth if it did happen—except from the old stories."

Paul deposited the fire wood in its box and now came over to pick up the radio, giving it a little shake as if that would subdue the blast of static.

"More likely some darned fool will set off a bomb somewhere and that'll be the end this time," he commented. "We go along just living on the edge of trouble these days. Seems like those who have the say should know it wouldn't do them any good to start such a war—be nothing left worth the claimin' afterwards and no one alive to do that claimin'—on both sides." He sat down and brought out his pipe.

"We wouldn't have any more chance of stoppin' a bomb coming over us now than we would one of those big waves, or a volcano, or the ground opening under us if it took a mind to. We're not as high and mighty, none of us, as we'd like to think we are."

Florence drew her sweater closer together. "That is chilling talk, Paul. What say we get out that old Monopoly game? It might give us something else to think about."

Something else to think about. What had they said in her "dreams"—that it was man himself, not nature, who was the threat this time? Gwen's fingers bit into her palms. Man himself—and could there be any stopping him?

13

It would seem that these dire weather predictions were working out to the satisfaction of the most pessimistic during the following weeks. There would be a milder spell during which Whitebridge resumed the limited winter life, only to face in turn another series of bone-freezing storms and high blizzards from the north. Some weeks Gwennan could get to the library only one or two days. However, business was brisk there when she opened—for the town was turning to books in the threat of a long winter shut-in.

Jim Pyron still burrowed in the Crowder papers, now and then lingering by Gwennan's desk to share some new discovery. It was he who brought news she would rather not have heard, stirring up memories she had thought well under control.

"Young Lyle showed up at Cranston's last night—" he told her. "I'd always heard that the Lyles had their own storehouse, but he did buy supplies. Though I think mainly that was an excuse. He was after something else—"

228

"Oh?" She knew her voice was cool, on the verge of snappish, but Gwennan wanted to hear no more of the Lyles.

"He—well, Gwen, he may have thought he was being smart about it, but I think he wanted to find what you were doing. He wrangled the talk around some, though he didn't come right out to ask any questions."

"Just what was he told?" Now her tone *was* sharp.

"Someone mentioned that you and the New-tons were sticking out the bad days together. Which is only sensible. You know, Gwen—there's something about that fellow. He wants something and he wants it bad. You were friendly with the Lady, weren't you, before she left? Maybe he thinks you know something she told you—something which he needs to know—"

Into Gwennan's mind flashed that last letter. She could remember every word of it—always would, she was sure. The letter and the pen-dant—it was the latter which Tor Lyle wanted. Perhaps if she gave it to him she could be rid of any further participation in Lyle concerns. That was one way—but even as she guessed that she also was sure it was not one she could follow.

"I certainly have nothing to tell him," she re-torted. "Did he suggest that I have?"

The fact that Tor Lyle was trying to check on her brought back with a rush the old uneasiness which she had thought she had escaped.

No! she was not going to remember, to start again any dealings with the Lyles, those wild dreams, hallucinations or such, which they ap-peared able to control.

"It isn't so much what he says." The girl realized that Jim was watching her closely. That she resented also. "It is just that he *is* fishing. Not that it gets him anywhere. He certainly hasn't the liking of the town. Arrogant cuss—though he tries to be agreeable. Only he's too impatient, I would say—and his temper gets away from him now and then. I'd be careful, Gwen. The Lyles have a queer standing in this town, always have had.

"None of them have ever thrown their weight around very much. On the other hand, no one has ever denied that they do have a lot of power if they want to use it. Most of them have kept their distance, the Crowder accounts make that very clear. It is as if they live one life and the town another—distant acquaintances, you might say. This Tor Lyle is something rather new — he pushes—too much at times. And there's something about him—as if—"

"As if he is laughing at us inside—" Gwennan returned without thinking, then was heartily sorry the minute the words were out of her mouth.

"Then you *have* come up against him! Gwen— be careful. I'm glad you're with the Newtons. You're altogether too isolated out on the far fringe of town that way."

"Why should I have anything to fear from Tor Lyle?" she demanded, her chin up, anger rising still higher in her.

Jim Pyron looked away from her, down at the two old ledgers he had collected that afternoon. "Perhaps you don't," he answered slowly. "It's just that fellow—well, he's strange, even for a

Lyle. Maybe he'll take off again soon. Few of them ever spend the winters here. At least," now he laughed, "this weather has gotten rid of the Devil for us—too cold for his Satanic Majesty—or his emissary. There have been no more chicken killings or bad smells around. Maybe the blizzards have done us one favor. About time you closed up, isn't it? Paul take you home?"

She nodded, very glad for the change of subject. Though she was going to make no comments about devils and the like. Again memory had risen in a surge which she wanted to push away. She had a momentary mental picture of that monstrous crew which had followed Tor's other personality in the green-lit world and perhaps had even answered to his drawing in this. Just how much was he responsible for what had appeared at her window that night? Why had such a creature sought her out? Was that also because of an order from Tor?

She spent Thanksgiving with the Newtons. Jim Pyron's guess concerning Tor Lyle's leaving town apparently had been true, for the last of the Lyles had not been seen again. Gwennan trusted that he had indeed disappeared, after the way of his clan, to seek a warmer climate for the rest of the winter.

As December began, the weather, oddly enough, for all its fury earlier, grew milder. Gwennan, back in her own home, kept to the round of duties she had followed for years. She made only one trip to the front parlor, bundling up the books there and taking them back to the library, firmly intent on seeing them returned through the interloan system to those establishments which owned them. She had left the papers of her notes, stuffed into a large manuscript envelope, lying on the seat of one of the very uncomfortable chairs, the same chair over the back of which she had thrown the cloak.

The scent that clung to it had grown sharper in the cold room rather than faded. That strange fabric, now fully exposed, gave forth continually its own odor, as might a blooming flower. And her first impression of the fabric, that it had once been a living thing and not woven from any thread she knew, persisted.

She found herself at times tempted to bring the garment out, examine it more closely. But she had strength of will enough not to yield to that temptation, congratulating herself on her ability to shut off firmly any further desire to learn what had influenced her weeks ago. Deliberately she kept to Miss Nessa's narrow routine.

Christmas had never been a particularly excit-ing or joyous season as far as her aunt had been concerned. Perhaps the very old New England custom of considering it a popish holiday, not to be celebrated in any way, had filtered down among the Daggert clan—at least to Miss Nessa's generation. Gwennan bought a handful of cards, realizing, as she spread them out on the table, just how few people she really knew—even in this village where she had lived for most of her life.

She dutifully addressed one to the family of each board member as was fitting, found one for Miss Graham and her mother, remembered the Newtons. And, having sealed and stamped that

small pile, put them aside. There were a few gifts
—to the Grahams, the Newtons—selected from
catalogues luckily far enough ahead so that the
recent tie-up of mail had not interfered with their
delivery. She surveyed her preparations for the
holiday, and, for the first time, saw them as limited.

Of course there was the baking. Miss Nessa at
least had seen that as a duty. The mince tarts
would go with her to the Newtons for Christmas
dinner, then there was her one timid recognition
of the season as far as the town was concerned—
the cookies for the plate she would keep filled in
the library during the Christmas week.

Though she was no such cook as many of the
townswomen were, Gwennan managed, as she believed, very well on the score of what she did—
again Miss Nessa's training. There were no deco-
rations to be put up in the house, of course—
but she achieved greens for the library, while
Miss Graham's class had sent class made Santas
and other seasonal cutouts which she placed to
the best advantage.

Midwinter day—

Gwennan stood now by the table where she had
carefully set out mixing bowls, cookie tins, all in-
gredients she had been gathering over the weeks
for this supreme effort.

Midwinter day—

The significance of that broke into her mind as
a painful blow. She put her hands to the side of
her head, cowered against the table. No! She
would not! She owed nothing to Lady Lyle—except memories now flooding through her with

force enough to set her shaking, sick, with fear rising cold in her.

Midwinter day—

She had not promised. She had *never promised!* Certainly she could not be forced to do as she had been instructed when she had given no promise! She had not asked for Lady Lyle's legacy—she wanted nothing but to be left alone. Left alone!

Midwinter day—

Even as Gwennan fought desperately, she knew that she had no hope of winning. She had been so very sure that she freed herself from the compulsion, that she was no longer any tool of the Lyle's. At this moment she learned how futile had been her attempt to build walls and barriers—that she had been allowed a shadow of freedom as a cat might allow a mouse to run a little before the lazy and powerful paw closed upon it again. She was not free—she was caught.

Weakly Gwennan dropped into the nearest chair. She had never been given to tears. Even as a child she had greeted both pain and sore disappointment with tight lips and an inner resolve not to cry. Now she felt her eyes filling as if she had no control over her emotions at all. These others had set their mark on her—she was as much a servant to the Lyles as the dark-faced, silent people she had seen under their roof on her few visits there. That was the other side of all the wonders that house held—this slavery—for slavery it truly was—which held fast those the Lyles wished to bend to their own service.

She fought, pulling on every atom of her own will and determination. Gwennan made herself get up, she did not even try to wipe away those slowly welling tears—let them run. She could still fight and she would. Her hands moved, uncertainly at first and then with greater purpose. She measured, stirred, cut out the fanciful shapes provided by the very old set of tin cutters she had found far back in the cupboard during a spring cleaning turn-out. She put cookies on the sheets into the oven, took them forth again, gold and crisp under their scattering of green or red sugar—and she fought—seeking always to twist and turn for freedom.

But, as she piled the cool cookies into the gay tin boxes set ready for them, the girl knew that she had already lost the battle with that first sharp stab of memory. Tomorrow morning she must do just as Lady Lyle had meant when that letter had been written. She would once again play a Lyle game and there was no escaping it.

That night she went early to bed—setting the alarm with fingers which were stiff enough to ache. Before she did that, she had gone into the parlor and taken up the cloak and the envelope which contained the pendant watch. As she clasped the latter in her hand once again, she saw that the dial was alive—that both sets of symbols, large and small were visible, that the light bars were dimly aglow. Though she would rather have opened the window beside her and hurled that thing out into the nearest snow drift, she lifted the chain and allowed it to encircle her neck once more. That warmth which seemed native to the silvery metal lay against her skin directly between her breasts.

Gwennan feared, expected, dreams to haunt her that night. Instead her sleep was deep, untroubled. She awoke before the alarm sounded, quickly and completely, as if a voice had summoned her. Methodically she dressed in her warmest clothes, nor did she stop to eat or drink.

Instead she caught up the cloak, and, on the doorstep, under the fading stars, she pulled it around her. Once more it enfolded her—eagerly —if one could say that of a piece of cloth (if cloth this was), closed around her as if she and no one else had ever been intended to wear it. The scent arose, now sharper. That was no perfume of winter but rather one which promised spring and the reawakening of the earth to new life.

The lane was only partially cleared when she turned into that path. Here were no signs that anyone had passed—at least no one from the Lyle House. The field wall was a mound, white and smoothly humped. Overhead the sky greyed, no clouds showing—a clear day to come.

A clear day and sun rising over the High Stone. Midwinter day—once a festival to which dark shadows clung. So much crowded into Gwennan's mind. This was the shortest day of all, when the sun must be coaxed back to serve the world—sometimes through cruel sacrifice. There had been blood spilled on the snow once when men, long lost to all but remnants of old knowledge, had tried to draw back the natural warmth and life of their world—bring life anew.

This snow did not pack nor cling to the hem of her long cloak. In fact the edges appeared to sweep aside any impediment offered by drifts through which it was necessary for Gwennan to make her way. She was at the wall which she had climbed across so many times in the past. The girl leaned forward using both arms, the cloak flaring wide, to sweep a way.

The fringes of the wood stood stark and black against the white drifts. Once across the wall, Gwennan paused to eye the stand of trees. They appeared so thick set that, even lacking leaves, this shadowed stretch formed a place of concealment—for what? She did not know except that she disliked that thought.

Knee deep in the snow she floundered on, keeping well away from the trees. There was the mound and the stones. Though they had wide tops snow had not crowned them, nor did drifts lie about the mound itself, as she discovered when she began to climb. Perhaps the winds continually scoured this small height, and kept it so uncovered.

There was light enough for her to sight the roof of the house. A single small trail of smoke arose there into the quiet air—the only sign of life visible. The wood was utterly silent.

Gwennan came to a stand between the two shorter stones—the third one towering before her. Reaching under the edge of the cloak she pulled down the zipper fastening her parka and drew out the pendant. That brightness of symbol which had showed when she first put it on was yet flashing—and the warmth of it reached through her mitten into her hand.

She raised it, dial out, towards those deep rose banners across the sky. The sun was rising.

At that moment the utter silence of the world was broken. A horn—afar, faint—sounding a call such as might have once summoned worshipers to a temple. It rang proudly, demandingly—

She started, looked to the wood below, more than half expecting to see something—someone— emerge from there in answer to that summons. But there was no movement. Then the dial shot forth a ray of light. Down that beam traveled a spiral of gold, aimed at the midsection of the tallest stone.

Where it met the surface it washed outward. Those markings which she had always known were there but could never quite plainly see came instantly alive. There was no show of erosion now. And they tugged at her mind—as if she knew but could not quite remember—not—

"Fal, Fal—Iaqua—trunc—

Aspex sim, dontpex—"

Out of nowhere words came to her. The twisting of the spiral of light fitted itself to the rhythm of them. Also she *knew!*

"Strength, Strength—give me of your bounty— Open to true blood, locks be broken!"

In answer the light of the dial's twisted beam bathed the whole of the stone, flooding upward towards the sky, downwards to where that wider foot was deep buried in the earth.

That pillar, which had appeared so rooted, was bending, canting away from her. Was the rock itself bowing to the rising sun? It moved very slowly, reluctantly, still it was plain that a force it could not resist forced obedience.

Gwennan voiced sounds which were no longer

words, rather formed vibrations crucial to this time and place—sounds which carried a power greater than any man might exert with either hand or tool. And the pillar answered to them.

The stone rested near on its side. Where it had stood was a dark opening in the ground. Gwennan's hand fell. The light from the dial now poured into that dusky well rather than upon the rock which had so long masked it. She sighted a step within, another below that.

Sweeping the cloak more tightly about her, she began to descend, still clicking with her tongue those weird, rhythmic sounds knowledge other than her conscious memory supplied.

Rock walls arose about her as rough-hewn as the stone above—there had been no attempt to smooth this path. A damp, earth born odor gathered, to be in turn banished by the scent of her cloak which freshened the stale air. She descended an endless staircase, for, as far as the light from the watch reached, there was nothing but the treads and the walls on either side.

A grating sound broke through her low chant. Gwennan was startled enough to look back and up, in that moment realizing the great folly of entering what might be a fatal trap. The stretch of sky she could see was narrowing. That stone which had bowed to the sun to allow her to enter was rising again. Before she could retreat it would wall her in.

Gwennan made an effort to break that compulsion moving her—too late. The rock had returned into its footing at a much quicker pace than it had opened.

Down and down went the stairway. Now she noted signs that it had not survived perfectly. There were cracks in the walls here and there, one large enough for her to insert a hand. Some of the treads underfoot were broken. There was one bad place where she had to turn sidewise, planting her boots edgewise on a step to negotiate four or five of them at all, they had been so clipped and reduced.

She became aware of the other light only slowly, her eyes being so completely attuned to that given forth by the watch dial. However, a dim break of the dark did show ahead, to one side. Gwennan reached the last of those steps to front an archway rudely chipped in a wall. Beyond that was the dull coloring of day—a cloudy, stormy day. She faced a hall or tunnel and the light came from squares of what looked to be dirty, much-seamed quartz set in the walls at intervals. It had a dreary appearance as might the inner ways of a prison and she thought of those dungeon halls which had run beneath the temple in Ortha's time and world. Still, even those had been brighter.

The hall was not too long, ending at another door. But this one was effectively barred by a slab of dark wood which displayed no latch nor hinge—a barrier past which she could not win her way. She thought of that sealing stone behind her and knew fear.

Impulse made her raise the dial, send its beam about the four edges of that door—just as one might use a cutter about the lid of a container. Where that ray passed there showed a line followed by a small curl of smoke. Twice more she made that pass about the edge of the barrier, deepening the line.

Then she cried aloud those same words which had come into her mind on the top of the mound. Some property of this dim, dreary hall magnified her voice, made the tone resound so that it had not the full semblance of a human tongue.

There was a loud crash. The barrier her light had severed fell inward, giving way to a light as bright as the dial, in which its rays were swallowed up. Gwennan smelled a strange odor, partly the richness of spice, partly chemical, nose wrinkling with its pungency.

So she came to a room or hall so vast, full of so much that it was hard to concentrate her sight on any one item piled therein. Color fought with color, and over it all shone the brilliant light. Ripples of light traveled through the air itself, pausing now and then to entwine this or that object as if bidding so for her attention. She was bewildered, a little dizzy, as she stood blinking— then rubbed her eyes with the back of her mittened hand. Too much to see—crowded, sacked, piled around her were things she could not view clearly because there was no order, all had been so ruthlessly jammed together. Still, as far as she could look, either ahead or to either side, Gwennan could sight no end, no other walls.

This was a treasure house, and also a storage place. There stood statues not unlike those which she had viewed in the niches at Lyle House, but their strange beauty was lost because they were piled so close to one another. Those things which

might have been machines—tubings of metal,
cogs and wheels were stacked in total disorder.
Boxes, chests, cylinders tightly lidded abounded.
The wealth or loot of a whole civilization—or a
greater part of it—must have been hastily dragged here, never to be freed.

Gwennan at last noted that before her opened a
wandering path or cleared way, where all else
was stacked tightly, to a height well above her
head, with the jumble. If she would advance she
must follow that. The passage did not run
straight, but made detours about some of the
larger machines. She had not gone far along it
when a glance behind showed she had already
lost sight of the entrance.

The light of the dial had died. Perhaps it was
not meant to compete with that which flowed
from bars set in a cross-hatching overhead. Yet
those floating, colored ribbons of light drifting
along did not appear to be born from that source
either.

Once or twice one of them, perhaps as long as
she was tall, would float beside her to the right or
left for a space, wreathing one or another of the
stacked objects as if so courting her attention.
But she never paused to explore that which they
would direct her to. The wealth about her grew
suffocating the farther she advanced. She could
admire the objects she had seen at Lyle House,
but here the mass pushed in about her, threaten-
ing her with the weight of all the riches a man
could be tempted to possess.

On wound the path. Gwennan so far had
sighted no farther wall. This was as wild a dream

in its way as the others she had known. She
wanted out—even just to see bare rock, plain and
of the earth she knew. Skirting an open chest in
which lay a tangle of gem-studded chains, the
edge of her cloak swept one from the top. It
jangled to the floor, the sound made her start and
look back anxiously.

But if there were any guardians in this place,
they did not appear. In truth Gwennan wanted
nothing of these treasures. Her desire was only
for freedom.

Yet the path led on, endlessly twisting until
sometimes the girl suspected she was backtrack-
ing rather than advancing. Perhaps this was a
maze in itself, a protection set up to mystify and
completely entangle any intruder. That being so
she would never come to the end of it.

Ahead two of the ribbons of the light hung in
the air. One was dark green, not unlike the shade
of her cloak, the other a rich gold. Even as she
caught sight of them they began to move, in a
twirling dance, one about the other. They still
hung above the path, wafting ahead only as she
approached them. Could she believe that they
were guides?

14

Drawn by those two interweaving streamers, Gwennan chanced upon a second narrow way branching off the main path. Turning into that she arrived once more at a wall concealed, until one came directly upon it, by the piles of treasure. Here was a door unsealed, for silently it arose upward even as she approached, affording a clear passage out into another and much smaller chamber.

Though this was not bare, it was far more orderly. The furnishings had been set carefully in place, not jammed without any design except storage. Seats were stationed at measured distances, before each a table or desk—Gwennan was not sure which. The wall to her left was not formed of native stone such as she had seen elsewhere, presenting a smooth surface resembling a very large mirror or plate of glass—save that nothing within the room was reflected on it. Facing that squarely was a single seat, apart from the rest, and very different in shape.

Gwennan shivered. She guessed now in a rush

what this meant and there could be no escape. What stood before her was the tripod stool of a seer. Only—she was *not* Ortha—she could not summon—

Nor could she, it would seem, control her body either. For she went to the stool even as she vowed within that she dare not. Stiffly, reluctantly, fighting her own body, Gwennan sat down.

All right, she was in the seat of a seer, but that did not mean she was about to play that role. She shifted her weight, trying to rise and leave—

That wall which was a mirror—truly a mirror —clouded. Even as Ortha had last viewed what was afar upon the billowing smoke and ash veil filling the doomed temple, so did Gwennan see the surface before her cloud, vapor rising to roll across it.

She half raised her hand, striving to cover her eyes, forgetting for the moment that she still gripped the pendant. The rich light of its dial rayed outward, but, before that beam touched the surface of that wall it was defused, became a haze clinging to the mirror, sinking inward to produce a change—objects gained substance within.

A square as tall as Gwennan steadied, to become clearly visible. She might be a child in a schoolroom faced by a blackboard, set to learn a necessary lesson. Markings darkened, starkly sharp. She recognized a reproduction of that same horoscope which had borne her own date of birth. But how could this be here? She wished she knew more (or had been permitted not to know at all—to have remained ignorant and free). Already she discovered she could not shut her eyes or

look away.

A pain grew within her head, a prying, a loosening. Gwennan crouched lower on the tripod and moaned faintly, partly because of the pain of opening a barrier that in her species had long remained closed, partly in fear of what might be freed at such an opening.

Before her was the key to life—her life. Stars wove their appointed patterns and the wheel turned—very slowly, hardly at all by the measurements of short-lived mankind. But turn it did. Thus it came full circle again after thousands of years, untold time. There was her life which had been once and now was again.

There had been no dream of Ortha, she had indeed *been* Ortha—and many others. From each of those lives she had carried onward a fragment of power—a portion of that which was greater than her human blurred senses could ever accept or understand. Now the full circle had been completed, she was once more to face, to do—and this time handicapped even more than Ortha, because through the flow of the past she had lost so much—

Tears of pain, of loss (for she had lost, Gwennan knew, all the safe, sure life which had been) were wet on her cheeks, dripped from her chin to the stiff collar of the cloak.

There was a change in the mirror which she must watch. Once more she viewed the dying world which had been, saw the survivors fall to the level of mindless animals. No, become less than animals, for in madness they did that which beasts did not do to their own kind, even to their prey. She saw the flow of death continue. Here and there would rise a man, a woman, who bore the look of that older race. They were quiet, cautious, secretive, striving to teach, to train, to reach those among the beast-people who could be influenced.

Some were proclaimed gods and goddesses in spite of their denials. Some failed their tasks, to accept such homage, using their control over the lesser for their own reasons. Some died—some grew weary and disappeared. But always they came to labor, and, nearly always, they failed. For a generation or two they might lift, teach, lead. Then men and women, having reached a point, did not progress farther. There followed wars, slayings, plagues, knowledge used wrongly —again a weary rise, to begin all over again.

Guardians, those strangers from the past deemed themselves. Their numbers grew less during the centuries. They produced few of their own kind, for it appeared that only a handful were fertile. Some, isolated in loneliness among those they strove to teach, took mates. There were a few, a very few children, of such mixed matings. In a handful of these offspring the old blood was strong. New teachers arose here or there, or people living obscurely had subtle influence, making better the time and place in which they appeared. Others—others were of blood and also of the Dark. They sought power to use in greed and pride. There were mighty conquerors among them, leaders of another kind— tearing down what had been so painfully built.

Never was this long battle over—only small victories won, which, within years, blew away, as formless dust and ash. It would seem that madness ruled the world and never would sanity or the light again prevail.

So Gwennan watched as time rolled by in huge waves of centuries. Now came history she knew through her researching, but how false was much which had been since taught, how far removed from the truth mirrored before her. Events hailed as facts were a coating of hallucination— sometimes deliberately reported so, sometimes altered in report because of the flaws in men's own minds begun with the first survivors.

Then, abruptly, as if that which controlled the mirror (it was certainly no power of her own which summoned this surfeit of defeat, death, and constant wrenching of lives) changed what it showed. There was no longer a wide panorama of action centering in at intervals upon one man, one woman, or one set of actions which had changed the whole course of the future. Rather she watched one of the guardians—and Gwennan knew her, in spite of the unfamiliar dress, the look of wearied, greatly wearied age.

This was Lady Lyle, more worn and more haunted even than the girl had last seen her. She moved slowly, painfully, as if with every step she took the strength drained from her as blood from a death wound. Here was a chamber lighted a cold blue. Down its center stretched a raised platform on which rested boxes of crystal which had the look of coffins.

Those closest to the doorway through which that woman had come so slowly were clearer

—the one at the very end totally transparent. Gwennan could see through the sides of two more though there was a cloudiness gathering to cloak what they held. In one rested a man, the other a woman. Both bodies were the white of frost upon the ground, their eyes closed, no sign of any breath or life about them. As the line advanced so did the murkiness of coffins grow thicker, until those at the far end of the line might have been wrought of marble not crystal, their occupants sealed away forever.

The woman who came, steadied herself with one hand upon the lid of the unoccupied coffin. Her back was bowed, her face so gaunt with weariness that much of its flesh drew tight against the bones. Her other hand plucked at the fastenings of her garments, a coarse, black full skirted dress with a wide white collar. She tugged and pulled until that fell about her ankles. The yellowish underclothing beneath were also discarded. Then she pulled from her head a tight, plain cap which had covered most of thin white hair, letting the locks loose about her bony shoulders. She was very old, her body near that of a walking skeleton, the spirit within her burning close to its final embers.

Leaving her clothing as it lay, the woman exerted what appeared to Gwennan to be a vast effort to lift up the lid of the waiting coffin. She climbed in. A shade of thankfulness, of joy crossed her face, she welcomed death eagerly—

She stretched out in the crystal box as the cover, without her touching it, descended. The woman's eyes were already closed. Gwennan could not see any lift of that breast where the bones showed so sharply.

Yet, though the entombing was past, the picture did not fade. Rather some voice she neither heard nor understood directed Gwennan's attention to the solidly white coffin at the far end of that line. The closing of the woman's refuge might well have been a signal. There followed a cracking across the surface there—one which spread in lines. Patches of solid material broke free, dropped into powdery fragments. The lid moved, ponderously, sending rolling from it the accumulation of centuries.

Gwennan could not yet see who or what lay within; however, there were movements along the edge of the box, fingers hooked there, a hand appeared. Slowly, stiffly a figure arose to a sitting position. A woman had entered the first coffin and gone to her rest, but a man aroused, sitting up for a long moment as if he must gather strength before he climbed out. He was young, his well-muscled shoulders twisted, moved, as he threw both arms wide, stretching, limbering up. Then he got to his feet and stepped forth.

At first Gwennan's breath caught—Tor? Then he faced her squarely as he left that time-embowered bed, began to exercise, stretching, bending, willing his body to life. He had the same brilliant golden hair—near the same cast of features as Tor Lyle, yet this was a different man, though perhaps a kinsman, one of a close-bred line.

He stumbled at first as he walked away from the line of coffins but his steps grew firmer and more assured with each step. Now he approached a niche in the wall and there opened a small grille from behind which he drew a bottle of rainbow bright glass. Pouring a small measure of its contents into a matching cup, he drank with a single gulp. Paying no attention to the line of coffins, he strode along until he came to the huddle of clothing the woman had discarded. There he stopped and shook out those garments. There fell something from among their folds, some object upon which he pounced eagerly. Holding his find in one hand, he gathered up the clothing in a rough bundle, to thrust the whole of it into another niche in the wall where it rested untidily for a moment before it flared up in flames to be almost instantly consumed.

The man turned and left the chamber, his find in his hand, and the mirror picture faded away. Only Gwennan knew now. The Lyles—were they the only ones? Or had there been other clans to know such renewing—rebirth? What of the half-lings—those whose blood were mixed? Did they renew? Or for them was it always normal rebirth, a reliving with all the loss of memory, the loss of even the faint shadow of the Power—a weary, rebeginning each time?

Once more the girl faced the chart of the horoscope—the turn of the star wheel. This insistence that *she* was one who carried the same potential as Ortha pressed upon her as might a physical burden. She felt as weary as that other Lady Lyle who had gone to sleep in her renewing coffin. And must recently have gone again—

Gwennan's head bobbed as if to reassure

another part of her. No death for the Lyles. They
went into their sleep to return once more, following a set cycle. What did they deal with now—
were they still teachers, covert leaders? What of
the warning that even as the star wheel had
turned for her, so had it turned for all the world,
and once more a cycle of disaster was upon
them?

A disaster wrought by man, not nature this
time. The threat of a final war had enshadowed
the world ever since Hiroshima had proved that
man could relearn old knowledge but apply it
only to strike out and destroy. So much had madness clung through the generations. War—and
complete destruction. So what could these
sleepers—even if they were all awakened and
spread throughout the world—do to prevent such
a catastrophe? Any more than they had once been
able to prevent the coming of the dead moon
world which had brought with it such destruction?

There was a vast despondency in her, a hope-
lessness which was as evil in its way as any of the
monsters Gwennan had seen prowl from another
plane. She looked upon the horoscope and
thought it mockery. What did it mean to her that
the wheel had turned? She was no Guardian—

Burning fire in her hand, a blaze to jerk her
attention away from the mirror to the pendant
she held. Now the dial of the watch was a glare of
light—no longer could she distinguish any of the
symbols, for bands of light which barred it spun
with such fury that they formed a single blazing disc. Half-blood—no holder of the Power—

Swiftly she attempted to deny what she held.

Gwennan shook, her body wove from side to side on the flimsy support of the seer's tripod. There was such a spin of half thoughts, of only dimly realized impressions in her mind that the pain there grew unbearable. She was aware of torment as a black wave rising to engulf her, then lost her last hold on the outer world and fell forward, far down, helplessly, into a dark nothingness.

Dark and nothingness, yet there was something to be sought, to be gained—to be held to. She was a seeker and she could not deny that, even though she now longed for the peace of a dark which would never stir again.

There was no road of thread to follow this time, no gates which stood for the signs of Power—and which did not try to hold her back. If she moved (she could not even be sure that she did) it was through nothingness where she was only a small lingering essence of self—fast fading—not caring—

Gwennan opened her eyes. Had the darkness only come because she had closed them in protest against the pain? Flowing through her, making her body tingle, her flesh prickle, was an energy which she could not have controlled even had she so wished. She no longer huddled on the tripod, nor had she fallen to the floor before it. Rather she was walking, and here was no mirror, no shining wall.

The corridor she paced swiftly, and with a purpose she only half understood, was not rough rock walled. Instead here was polished masonry in huge, strangely angled blocks, each fitted so carefully together that there was no sign of any mortar to tie them so.

Overhead the ceiling hung low. Gwennan could have reached up an arm, run her fingertips along the stone slabs which formed it as she went. There was no light except that which she carried with her—which radiated from the pendant in her hand, flared also from the floating cloak about her shoulders. She walked in light—she—was—a carrier—

Gwennan now lifted her free hand, held it up and out—

The Voice! No, *she* had no Power. Still from her fingertips threaded ribbons of light—pale in color, possessing none of the brilliancy she had seen evoked in Ortha's temple. She waved her hand, spread those fingers. The light ribbons floated lazily, weaving about her as she went.

Even as she so played, child-wise, with what now filled her, she sought to fit one small portion of knowledge to another. The leys—that old belief was the truth! Within the earth—like the veins within any living body—ran those lines of energy. Man had known them once—drawn upon them for healing, for defense, for the well being of the world. Then they had broken, diverged—and only the legend of them remained. Yet they were not dead, only rebuilding, renewing within themselves. Once more broken ends joined here and there, channels formed anew—perhaps a fraction less strong because of their half destruction—but ever growing.

There had been those (the guardians and those

whose minds could be reached) who had built new temples once, rough and without beauty, but encasing, fostering, aiming the energies. Knowledge lost, knowledge half found, knowledge lost again—a pattern so often repeated. There was energy here where once had stood a great temple. As yet it was a feeble burst, when compared with what had once flowered upon call—but it was here!

The strange and massive walls about her were broken by insets of stone which were blue, or which were studded with quartz in rough clumps. There were holes in some of those plates, small enough to accept only a finger, large enough to engulf a hand to the wrist. She avoided those because she did not know enough, not yet, perhaps not ever. Hers was another task, one which she did not yet understand and which perhaps she could learn only bit by bit.

Once more Gwennan was faced by a door and this was a wedge of rock, triangular, point meeting the surface of the pavement—a little wider than her shoulders at its greatest. The girl slipped the chain of the pendant around her neck to rest on the folds of the cloak where those smoothed only against the rise of her breasts. She put forth both hands, laid palms against the stone. However, she did not seek to exert any strength, either to push or slide, she merely stood and let that which gathered in her flood into the stone. And the force did seep into that. The rock of the barrier was like a sponge greedily sopping up spilled liquid.

There came a harsh grating. Gwennan sensed

resistence to her desire. Still she was not to be
refused. The stone lifted until her arms were
stretched well above her head. She threw herself
forward then, knowing the danger of what she
did. The stone crashed once more, to bury its
point against the pavement. But it had not caught
her in its fall.

Thus she came out of the place of ancient
masonery. More stone walls—but these were like
any to be seen in a cellar. Arranged around them,
and in rows forming aisles, were shelves of unfinished lumber, hung with cobwebs, grey with
old dust. There were jars and bottles grimed and
thick with more dust sitting there. The place was
very dusky, near complete dark. That energy
which had filled her, flowed outward from her
had drained, was dying down, leaving her weakened as she remembered Ortha had always been
weakened after her bouts of farseeing.

There remained just enough glare to show a
flight of steps ahead. Gwennan turned to look
backward from the three cornered door. There
was no sign of it—only a fieldstone wall. From
this side it was well concealed. One of those
new parts of her mind supplied, without her
conscious direction, the secret of its opening
once again. One stepped to the left, one pushed on
a stone thus, then pulled again, downward on an
edge of shelf. That would not open the door, no,
but it would reveal it to the seeker.

Gwennan had no desire to return, the way was
before her now and not back. She crossed the
floor of the cellar, climbed the wooden steps,
needing a hold on the rough bannister for sup-

port as she went. It was more and more an effort for her to keep moving.

There was another door at the head of those stairs, one with an old iron latch of the kind which had been in use two centuries ago. The girl grasped it with what firmness she could, bore down, so came out into a tall ceilinged room which she knew. This was the library of Lyle House—nor was she surprised that her journeying had brought her here.

In the wide fireplace wood burned with a blue flame from which came the strong scent of the same kind of incense which had clothed the globe in her own home on that night when Lady Lyle's talisman had come into her hand. There were tall candelabra, glinting with gold and jewels, the main portions of which were fashioned, one as a man, a warrior for he held a bared sword and there was on him the seeming of a mail coat, though he wore no helmet—rather the finely depicted curls on his head were half hidden by an oddly shaped crown which could be the branching antlers of a stag woven together. There were green gems set in his finely featured face for eyes and those were live in the firelight.

Fronting that candelabra which carried five red candles aflame, was the other and it was formed as a woman whose body was hardly concealed by a short tunic she wore, one baring her arms and much of her breast. In the hollow between those half-revealed breasts hung a pendant twin to the one Gwennan carried in her hand, and on the high held head of the woman was a second representation of the full-half moon wrought into

the forepart of a crown. Five candles she supported also, but these were blue, and the flame
which danced from their wicks was pale and
silvery in contrast to the rich gold of the red ones.

Both the candelabra stood on a table, a solid
unornamented slab of wood, a crosscut section of
some tree so giant in girth as to be beyond
modern imagining. The wood was highly polished
so that the rings showed—and of a dark honey
color within an outermost section of deep brown
bark.

So polished was that surface that both the
candelabra were mirrored in it, yet their reflec-
tions were broken and obscured by three objects
between them. There was a cup—or rather a
chalice—of a red color, its stem a single long
crystal, octagonal in shape. Before that lay,
blades crossed, two knives or daggers—their
hilts of some dull, dark stone but finely wrought,
so that one was the head of a wolf (or was it both
wolf and man in a terrifying mixture of one
nature with the other?) and there were red stones
for the eyes.

The second knife bore another head which she
knew only too well. This was that owl-faced thing
which had been one of the monster pack. It was
fashioned of grey, dirty-looking stone. Its two
eyes were red and alive.

As the girl stared at the table both her hands
moved to the pendant. It seemed to her that the
cloak stirred of itself about her, enfolding her
protectively. For what lay there, bright and
shining as it was, held—the Dark—the old Dark—
in all of it. In a way this display profaned the

room, bringing a shadow to soil what should be light.

Somehow she dared not turn her back upon it. A quick glance at the near wall showed her the door through which she had always entered on her visits here. That opened into the hall—then it was only a short distance to the outer portal and she would be free. There had been a change in this house—her heightened senses were aware that below the fresh scent of the incense gathered a sickly-sweet taint of corruption.

Tor's mark! She believed it as firmly as if she had seen him offering an invocation here. If Tor was the newly awakened Guardian for this time —then indeed fear must be faced. And he was greater than she—even if he was half-blood. His learning must have taken him very far along the road of knowledge—light or dark. She was something he could indeed mock. Why had Lady Lyle seen fit to pit her against him? The old line must indeed have come near to extinction to have only such a desperate choice.

Gwennan moved, ever facing the table, listening, sure that Tor had only momentarily left the room—that at any moment he would return to carry forward whatever invocation or ceremony he had planned. When she reached the door she had to lean against the wide panel for a moment to gather strength before she dare open it.

Her fingers closed upon the latch as her nerves triggered her next move. Throwing open the door, she lurched into the hall.

Though there was no one in sight she waited,

listening. To cross those last few feet to freedom was one of the hardest things she had ever attempted. She saw the sly eyes of the woods-maiden catch a glint of light. Those followed her —even as did those of the other statue. She flung herself at the outer door, dragged it open. Luckily it was not locked as she had feared. Then, breathing as hard as if she had been running, she pushed into the weak sunlight of what must be early afternoon.

15

There had been no effort here to clear away the snow, nor was there any track across drifts to suggest that anyone had recently gone in or out. Floundering along, Gwennan glanced apprehensively back over her shoulder. The deep-set windows with small diamond-shaped, lead-set panes looked dull, like eyes from which the spark of light had departed.

Still a fire had been burning on the hearth, someone had lighted those candles. Yet, now as her fear faded in this open, the girl was aware that there had been a curious emptiness in that house. The servants? Always before on her visits here they had been within sight sooner or later, moving after their silent shadowy fashion. They had had, she sometimes imagined, their own secret world, from which they emerged only at call from the head of the house.

Where could they be now? And Tor— Surely it must have been Tor, the new master, who had set ready that altar table. Yet she had seen nothing of him. But the house was large, she had never known how large, and it must have many rooms above, behind those she had visited. Except—all had been so quiet.

Gwennan had to wade through two unbroken drifts to reach the rough pillars marking the lane. Even here there had been no recent plowing. However, the walking was better. She refused to look back again, nor, as she moved along the buried wall, did she allow her head to turn to glance to the stones on the mound crest. There sounded a harsh cry from that part of the woods closest to the wall's boundary. She flinched and then took herself in hand—only a bird's call. Though as much as she knew of the wild life about she had never heard such a sullen, loud-carrying cackle before.

The lane curved, she sighted her own house, the stand of trees between it and the Newtons. Gwennan began to run, slipping and sliding, but determined to reach a place which meant return to the sane world. Once she had gained the open that domination which held her since her journey forth in the dawn was defeated, or withdrew, allowing the reality she had always known to rise and claim her again. She was two—and in her those two vied for rule—

The door was unlocked. She must have left it so when she ventured forth. A whole day near gone and how could she account for those missing hours if she were asked? She shut the door behind her. There was warmth in the hall. Dusk gathered as she turned and shot the bolt.

Gwennan realized that she was hungry as well

as tired. At least the pain in her head had subsided into a nagging ache, but it left a weak feeling. When she reached the kitchen she was forced
to sit down for a moment, staring thankfully
about at the familiar—drawing into her once
again that feeling of safety which was a part of
this house. The loosening of the eye brooch allowed the cape to slide from her shoulders, nor
did the fabric now try to enfold her, to cling.

Shuffling the wad of material into another
chair, shedding her outer clothing, Gwennan got
to the business of frying eggs, turning thick slices
of country bacon, filling the coffee pot.

She ate as if she could not get enough food, ending with a handful of those cookies, broken or a
little too brown, which had been discarded from
the library tin. Tomorrow was Sunday. She
would call the Grahams, say she could not make
it into town. She wanted nothing more than to
sleep—and sleep—and sleep—

To sleep—but not to dream! The thought of
dreams roused her quickly from drowsiness as
she made herself clear the dishes away. No, no
dreams!

Yet, even the fear that the very thought of such
awakened in her could not stem the full tide of
fatigue bearing her to the bedroom, to her
burrowing down under the bed covers. She had
drawn the curtains as far across the windows as
she could jerk them. This room was all she
wanted to see, no hint of what lay without its
time-seasoned walls.

Still as Gwennan undressed, she did not slip
the pendant from her neck. It had become a part

of her, she could no more think of putting it aside now than she could of separating her hand from her wrist. The dial had faded once more, the markings on it were not even visible in this dusk. It was early to go to bed, yet she could sit up no later—even though the sky still held a glimmer of sunset.

Sleep fell upon her very quickly. And there were no dreams—just sinking into a warm and waiting darkness where no doubt, fear, or memory followed.

Gwennan awoke into a dark where only a faint edging about the curtain marked the nearest window. There was a hissing against the pane— snow again! But no wind howled or drove blasts to beat the walls. Then—she stiffened on her pillow, her hands caught convulsively on the quilts and comforter over her.

A cry had pierced the soft sound of snow, entered through walls, rang as sharply as if a window was open to the night. It was that same hoarse, harsh croaking which she had heard coming earlier from the wood. Surely, that was too loud, too strong in timbre to issue from the throat of any bird. Owls she knew well, and this was no formal night hunter.

Against her flesh the pendant warmed. Gwennan pulled down the collar of her quilted pajama top to look. The dial lay against her skin, hidden. But the metal of the outer casing was agleam, alive.

She had no defense in this moment of waking, against that new knowledge from which she still shrank. Even the illusion of safety which the house had given her was now broken. Gwennan knew what cruised overhead. In her mind formed a picture as clear as if she viewed it with her physical eyes.

What beat wings across the sky—yes, and what was padding across the fields, leaping through white snow which fell away from a misshapen alien body. The hunter was out—not moving through that green-lit world but in this one, and his monstrous pack ran—flew—crawled free.

Even in the ancient days of temple Power the forces of the Dark had been known, had been fought, and had been kept at bay. There had always existed those cracks between worlds through which such things prowled while perverted minds know how to summon such. The Arm—surely it was the Arm who had in the final days opened the door of Ortha's world. Now—

"Tor!" Gwennan whispered the name, the hiss of her voice was echoed—perhaps not in her ears but her head—

"Tor! Tor! Tor!"

She huddled in her bed, listening not only with her ears, but with that newly awakened other part of her—using the sense she could not name. The Dark was broad—it cast—it sought— Why did that pack not come then to attack? Men in centuries past had tried hard to build defenses against that which was now cruising the night. They used rituals, even water they thought blessed, herbs which the Dark ones were supposed to hate. They had built churches and holy places. Some relied upon blades of silver, on words older than time they themselves might reckon. Others clung to artifacts of religion. But all, in their heart of hearts, feared, and by that fear they left a chink in their defenses.

It was fear itself which was the greatest weapon of the Dark—that had always been true. Her species were born with a kernel, a seed of fear, buried within them. Given support that could grow, bud, flower. Fear screamed, ran, scrambled through the night out there now.

Such crude fear might slay, even as talons and fangs cut off life. These night runners were the messengers. Only by reaching behind them could one fight a true battle, stand against the enemy. And she—what was she against Tor? He had boasted of his knowledge, she could not deny that he had such. Half-blood he might be, twisted he might be, if the Arm had succeeded in gaining shelter and then had fathered a child on some survivor. Yet he was as far ahead of her in command of force as perhaps the Lady was to her, Ortha, Gwennan—whatever name her true identity wore.

Lady Lyle must now lie in that place where Gwennan had watched the earlier Guardian return for renewing. How long did such renewing take—for the old to become once more young, able, a handler of Power? Years—how many—? Generations—centuries? How deep into the renewing slumber had the Lady already fallen?

But—

Gwennan's eyes opened wider, though all she could view with them was the dark. When she had witnessed the renewal process the woman had gone to her "coffin" *before* the man had come forth! Yet Tor had appeared weeks before Lady Lyle had gone to her rest. She had spoken in her letter of factors which had hastened her withdrawal—though at the time the words had meant little to Gwennan.

So—Tor had not come forth from any renewal chamber as Guardian by right. Then who had? Somewhere on earth Lady Lyle had been replaced —she must have been. Tor was not the one meant to draw upon the mended earth force. Nor was she—Gwennan. Still there was a pattern behind all this. The girl could sense the lines of weaving —only she could not follow those threads to their source, nor even know the design.

She had been chosen to be part of it—to stand against Tor. Surely the Lady—the Voice—would not have drawn her in unless there was at least a small chance of her working out an ending which was of the Light. Tor wanted her—not as an enemy but an ally. But he believed her share of the old blood so thin, so meager, that he could rule her easily through fear. He must believe that or he would not have upset the gatelocks, loosed this which came.

Gwennan crawled out of bed and began to dress. She gave a shudder which she could not suppress as she heard again a cry of the flying thing, as close as if it would dive against the roof over her head—so force her out into the open for its master to find. There was a way—yes, certainly there was a way.

She knelt by that cupboard in the kitchen into which she had shoved the tray, the globe. The light over her head flickered but she had taken

the precaution of bringing out the battery powered storm lamp, putting it in the middle of
the table. Under it was spread the cloak, for she
had the feeling that she must bring into use anything which could add strength of one kind or
another to that she would attempt.

The tray still had some unburnt crystals a-
round its far edge. Gwennan pushed these inward,
about the base on which she placed the globe
with care, after she had once more set in concealment, just as she found it, the pendant which
slipped easily into the waiting hollow. The globe
was secure. Gwennan reached for a match and
then shook her head. She was searching her
mind, trying hard to remember. Did those fleeting fragments of thought come from her long
time reading, or were they born of her sessions of
far memory? It did not matter now—what did
was that they reached her in this need.

Lamp in hand she went to the wood box. Ash—
there had been two downed ashes which had been
split to feed the stove. She dug until she found
one and, with a knife, she hacked a long sliver
from the side. Its tip stirred into the newly fed
fire, blazed up. With that she lit the blue crystals,
hoping that there were enough of them left to aid
in what she must do.

That which flew above screeched. To Gwennan
there sounded the ring of a summons in that
sound. When the fumes of the incense began to
curl up from the crystals, she blew out the ash
stick, went hurriedly to the two windows. The
falling snow was thick, forming a curtain. Her
hand moved, and she drew, with the blackened

point of the stick on the glass the looped cross, making sure each pane was so guarded.

Another weapon of men who had forgotten. However, because they had believed in it for generations power gathered to it—giving some frail advantage against what wandered out there. Faith was the seed of strength, and symbols of faith did protect when used in the name of the Light.

She slammed shut the door to the woodshed, and that to the hall, inscribing that symbol on each. There was no visible marking left from her tracing but that did not mean that it would fail. The eyes did not always see what was present.

So, having set what walls of defense against the hunter that she could, Gwennan once more approached the table, taking her seat there to lean forward breathing in the smoke, steadying her head between her hands, her elbows planted firmly on the folds of the cloak. She stared at the globe beaming tentatively, to grope as a child new at school would struggle with half understood words, for that which had once been so easy for Ortha—the second part—the stronger part of her life.

Gwennan struggled to bend all her will to this purpose, to empty her mind to all but her need.

The smoke might be a drug; seers through many ages had used such to loosen their bonds with the here and now. Its rich scent did not make her sleepy. Rather it pulled her on into a new kind of wakefulness, she was aware in another part of her which she did not recognize.

There was a clouding of the globe from the

smoke—rather a billowing within the confines of the crystal, a rising of force.

"Show me!" Gwennan's demand was fierce, sharp— "Show me where!"

There was a door in the crystal, save it was not the globe—it was another place and she was there also, not as an onlooker, but one who acted. She knew that door—it was the vast, age-darkened one of Lyle House. There was the heavy knocker but she need not lift hand to that—rather she pushed ahead with the same fierce desire to be about what she must do as had filled her from the first.

The wood swung inward. Before lay the hall but it was a blurred, an only half-visualized vision of no consequence, not what she sought. Nor did she turn to the library where Tor had left what she believed was meant to be a trap, but not one by which she could be captured. No, her way led ahead, back into that portion of the house where she had never been before.

Another door, another hall, more half-opened doors here and there. Then a wall, paneled in heavily carved wood which had been painted, though the colors had worn away and still clung only in the curls of leaves, the entwining of boldly wrought stems. For it would seem that the artist had attempted on this one room side to create a section of heavy vine, stem, plant, beginning at the floor line and extending up to the ceiling.

So embossed was that design that one could hook fingers into it deeply in many places. Yet there were only two such places which counted, one the center of a half circle of leaves. Yes, as she looked closer she saw there a small head, a laughing face with eyes which lived, pointed ears standing from among curls on the head. The whole was hardly larger than her thumb nail and yet perfect. And, not too far away, was a second twisted leaf, this one hiding the head of a stag—proud as that animal the huntress had ridden in the green world.

Press—she did not press with her hands—she only sent a thought hurling at the two points. There followed a shaking, a trembling, throughout the wall. The whole of the carvings there tingled with life, and would be free. Then the surface split along a line between head and stag, the vines and leaves so cleverly set that none of them were riven apart by the opening.

A door—so narrow that she might have to turn sidewise to pass it—Gwennan did not remember entering, she was just beyond. Here were steps even as there had been beneath the stone in the meadow. Save that they were not time touched, but straight and sharp edged, and she followed them downward again.

It was dark and still not dark to her sight which was of the inner not the outer world, while she passed far more swiftly than she could have done had she made that journey in body. It would seem as though she was seeking the center of the world, descending endlessly. To every action there comes an end. She was again before a door which swung open as had the one of the treasure house, yielding easily.

This room she had seen! This was what she had come to find—the heart of the Guardians' life—or the place of their deaths. Here were ranged those coffins, crystal deepening to opaque. Gwennan knew who lay in the first of that line. Lady Lyle rested as a smooth faced statue, the clouding of the crystal about her well begun.

There certainly could be no wakening for her, once she had entered this place and surrendered her body to the renewing. Gwennan looked upon her longingly for a moment or two—wishing that the process could be reversed, that the Lady might be summoned forth. No, it was the other coffin which she must see—that solid one at the far end of that line. Thought alone wafted her there, she stood beside it in an instant. Solid as any stone, no sign of the flaking or breaking of the outer shell, as she had witnessed when she watched from the seer's stool.

Did the renewal then sometimes fail, and that lay within that shell—was it indeed dead?

She stared down at that portion which was meant to cover the head. A skull beneath—or someone who had slumbered past the awakening time? Some very ancient mechanism could have at last come to a final halt.

It was then that she sighted what lay on the surface above what might have been the heart position of the sleeper. White as the encasing of the coffin, near invisible against it, only the longer she focused upon it the clearer the form of it became. A symbol—not unlike one of those two daggers which had lain crossed on the table in Lyle House—white like frosted ice and as deadly in its life-refusing chill. The one who should have arisen was so sealed within. Unless that evil thing be raised the rightful guardian would remain a prisoner.

Tor—only Tor could have done this. Gwennan fastened her mind power upon that white, near invisible, knife—strove so to fling it aside, even as her will had freed the upper door. But she could move nothing. This was not a matter of will (or at least *her* will); she had not the strength of old Power in her. Neither could she reach forth a hand—for that essence of her which had made this journey had no hands to grasp and take. No— she must come here in body for there was no doubt that the only hand which would serve was hers.

She had been shown the way, the problem made plain to her. The rest depended upon her will, determination—and her courage! For that Tor would allow this threat to his power go un- challenged she did not believe. By her very act of learning this much, of coming here, she had bound herself to action. There could be no retreat.

Even as she accepted that, Gwennan was again before the globe in the warmth of her kitchen, trembling from the effort, too tired to move.

The inertia which held her was broken—by a sound from outside. Not the screech of the hunting beast, but a clangor which startled her so she gasped. There was shouting, faint but increasing in strength. Again a siren which could only be the sheriff's car—

Gwennan stumbled to her feet—wavered to the window then realized that she could not see the outer road from the kitchen. She made her way down the hall, steadying herself with one hand against the wall to open the front door. There was a confusion of passing vehicles, of the warning lights revolving on cars. Half of Waterbridge was coming up the road, headed past her house, on towards the narrower lane.

The sky was alight—not with dawn rays but rather the glow of a fire lying to the north. There was only one place which could show so easily here. That was not the sign of fire at any outlying fire—but rather at Lyle House itself!

Set by those candles left burning on the table in a house she had thought empty? But that was hours ago. However, the house's inner paneling was of wood—very old, oiled, polished into being good tinder. While the walls might not be breached for they were stone and very thick, the inner shell could easily be gutted.

She raced back, caught up the cloak, thrust her feet into her boots. There were people coming along on foot now in spite of the hour and the cold, she slipped out among them and heard their excited voices—telling of a phone call which had sounded an alarm, though no one was sure just who had called—of the destruction of the house unless help arrived in time.

Would Tor have done this to conceal the resting place of the Guardians? Gwennan believed that no true Lyle would be able to destroy their refuge, the place to which they had clung for centuries. But Tor was half-blood—the house could mean very little to him against what he thought he might gain from it. Had he been able to sense her own penetration by thought into the secret which lay beneath and so acted hastily but ruthlessly, before she could carry out that which she had just found she must determine to do?

The fire engine—bought largely with Lyle money the girl remembered wryly, had reached the house, followed by the sheriff's car, by two truckloads of men who jumped out to mill around. The high snow might well be such an impediment to their efforts as could spell disaster.

Standing half open, the front door allowed a view of flame and smoke. There was no sign of the servants, were they trapped within? That appeared the opinion of those who had come to fight the fire. Two of the new heat suits were being donned, volunteers wearing them stamped on through the door under arch of water, from the pump truck, water which froze as it gathered around them.

Gwennan stared at the glare flickering behind the front windows. What treasures were being lost in there! If the house were consumed she might never perhaps find that inner doorway the globe had led her to.

There was shouting as the two men who entered returned supporting a third between them. He whom they had rescued was plainly unable to help himself as they bore him forward. While there was no mistaking the brilliant color of his hair, even though his head was turned away from her.

No matter who else might have been in the house, Tor Lyle had been caught and— Gwennan studied that limp form they settled on a stretcher. One drew a covering over him. Dead? No, they lifted him into the back of the sheriff's car. He was bound for the station house where the medics would be able to call in a helicopter to take him on to the hospital in Fremont—if he still lived. The way his body had sagged had made her wonder about that.

Gwennan felt only wonder at first, and then her feelings became stronger. She was inclined to believe that he might have brought about his own death, perhaps because of his hot ambition—that need to be in command of the Lyle secret. Tonight he had opened a gate for those creatures from other worlds, of that she was as certain as if she had watched him at such summoning, still to meet with death—no! There was another answer somehow—If his death was meant to be, Lady Lyle could have caused it herself. She who had once been the Voice was ruthless for the triumph of the Light as Gwennan herself could testify. To face, to remove, the menace Tor represented was for any Guardian an outright duty, nor would Saris Lyle flinch from carrying that through.

So no affection had bound the older woman to Tor—rather a need to work out a desired pattern. Time had failed the Lady, therefore she had done all she could to make sure that her mission might not also fail. She had suborned Gwennan, awakened, used her, to achieve what she herself might not do. Tor was not a thread to be pulled loose and tossed aside, he was still one who mattered to time's weaving.

Therefore if he were dead, there had been partial failure not a triumph for the Lady, unfinished action still remaining. Gwennan watched the firefighters, more intent upon her thoughts than their actions.

The glow behind the window now, certainly that was much lessened. Finally the men tramped out pulling out smoldering tatters of cloth behind them to be tossed into snow banks. The acrid smell of smoke hung heavy. Gwennan heard the news passed along that the flame had been largely confined to drapery and a section of carpet. That the fire crew themselves were surprised that so little real damage had been done.

Young Lyle, the story went, had collapsed from smoke inhalation after fighting the blaze on his own. There had been no one else in the house.

16

So far Gwennan had gone unrecognized in the crowd. People were still straggling out from town. The fire must have roused all of White-bridge. She had seen enough, wanting to get away —to think, perhaps to call once more upon the globe. Tor was for a space removed from the board on which he would play his game. Now might be her only chance.

She slipped away among the brush of the shrubs which helped conceal most of Lyle House from the road. They would surely leave a guard on the house. What she must do—if she could— would be secret.

What she could do—

Suddenly realizing that her time might be very short before she might be seen, or precautions taken to lock up the house beyond her pene-tration, Gwennan pushed through the shrubbery, heading towards the back of the house, away from the lights and confusion of the trucks and people in the fore yard. She had never explored the grounds here, nor was she sure that she could discover any unguarded entrance to the side or back of the house. The absence of the servants continued to present a question. Had Tor sent them away? Or had they refused to serve a master they believed in a false position? Gwennan was not even sure how many of them there had ever been. The woman who had been the lady's soft-footed attendant, a man who had tended the door, been seen in the yard at intervals—another older woman who waited on the table for their dining —those were all she personally knew.

Though the snow was not drifted here, a thickened growth about both the side walls of the house and a series of shrubs and hedges of bare branches acted with the persistence of a maze to keep her from a straight path. Gwennan was continually having to turn right or left to avoid some such obstruction, many looming well above her head.

She had made some progress when once more the cry of the flying thing shook her. Instinct took over, forcing her back against one of the lengths of hedge. The tall, overhanging branches here would, she hoped with a fast-beating heart, conceal her.

That stench of an Outworld thing enveloped her. She heard the beat of what could only be wide wings. More than half of her screamed silently to run—to get away from this place. Tor had set his own guards! Against the monsters of his pack—what weapon had she? The flyer might not be able to reach her in this entanglement of shrubbery—but there were other hunters out this night—and perhaps that impatient cry from overhead summoned those!

Would the house itself provide any defense, be a refuge? How could it? Even in the most sacred temple of Ortha's time, the beasts from outside had prowled—prowled to slay.

Yet the house, its thick walls, seemed to be the only refuge she dared hope to gain. She was somehow very certain that what was alive in the night wanted no dealings with the others. No, *she* was the intended prey—Tor's prey!

The girl dared not move into the open, so she caught at handsful of the icy coated branches to draw herself along, support her over the roughness of ground she could hardly see. Thus Gwennan reached the back of Lyle House, saw a wall forming a barrier, then a door. Shrubs grew close enough that she could follow under their overhang so that moments of being in the open, vulnerable, were very few. Success depended now on whether that door was barred. If she reached it and could not win through—

Gwennan ran clumsily for the wall gate. There was no latch, no handle. While above she heard the beat of the wings—the foulness wafted by these made her choke and gag. She threw out both hands, beat upon that resistant surface.

The pendant swung loose from her half opened parka. A thread of light shot from the crescent moon on its top, not a full ray such as the dial might have offered, yet visible enough as it struck on the door.

Oddly enough it slanted downward of its own accord, though she had not attempted to aim the ray, that finger wide beam found to enter a hole in the dark old wood.

Gwennan dared not look up over her shoulder.

That which swooped upon her out of the night was monstrous. She need not actually sight it to know that. It flew silently, avidly. Were beak and talons already reaching for her? The door swung back to allow Gwennan to throw herself inside, catching at the stout slab with both hands. She slammed it shut, to stand gasping for breath—her fear and the terrible fetor mingling, to leave her so shaky she doubted for a fraction of time her ability to move.

There came a shriek filled with hate and rage—rising until the high whistle of it was a pain in her head, passing at last beyond audible range. Something heavy slammed against the wall and there were sounds as if great claws strove to rend the thick wood of the door, the stone of the wall, into splinters and rubble.

Gwennan waited. That thing need only rise to wing again—take off and coast easily across the wall. Yet it continued instead with blind fury to attack at ground level. She looked to the dark bulk of the house. This was a courtyard such as she had seen pictured as part of very old buildings overseas.

The house formed one side of a square. That wall through which she had come was a short one, joining, not too much farther on, two one-story buildings which formed a corner, and were attached in turn to another and much larger two-story, box-like structure. In this dim light the girl could only see the general pattern, for there were no lights within. Another low building made up a section of the square on that side, the roof of that glittering a little—save in one place the structure

divided on the lowest floor to form a wide gate-
way arched above.

The house was what mattered. Gwennan, hearing the continued fury of that creature who
fought to reach her, ran toward that. She must
find an entrance. There was no snow on the pavement here; efforts must have been made to keep it
clear. At least she need not fear any ice patches to
bring her down.

Windows formed dark squares at intervals
along the side. Unlike those at the front of the
house these were heavily shuttered, and she did
not doubt that those shutters were barred within.
However, there was also the door she sought, as
solid and forbidding as all she had earlier en-
countered. When she stood before it she saw that
this also had no latch, no visible hand hold. The
pendant—?

However, when she raised that this time no
pencil thin beam answered. Gwennan bit her lip.
The thing outside had not abandoned its assault.
Sooner or later wood and stone *must* give way
under that fierce attack. Then—

She heard something now—a low growling, not
the shrilling of the flyer's voice. Another of the
night hunters must have closed in. The house
door—! Gwennan beat on it with both hands
before she could regain control, sheer panic
rising in her. To try to take refuge in any of those
other buildings around her she sensed would be
fatal. Only within the house where Power had
gathered could she hope for any safety.

At last, because she was no longer able to think
of anything else, she stooped to set the horn tips

of that moon carving into which was indeed a wider hole than that one on the gate. They slipped in as easily as if that opening had been contrived to contain them, and Gwennan, as she might have done with her own house key, gave a turn. The pendant obeyed—and the door opened!

She was through it in an instant—into a hall thick with acrid smoke. Once more she slammed a portal tightly behind her, to stand listening in the dark, reaching out tentatively with that newly revealed sense of her—striving so to pick up any suggestion that there remained life under this roof.

If she only had a flashlight! This part of the house was unknown territory, but she believed that there was no one here. She could hear some distant sounds which suggested that there was activity towards the front—that the firemen or the sheriff's deputy were still in possession of the building.

Using her hand along the wall for a guide, Gwennan crept forward. What she sought lay beyond these service quarters, and it would depend upon continued presence of those others whether or when she could reach her goal. Her fingers slipped from the stone walls (there were no wooden panels here) across what could only be a closed door.

The thought of locating a source of light made her try that. It opened easily enough. Not only opened, but there *was* a gleam of light which startled her into immobility. Before her stretched a huge room possessing all the furnishings and characteristics of those great kitchens which had been scenes of activity two centuries or more before her own birthdate.

The large fireplace, in which nested the source of the light, a fire hardly more than the ember stage, was equipped with a spit, dangling hooked chains to support pots, a side oven of brick. Nowhere was there any sign of a modern stove. But by the dying fire Gwennan sighted a candle on a table, a ruffle of melted wax still about its wick. It was only a moment's work to light that from the dying fire.

The walls were pegged and on those pegs rested pots and pans of metal, brightly burnished. Not only must this antique kitchen have still been in general use, but also most carefully kept. Yet there was about it now an aura of desertion, as if those who had lived and worked there were gone.

Candle in hand, Gwennan slipped back to the hall. However, instead of going forward, she returned to the door by which she entered, pressing herself against it tensely to listen. There was nothing to be heard. If the creatures had at last won inside the courtyard, the thickness of these walls deadened any warning. Not knowing how much time she might still have, she hurried now, trying to pass as noiselessly as possible.

There was another half open door where the smell of smoke was even more pronounced. From beyond Gwennan caught the murmur of voices. Then the sound of a starting engine, a crunching of the truck in the outside snow followed. The siren of the sheriff's car clamored. Gwennan wondered if they had been alerted to the monster pack. Surely the screams of the flying thing had not gone unheard.

"See yuh—" That was the sheriff. And he did not sound as if he had been alarmed by any manifestation out of the night. Instead he was tramping heavy-footed down the hall nearby— searching the house a second time? Gwennan shielded her candle with her hand as she glanced around. Were the night monsters only made known to those they hunted? she wondered for a moment.

A hiding place? There could be a hundred such here and she would never find them! But *she* must not be found! The kitchen?

The girl sped to that very wide fireplace. It possessed such a width of hearth. The fire, which by its present remains had not been large, had also smoldered well down, so that Gwennan was able to edge into a cavern meant to accommodate full logs. Pressed back against one wall perhaps she might pass unseen. Reluctantly the girl blew out her candle, entered the gaping mouth of what seemed to her a small, sooty room. Flattening herself as best she could against the ancient bricks with a fleeting wish she might indeed be swallowed up by them, she wondered how visible she might be.

Steps sounded loud on the uncarpeted floor outside the door she had left ajar. Then the flash of a strong hand light aimed into the room, making a full sweep of the kitchen. Gwennan clung tighter to what was certainly no true refuge as the light passed across the mouth of the fireplace. She expected the beam to center on her, to hear a demand to come out—to be forced to explain—

However, her simple maneuver worked. The circle of light slipped on leaving her undiscovered. Finally the door closed with a snap. Gwennan let out her breath in a little gasp, emerged to pick up her candle, relight it. She need only wait a short time longer, she was sure. After a search of the house there might be a guard left outside but it would be the duty for such a one to remain close to his car radio to catch any signal.

Now—to find the room she had seen in the vision the globe had given her! That chamber could not be a part of the serving quarters—though she believed not too far beyond. Back once more in the hall, Gwennan moved only a few steps at a time—listening to other sequences of sounds—closing doors, a footfall here and there where there was a bare flooring.

She counted to a hundred, once, again, and again, growing more impatient with every tally. At last she heard the firm slam of what could only be that massive front door. Now she hurried through into the main hall. With the flame shielded as best she could against drafts, she at length flung open a door to discover the room she sought.

This *was* it! Though by the very poor light Gwennan carried, that deeply carven wall was a mass of shadows. She tried to recall just where she stood in her vision. There were so many curled leaves, such a confusing massing of those and the entwined vines. At length she had to hold her candle within almost touching distance of the panels and peer very closely indeed. The face— that was it! Now for the stag—but once she had the one in line the other was not difficult to find.

Placing the candle on the floor between her feet, Gwennan set a thumb hard on both of those minute carvings, pressing inward with all her might.

For a long moment she thought that she had failed—unless the globe vision had taunted her with a hallucination, for nothing at all happened. There was no appreciable give to the two knots of carving on which she concentrated all the strength she could summon.

Then came a sound—not unlike a long drawn out sigh. Her hands slid apart, being carried by the carved portions she still pressed. Immediately before her opened that parting of the pattern in the wall. The aperture appeared so narrow that she wondered if she could squeeze through and her passage was something of a task, muffled as her body was by heavy clothing.

Candle once more in hand, she stood at the top of that flight of stairs. Before she began the descent, Gwennan dragged off her scarf, wadded that into a roll, which she planted between the leaves of the concealed door, for she noted no latch on the inner side. The wool resisted the closing of the panel, leaving a strip into which she could get her finger. That seemed her best precaution against being sealed in.

This stairway was in far better shape than that beneath the stone. She was able to move faster without having to watch for any broken steps. So Gwennan came at last into that room of the coffins. For a moment she paused beside that of Lady Lyle. The serene beauty of the face, which was still to be clearly seen, mocked her. Such perfect rest—and all this trouble left behind for Gwennan to deal with. Nor could the girl ever be truly sure that any decision she might make was the right one. Why had she been pressed into service? And who was the rightful guardian, the one whose power Tor so coveted that he had used forbidden methods to obtain it?

Not that he had been successful. Gwennan had considered him all along as one against whom she had very little chance. But was that truly so? She frowned down at the sleeping Lady Lyle. Even if Tor had summoned the monsters, so far it appeared that those were none too efficient as a weapon. They could generate fear, yes. That had worked with her, as she could not deny. But what else had he been able to do which had raised any real resistance to Lady Lyle's plans? If it was through Tor's meddling intrusions that one of the Lyles had been forced to enter renewal ahead of time, then she had taken what precaution she could against his bid for power. And the foremost weapon was apparently Gwennan herself.

The girl still did not believe she was a fair match for Tor, no. Yet, in his confronting her he had so far shown himself surprisingly inept. Her hand went to the pendant. Was *this* the ultimate protection against him, or was there indeed truth in the Lyle talk of a wheel of the stars and return of certain patterns under which Gwennan herself could flourish and stand for more than she thought?

Questions to which she might never gain any

answers. What she needed was the final solution —or what she believed to be that. *That* must lie in the last coffin of this line, nailed fast within by Tor. That much she believed he had been able to accomplish, perhaps after Lady Lyle had been forced into premature retreat.

Down to that opaque coffin Gwennan went, still fingering the pendant. Exactly what she had seen in the vision lay there. Though she did not touch it (having a healthy desire to learn more before she meddled) she leaned close to examine it. The knife or dagger looked (she could see well for each of the coffins carried a glow of light about their shells) as if it had been so affixed to the lid as to now be a part of that—not just to be picked up or pried loose.

Pried? Gwennan studied the blade carefully. Was there or was there not a slight indentation between the point of pseudo-knife and the surface of which it looked a part—a notch into which a knife point or something of like nature could be worked to use as a lever? Only she had nothing of the sort. To go back up into the house in search of such—no, the feeling of time's pressure was far too acute. She must do what she came to do and as quickly as possible—or there would be no reason for any of it—Tor would win!

Pry—the idea haunted her. At last she tried the only way she could imagine, bringing up the pendant to set its two moon horns against the surface of the coffin. Instantly a chill as intense as a freezing bolt of ice shot up her arm. The girl almost dropped her hold on the metal disc. Her fingers were already numbing, in another moment or so she would lose all feeling in them. Quick—!

She joined her second hand to the first. The same intense cold attacked those fingers, but not before she had fitted the curve of the moon into that crack (and there was a crack there!) between the point of the dagger and the lid. With all the strength Gwennan could summon, even as the cold flowed up from her fingers, through wrists, into her forearms, she dragged the pendant towards her, seeking to use it so to break that bonding.

Not only were her numbing hands locked into action, but also she brought her mind and will to concentrate on what she would do. She was aware of a similar numbing within her head, a seeking to dampen, to defeat. Tor must be fighting, even though he lay miles away and perhaps unconscious—a part of him was tied to this struggle.

Gwennan could not hold much longer. She had no feeling in her fingers, soon those would lose their hold on the pendant. If she was so defeated, the girl believed, there would come no second chance. So she pulled and willed—

There followed a burst of sound. Perhaps she also screamed—for with that noise the pain in her hands and her head became near intolerable. Only that knife which had been welded to the coffin broke free, flew off the lid, to shatter on the floor. Gwennan staggered back, away from that line of sleepers in the boxes, until her shoulders met the wall of the chamber, supporting her so to keep her feet.

As she had seen in her first vision so the same action followed. The opaque coating on the surface of the coffin developed long cracks, shards fell away, to display the clear crystal below. For a moment or so that remained inwardly clouded still.

The cover arose to fall back in the opposite direction from where she stood. Now—yes, there was the hand appearing out of the depth, groping for a hold on the edge. Then fingers closed upon the other side. So aided and steadied the occupant drew himself up.

Gwennan gave a cry of sorrow or defeat. This was—Tor!

He did not turn his head in her direction, his eyelids lifted very slowly as he drew in deep breaths just as might one who needed to fill his lungs to their utmost capacity over and over again. Then, moving slowly and carefully he got to his feet, his slightly bronzed body (as if he had lain in a place of warm sun) was as perfect as that of any statue she had ever seen. He turned—

Their eyes met. His widened for only a fraction. It might so have taken no longer than a single breath for him to learn and understand all which had happened—to recognize her and be aware of her part in all this.

"Well done—" he said and his words echoed.

The girl slid along the wall away from him. So it had not been Lady Lyle's game which she had played after all—but Tor's. He had brought her here through some trickery to free him! Though —she was sickly bewildered—she *had* seen him carried away. When, an hour, two hours ago? He

had been unconscious— Then how could he awaken in the guardian's own place? Hallucination—or was she caught in another of those visions meant to deceive and bewilder her? They had played with her, the two of them! She knew dull anger—only strength to fight had gone out of her.

"Tor—" She repeated his name in sullen resentment of her own folly.

"Tor—?" He shook his head. "Not the half-blood—not yet—"

She had no idea of his meaning. What was he going to do with her now, since she was undoubtedly of no more use to him? Would he call in his otherworld things and let them make an end?

"You are afraid—you are—" He shook his head before he smiled and held out his hand to her. "Kinswoman—such fears are unworthy in you."

"I don't know what you are talking about," Gwennan burst forth, her despair and anger giving her strength to flare up for perhaps the last time. "You are Tor Lyle. But I do not understand what happened—you were injured in the fire—and now you are here. I—I turned you loose —I thought I was doing as I should—"

He nodded, took a step or two towards her. She pushed farther away. Then her will broke and she turned and ran for the stairway, stumbling, pulling herself up it. She wanted nothing but to get away. The failure had been so great, so devastating to her, that she was reduced to nothing but a raw desire to set it behind her. She had been used, over and over again. All her belief in herself was wrung out of her.

There was the crack of the door she had wedged open. She rammed her hands into it, dragged and tugged. The sheer force of her fear and anger gave her the strength to send the sliding panel back so that she fell forward into the dark room beyond. For a moment she lay there sobbing dryly. Then, because she had so little strength left in her, Gwennan began to crawl, drawing herself along by her fingers hooked in the rug on the floor, pushing feebly with her feet—wanting nothing but to be free of this house.

Hands fell on her shoulders, gripped tight. In spite of her feeble struggles she was pulled up to stand, leaning back against another behind her and whom she could not see, but who she knew. There was no escape now, perhaps there had never been any from the first morning when they had met by the standing stones. She could fight no longer.

"I am not Tor—"

His voice came close to her ear as his breath stirred wisps of hair which had worked free from under the edge of her cap.

"You shall see—"

17

He swung her up as if she was of no weight at all, carried her swiftly to the next chamber where furniture loomed darkly against the walls and she knew that she was once more in the dining room where Lady Lyle had once sat enthroned. It was to that same chair this stranger brought her now, settling her within it. She struggled for self-possession, for the energy to (once his hold was off her) get away. But it was as if she had been bound with cords and she suspected that his will made that so.

Even in the dark his body was visible, he seemed to glow faintly as had the stones—not with their white light, rather with a faint haze of gold. She watched him wordlessly as he went to the doorway again and passed through, leaving her alone.

Gwennan was cold. Her body shook still with that chill which had crept up through her hands, her wrists, her arms, during her labor to open the casket. Her teeth chattered in spite of her struggle for control. Within her boots her feet

were as numb now as the upper part of her body
—she might be congealing into ice.

There was no sound through the shadowed
house. Only on her breast the pendant glowed.
Somehow she managed to break the hold of her
icy, stiff fingers on the arms of the tall backed
chair—the hold which kept her where she was,
not suffering her to slide to the floor as a bone-
less heap. With an effort Gwennan brought her
two hands together, cupping the pendant between them.

The silence was not that of death—of an end; it
was rather one of anticipation, a pause before
action. She realized that slowly by the aid of that
other awareness. Her hands were warming, life
was returning to her. However, there had come
no added strength with that life, rather her sense
of being a prisoner grew the stronger. A prisoner
to another's will—to fulfill a commitment she
had never made—not consciously.

She could only fight for control of her inner
will, as her body responded to the power enclosed in that piece of alien metal. Her breath
came in deep, long inhalations equalling those
the awakening Guardian had taken before he
moved into action. As her frantic beating heart
slowed, the warmth spread through her, Gwennan listened.

Nothing to be heard, not even the faint stir of
air. There lingered an odor of the smoke. In this
chamber she could not see a window. Long pieces
of tapestry were drawn over those. Candles—on
the table—on one of the tall chests—but she did
not have the strength to rise and light those.

Gwennan shifted in the chair, transferred her hold on the pendant to one hand, with the other tried to push herself up. Light at last! Her head snapped around so she could gaze squarely at the glimmer growing brighter at the doorway through which her captor (for she must consider him so) had vanished.

The light did not sharpen—rather remained a diffused radiance. Then he entered—that other Tor. He held his right hand outstretched. In the cupped palm rested a sphere, twin to that which had already given her windows on strange places, shown her at last his place of rest.

He was clothed now—Tor's clothing—and it made him look even more like the one she feared. Still, when she gazed up into his face, there was a difference. The gem bright eyes were as far seeing but they were now half closed—forming shields for what lay behind them. There was no sly mockery about his mouth as he smiled at her. His lift and curve of lip was like that of Lady Lyle, meant to—charm—entice—? Gwennan settled farther back in her chair.

"We have little time," he broke the silence. "Doors are opened which must be closed. However, only he who summons can also dismiss—"

"You—" the girl had to moisten her lips with tongue tip before she spoke.

"No." He seated himself in the chair at her right and laid his hand on the table so that globe was between them, flowering like a small bit of sun. "There is Tor— Look!"

She could not have resisted that order any

more than in this moment she could have arisen to leave the room. There was the familiar swirling of haze within the globe he supported and her eyes centered on it. That took form—a form—

On a cot lay a man, his shoulders and arms swathed in a thick green covering—a treatment for burns. His eyes were closed but his head turned from side to side as if something within him sought escape.

"Call him!" That was a command. Again there was nothing Gwennan could do to stiffen her will so she need not obey. She was forced forward, there might have been a vast compelling hand set to her back, pushing her so.

"Call him!" The command did not ring loudly, but it was one she could not evade.

"Tor—" At first that name came as a ragged whisper. Then she spoke it more loudly as if she did indeed stand beside the injured man demanding him to return to consciousness.

His eyes did not open, but his movements became more restless. Where he was she could not tell, but she thought perhaps he was still in the village—that they had not yet transported him to the hospital for treatment.

"Tor—!"

He did open his eyes now. They were dull, unseeing—

"Tor!" For the third and last time Gwennan called. Then the haze arose, the picture was gone. The ball moved from the hollow of the hand which held it, rolled out upon the table—though it did not lose its glow.

"He will come—" There was assurance in the voice of the one who sat beside her.

"How can he?" Gwennan had command of herself again enough to ask. "He's hurt—burned—they'll stop him—"

That other shook his head. "It is laid upon him —no one can stop him. Come—" This time the summons was for her, and not Tor. He held out the same hand which had cupped the globe, making no move towards picking that up once again.

She found that, without thinking, her fingers had reached out, to be enfolded by his. There was an instant flow of strength and vitality borne by the touching of their flesh—an in-flow to her. She remembered how Ortha had watched the Voice weave the Power into that which comforted and brought peace. Did she want such comfort, such peace? A small part of her cried out against taking anything which was not of her world. However, she had gone too far down that other path, been drawn into a slate which was now removed from all she had been and done.

He drew her up from the chair and she discovered that she had lost all weakness and gnawing fear which had ridden her for so long. Then, hand in hand, they went through the house, not towards that front portal, but the back way by which she had come so secretly in the dark.

When they stood together in the courtyard outside Gwennan discovered that in some unknown fashion her eyes had adjusted to the dark—that she could see much which had been hidden before. See—hear—smell—!

That which had followed her to the wall gate no longer battered nor screamed, still it waited beyond. More than one of those alien things lingered outside.

"He is coming—" The earlier promise was stated as fact by her companion.

"What can he do—?" she dared to ask.

"What he must," was the answer. "The calling was his—so now he must also face that which was called. For every action there is a summation. One faces that willingly—or unwillingly."

"Who—who are you?" She had had to accept that he was not Tor. But who or what he was she felt she must know.

"I am he who has the Duty. I am he who must wait—"

Evasive enough, but she dared not at present try to learn more. She was as much in awe of him as Ortha had been of the Arm in ages past. Tor possessed powers beyond her reckoning, she had always guessed that. But this man (if he were man at all) was greater by far.

There was an absolute stillness when he finished speaking—a stillness which waited—as the house behind her waited. Gwennan strained to hear even the smallest sound which hinted that the end of that waiting was nearer.

A grunting growl—so deep and menacing — broke that silence. Gwennan started. The clasp on her hand tightened.

"It is time—"

He who stood with her went forward, confidently, as though there was nothing which could touch him. She, too, was so drawn along, matching her steps to his. They were at the gate of the courtyard. His other hand pointed. That barrier swung inward and they stood waiting until the force of that swing thumped it against the inner wall.

Her night sight held, but now she wished it had not. That milling, monstrous crew before them were much the same as had accompanied the hunter in the green-lit land. Here was he of the owl's head, and the arm-wings, the wolf-man, the haired creature—and others—such a splotch of evil and the Dark as she had never faced, even in the worst of her nightmares.

Yet there was utter confidence in the way that he whom she had freed went forward with the same firm steps. Those creatures from Outside drew back, forming a lane. Down that open space the Guardian led Gwennan.

That calm which had flooded into her from his first touch held. She knew rather than saw that the creatures drew in again behind them, to follow. Yet they did not menace, nor did they utter any more sounds.

Through the massive growth of the garden the two made their way. Gwennan had a sudden guess as to their goal—the stones! It could only be the stones! Where her adventure had begun there also it must end. There was more than one wheel which turned in its own time.

There was no wall to be climbed now. The snow lay unmarked as they came through the wood along a path, hearing the rustle of the monsters padding at their backs, smelling always the foulness which was the mark of those spawned by the Dark.

The stones were alive. From their crowns arose those flaming wicks of light Gwennan had seen once before. It was straight towards those beacons that she was being led. The darkness of the night was on the wane, the greyness of before dawn arched up the sky.

Side by side they came to the mound. Snowdrifts arose about their legs, nearly to their knees, yet they walked steadily, as if those white banks were nothing, giving away as easily as water. Up the mound they climbed—came to stop only at the foot of the great stone.

On that was clearly visible all those markings she had half-known were there—having been hidden both by time, and the forgotten art of those who had wrought them. Gwennan understood that she could read them if she willed, that to her now there could be no more secrets. Still she did not try. There was too much expectancy in the air—too much excitement stirring in her. Something was about to happen which would be not of her old world and which, in her half-awakened state, she shrank from, yet half welcomed, aware that it must be accepted.

The two turned at the foot of the tall stone, looking steadily towards the lane. Between them and the field wall was the snow—a brilliantly white carpet—the very purity of it making it shine. Sound again, low growls, twitterings, a coughing thick and foul. Those who had followed them flowed about the base of the mount not setting foot upon its rise, but gathering in around the sides to also face the lane.

Gwennan nearly flinched from full sight of some of those abnormalities that crouched, shuffled, sat, or stood, waiting. Here were gathered things like the visions of men of the past who had attempted to draw upon the darkest side of imagination, summoning up their personal devils or monsters. The worst was that all these dark distortions were mingled with the human, so that one might see what man could become when sinking to the lowest within himself.

Movement on the lane brought the creatures creeping inward. A wolf-man bounded forward, nearer to the wall, throwing up his narrow head and widening his jaws as if to howl. Still no sound issued forth—unless it was one too high for human ears.

He who walked down the lane wove from side to side, stumbled and wavered, yet kept always on his feet, though his head fell forward, chin near against his breast, as if he did not watch where he went but rather was drawn by that he could not resist. At the wall he fell as he strove to climb, and was several moments floundering in the snow before he unsteadily arose again.

Tor—coming in answer to her summons. How he had eluded those who had cared for him Gwennan could not understand. He moved so clumsily it was plain he was weak, probably in pain, still he came. The wolf-man moved beside him, its stance that of a hound waiting for orders, but Tor never raised his own head nor looked to the thing which matched his march towards the stones.

The creatures opened a way, even as they had outside the gate for Gwennan and that other, leaving an open space at the foot of the mound. In that Tor staggered to a halt, stood swaying, his arms hanging loose, his burns visible beneath the dressings. Now his head came up at last and his eyes—those dead eyes, gazed to the two above him.

His lips writhed into a snarl as pronounced as any on the animal-man face of the thing who crouched close at his feet. Life began to flow into him. There was a fire which was not of the kind which had seared his flesh—rather it burned inside him. Upon that he drew deeply and willingly.

"I have come—" His voice was not weak, nor strained, nor even touched with pain, rather it was a challenge.

"You have come—" Gwennan's companion returned.

"I am of the Blood—" Again there was pride in that, force. He no longer wavered, his back was straight. He bore dreadful burns but they seemed no more to him at that moment than clothing he could take from his body and throw away.

"You are of the Blood—" For the second time there was acknowledgment.

"I command—" Tor raised his arm. There was a guttural answer from those things crouched about him. Their red coals of eyes swung to the two above, they waited only for the gesture or the word which would send them bounding up to destroy.

"*I* command—" The hand which had held Gwennan's for so long, instilling in her warmth and serenity, loosened itself from hers. He moved from her side, passed between the two shorter stones, began to descend.

The girl would have cried out, tried to restrain him, but she knew that would be no use. This was between the two of them, those who looked so much alike that they could have been the same man reflected from one to the other, had it not been for Tor's visible injuries.

Tor's eyes were only on the one who approached. The beasts shifted about hungrily. Still whatever held them in check was still in force.

The guardian reached the foot of the mound, passed between two of the monsters, and stood only an arm's distance from Tor.

"You cannot take—" Tor said. There was none of the old mockery in him. Anger blazed so that his eyes were as much afire as those of his pack of beasts.

"I cannot take—" the other agreed. "Only you can give."

Tor's face twisted in a grimace which must have torn at his burns. He raised his arms high, his hands clenched into fists, if so he might bring them both down in a shattering, killing blow on the man standing so quietly before him.

"No!" He screamed in a denial, which could have been twisted out of him by a torturer's skill. "I will not! This time it will be me, me!"

While all the time that other only watched. Gwennan had unconsciously moved forward.

"You cannot use the Power against me!" Tor cried.

"I shall not use it. The choice is yours—as it has always been—yours!"

Tor's arms fell to his sides, his fists uncurled. There was weariness about him like a cloak. Still his eyes blazed.

"You cannot bind me—"

"Only the Blood can do that. Which is why you did not want to face me—is that not so? The Blood is strong—it binds—"

Tor gave an inarticulate cry. "To go—I will not go! I am free—"

"Are you?" Two simple words, yet Gwennan saw Tor's shoulders quiver.

"I am free—" his voice came muffled because both his hands now covered his face. "I will not be—taken— I am—"

"You are master of such as these," the other made a slight gesture at the monsters now in circle about them. "Is that what one of the true Blood wants? Will you come to Power by Dark Ways?"

"There are others of us—we stood free—"

"Free? Ah, no. you were more tightly enchained than any man ever was in any time. You wear your chains within—not without. Those of you who took the Power thus: how did it serve them? Think—remember—how did it serve them?"

Tor stood, his face still hidden. "You cannot—"

"Had the wheel not turned, perhaps not. Look upon me!" Now that voice was sharp, cracking with an order which even Tor could not disobey.

He dropped his hands to stare eye to eye at the other.

There was something Gwennan had never seen before in his face—a pain which was not pain of body, a softening, breaking of spirit.

"Had it not been *you*—" he said in a low voice. "You and the time."

"Yes, the two of us—and the stars which spell the time. It is your choice still—"

.

Tor made a small gesture. "What choice have I? Already you have set the mark on me. If I could have kept you fast until—Saris—she has won. She called up that other half-blood—" For the first time he glanced at Gwennan— "and against the two of you what chance have I? Have it then as you wish—"

The other shook his head. "Not as *I* wish, no. The wish must be yours. There is no defeat, no victory. Only that which was rent must be mended—that which was sent on a wrong path must be turned aright."

"And the darkness which is to come—does that mean nothing?" Tor demanded. "Once more the dark, perhaps a slow climb and again a fall, will this then go on forever?"

"Nothing is forever. Nor is even that darkness complete. Which also you know. You cannot achieve any pattern yourself. It needs many to make, with none to claim to be the master weaver."

Tor turned his head slowly from side to side. He did not look to his monsters, Gwennan believed, but rather at the snow-covered world about them. Then he held up his right arm and pointed to the woods. There was a stirring among the monsters, whines, growls, cries, as if they would dispute whatever unheard order he gave. Then they turned and went, with a fluttering of wings, a padding of paws, a stumping of feet, of hooves. Overhead the grey of the sky darkened with clouds drawing together and Gwennan heard the first roll of thunder.

The monsters reached the edge of the woods.

Tor brought down his arm in a sweep as if flesh, blood and bone were a weapon to cut through an unseen barrier. There followed a burst of lightning near eye-searing. Gwennan blinked and blinked again. The creatures were gone. She could see the staining of the tracks in the snow —and then nothing but unmarked whiteness. They had gone Outside.

Tor grimaced again and staggered. "It is done—so let us finish. I am tired—"

"Not so. This is no release for you. A beginning, not an ending—"

"An ending for what I am. Who knows what I shall become? I am myself—all men hold to that —even you."

"Even I," the other nodded. "But I say it still —this is no ending. Come and see—" He held out both hands palm up.

Tor looked from the stranger's face, to those waiting hands, and then back again. Slowly, so very slowly, his own arms raised, burns red and angry along the one. Then he reached forward. Gwennan saw him set his mouth as if he knew that he walked a way which he feared and yet had no other resource than to follow.

"I come," he said heavily, laying his hands on those which waited.

So they stood for a moment which seemed to stretch out of the counting of time itself. Tor crumpled, nor did the other attempt to hold or aid him. The body curled in upon itself in the snow, head resting on one arm. In spite of the burn marks it was peaceful—as peaceful as she had seen Lady Lyle in that casket of renewing.

"Is he—" She had come down the rest of the way to stand beside the Guardian.

"Dead? No—look at me!"

She looked, and her hand went to her mouth as she backed a step or two, glancing from the body on the ground to the man standing under a rapidly clearing sky.

"You are—"

"I am whole. The wheel has truly turned. I am both parts—that which held the ambition and the will and the need for power—and that which was perhaps a wiser essence. Half-blood he called himself. No, he was rather half-part, though he did not know it. We did not altogether escape the madness of the Day of Ending. Some of us were affected by it in other ways. So I was—"

"You were the Arm—and Tor—and—"

"Others, many others—always lacking part of what should have been the whole. Now it is whole."

"Tor—"

He laughed and there was a joyfulness she had never heard in any voice before—or so it seemed in that moment. It was his turn to fling wide his arms, as if he would draw to him the whole of the world about, make it his, and him its in every way. He was indeed whole in a strange way which she could not describe, yet she knew it was a state of being which the world had seldom known since that day when Ortha saw death come.

"That is my name in this time."

"And him—" She looked to the burnt and battered body and gasped. It had shriveled, fallen in upon itself, darkened. There was no hint of

corruption in its disintegration, merely a return to ashes, as if some tree had been burnt by an all consuming fire.

"That wornout clothing is no longer needed," Tor told her. "Two are made one as was promised —and the wheel has turned. We have that before us now—and this time we may deal better—"

"We?"

"The Blood has found its way across the world," he told her. "And the Blood always rules. Kin knows kin no matter how far apart the years of birthing and dying have separated them. This is so—you know it now. Open your heart—and your hand—and see!"

He held out his hand and once more she took it, this time with her full will, feeling again the rise of the tie warm and strong between them.

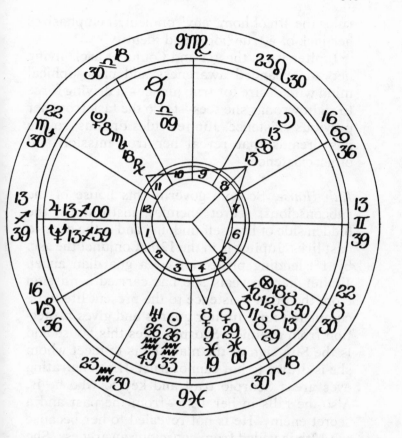

1st House: **Sagittarius** ascendant (rising). Sagittarius gives height—makes one tall and well-built. Jupiter Conjunct asc. (just as in 12th) gives added height—Sun also is tall. Possibly red hair.

Neptune in 1st in Sagittarius gives her mystical aspects and thoughts of fantasy. She daydreams a lot and often feels alienated and not belonging. Neptune here makes her an orphan and, as it rules the 4th of home environment, it emphasizes her lack of a true home and identity.

Jupiter rules the 1st and Conjunct asc., giving her an expanded awareness and philosophical mind with desire for true justice—a driving force to right wrongs she sees—to do the task from her previous existence. Jupiter rules dreams, so she has dreams that reveal her true mission and other existence.

12th House: Scorpio governs this house of the subconscious, secret enemies, institutions, the hidden side of life, self-undoing and is the door to past lives. Jupiter is in the 12th (Conjunct the asc. by 1°) lending protection as a guardian angel. Jupiter here reveals she has carried a mission from the other existence to the present life to be completed now Jupiter guards and gives protection from enemies. Scorpio rules this house and is the Sun sign of the man she is to meet whom she is drawn to but cannot trust. His penetrating eyes are a Scorpio trait and key to who he is. Also, he falls in her 12th—from the past and a secret enemy. He is not revealed to her because the 12th is veiled from conscious awareness. She will have to learn to beware of him.

The ruler of the asc. Jupiter fading in the 12th makes her tend toward a reclusive life.

8th House: Is Cancer ruled—Cancer is a psychic sign and its ruler—the Moon is also in Cancer in the 8th. While Capricorn governs her 2nd house of finances and shows restrictions of money—the eighth house is inheritance and legacies. The

Moon here and in positive aspect bestows a legacy upon her. The Moon here gives her psychic abilities which is enhanced by it being part of a grand trine. This indicates she will survive the crisis in her life and experience a natural death. Jupiter and Moon help her go through the karmic experience.

The grand trine is in the element water from the Moon in Cancer to Pluto in Scorpio to Mercury in Pisces. A grand trine is abilities, talents and gifts from another life brought into this one.

Pluto is in the giving her a friend who will benefit her—the legacy from the friend. Pluto is well placed in its own sign of Scorpio and rules transmutation or metamorphosis, all vital parts of her and that which is called death, present life experience and mission.

The 3rd part of the grand trine is Mercury in Pisces in the 4th house. Mercury is communication and in Pisces, which is other realms, she is able to communicate and further exercise her psychic abilities. Mercury governs travel and in Pisces as part of the trine she will travel through time and space.

3rd House: Is Aquarius with her Sun and Uranus therein. Being an Aquarius with its ruler Uranus in close Conjunct, she is exceptionally quick and bright with sudden flashes and insights into the future and past. Uranus rules the future.

The 3rd house is the mind and journeys—Uranus gives her sudden and unusual journeys.

Uranus governs lightning.

One of the most significant configurations in the chart is the Yod or Hand of Destiny. It is drawn to look like a giant "Y" between three planets which must be specific degrees from one another to form this configuration. It is a rare aspect and indicates the person will experience some event that completely changes their life into a different direction. In this chart the Hand of Destiny points to the 12th house of karma—the house of secrets; doorways to other dimensions, the key to other lives.

This may be activated by the transitting planets as they touch the points of the planetary positions.

The Moon, as part of the Yod, is at 13° Cancer exactly on the degree of the Star Siribls.